H.J. ROBI

HAESEL
THE PROPHECY WITCH
Conspiracy Of Fates - Book 1

Copyright © <2022> H.J.Robertson
Haesel
The Prophecy Witch
Conspiracy Of Fates Book 1

All rights reserved. No part of this publication may be reproduced, distributed or transmitted in any form or by any means, including photocopying, recording, or other electronic or mechanical methods, without the prior written permission of the publisher, except in the case of brief quotations embodied in critical reviews and certain other noncommercial uses permitted by copyright law.

This Urban Fantasy Novel is a work of fiction. An Urban Fantasy is by its nature a mix of modern day life and fantasy. Names, places, characters and incidents are either the product of the authors imagination or are used fictitiously, and any resemblance to any actual persons, living or dead, organisations, events or locales is coincidental or a product of imagination for the purpose of the story.

Warning: the unauthorised reproduction or distribution of this copyrighted work is illegal. Criminal copyright infringement, including infringement without monetary gain, is investigated and punishable by up to five years in prison.

Warning: Contains graphic scenes which some readers may fine upsetting.

Cover design by Emily's World of Design
Formatting by Tapioca Press

For my children with love

Imagination is a wonderful thing.
Use it for comfort, to ease fears, to inspire and empower you, and to
bring you the confidence and strength to ask all the 'What if's' in life.

1

Staring into the molten, red orb, I became transfixed. Unable to drag my eyes away as it pulsated with a heartbeat rhythm, drawing me in and keeping me captive. I could feel its pull on my soul as the black endless depths of its centre flicked in darting motions and tightened its grip.

Images flashed before me, distant screams and smouldering remains littering the ground, the smell of burnt flesh, repulsive, as it was drawn down my throat with my need to breathe. The heat increased coming from behind, and sweat ran freely over my body, stinging my eyes. I tasted salt as the edges of my vision blurred into orange, and I screamed as the flames engulfed me.

This was it. I would die now. Unable to fight as the searing heat took over…and then I would wake up.

Only I didn't.

This time it continued, and a surge of energy built in strength from deep inside my chest. It spread like liquid lava through every cell in my body and radiated out in continuous waves. I shook with its force and turned, only to stare into enormous, gaping jaws. Heatwaves shimmered from the glowing throat as the lethal rows of teeth closed around me.

My eyes sprang open, and I sat bolt upright, gasping in huge lungfuls of air.

My mind raced. I had been having this same dream, on and off, for the last two years, but recently it had become more frequent, and this time, for the first time, it hadn't ended when I screamed. There had been more to it.

Admittedly, it could have ended better...but it had moved on.

Inhaling deeply, I stretched my shoulders back, causing several satisfying cracks, then stripped off my soaked PJs and made my way to the shower to rinse off the thin layer of sweat that was lying cold on my skin.

Downstairs, with the radio on and my hands wrapped around a cup of steaming herbal tea, I sat at the wooden table in the kitchen-dining area of my modernised white rendered cottage, still pondering the dream. It was a stress dream, I had already decided that. Like the dream where you are trapped, or you're naked in front of a crowd of people, but what did it mean? I glanced up at the worktop. "Alexa, stop." Alexa lit up blue and cut off the news reporter mid-sentence. I'd heard enough for today.

The killer virus spread by flies had upped its pace and was killing cattle at breakneck speed. It had been all over the news for the last three days, and scientists were racing to come up with a solution.

The information didn't quite add up, and something about it didn't feel right to me. I couldn't explain it, and I couldn't shake it off. The underlying tightness in my chest embedded itself deeper and made it harder to breathe. I felt like I was waiting, watching, and I was sure there was worse to come. I reasoned that it must be this anxiety that was causing my dreams.

I looked to my left at my newly-extended, open plan kitchen and pushed the thoughts to the back of my mind. It was peaceful here, and my breathing calmed. To my right was the beautiful garden room with bi-fold doors on two sides so that when they were both open, my haven, the garden, was in full view.

The garden was my whole life and the reason I bought the house. I had attained a Bachelor's and Masters science degree in molecular plant science and botany, along with a degree level course in herbal medicine with the NIMH, The National Institute of Medical Herbalists, a good few years ago. With two walled acres of nature, plants and trees, and a rather sizeable herb and vegetable plot, it was bigger than most and contained two polytunnels, the produce of which supported my herbalist shop in the village. The whole garden backed on to an amazing ancient wood where there were hundreds of species of plants and trees for me to study and utilise. Perfect.

I mentally shelved my thoughts of the virus and turned my attention back to my notes. Tapping my pencil absently on my notepad, I reviewed an article I had found in the Journal of Restorative Medicine. I was working on a new skin healing range to treat acne and psoriasis and jotted down the ingredients, making notes as I went. Increased levels of endotoxins in the gut had been associated with these conditions, and I added artemisia and sarsaparilla to the list. Both were proven to be anti-inflammatory, binding to these endotoxins in the gut and eliminating them.

Reaching for my tea, I finished the still warm liquid, enjoying the relaxing warmth that flowed down my throat. Pondering on the ingredient combinations now on my list, my eyes drifted to a meandering line on the wall. The newly painted extension had dried out, and the inevitable cracks had appeared in the paintwork. *Oh well, I might repaint it anyway*, I mused. I wasn't too keen on the pebble grey that I had chosen. Maybe a pale mossy green would look more in keeping with the colours of the garden, bringing the outside in.

My eyes followed the crack in the wall up to a tiny hole in the corner under the coving. I was staring straight at it when the brightest of blue lights flashed out, for a split second only, then was gone.

My eyes widened, and a tight curiosity balled in my stomach as I stared at it. This seemed to have been happening a lot lately. Mostly when my mind drifted off, and my eyes were staring blankly at something. However, I was a logical person and explained it away as the water in my eye settling, then catching the light as it moved just a fraction, and yet, I still felt something, a strange feeling, unsettling me. I shook my head to stop my imagination that still wanted to explore all the ifs and buts of what it might be.

My mobile rang and vibrated loudly on the table next to me, making me jump and bringing me back to the present with a jolt. Rowan, my daughter's name, was displayed on the screen and brought an automatic smile to my lips as I picked up.

"Hi, sweetheart, how's things?" I asked.

"Hi, Mum. Yeah, everything's good. Just wanted to say sorry, but I won't be home this weekend. I'm going to stay with my friends as we have a project that needs to get finished, and I really need to spend the time on it." Her voice sounded anxious, and I made an effort to make mine sound brighter than I felt.

"Oh, that's okay, don't worry. Get the work done and make it brilliant," I said, forcing a smile.

"Ah, thanks, Mum. I'm really sorry, are you okay?"

"Yes, I'm fine. Honestly, don't worry, I'm on my way to the shop soon. I've got to prepare more supplies, so I can catch up on that this weekend instead. I'll see you the weekend after?" I asked hopefully.

"Yes, pinky promise. Thanks, Mum. I've gotta go, love you, bye."

"Okay, love you, sweetheart, see you soon."

I hung up, slumped back in my chair and blew out all the air in my lungs through puffed out, lazy lips, mentally and physically deflating. I had been looking forward to seeing Rowan and had planned for us to go out for a meal together, but I understood. I was so proud and pleased that my daughter had started on the path to doing what she loved, studying animal behaviour and zoology at Cambridge. Animals were her passion, and she had a natural affinity for it, being calm and kind in heart and spirit.

I glanced at the clock. I had to open the shop at 10 a.m. It was now 9:15 a.m., and Fridays could be busy. The walk to my shop in the village would take me twenty-five minutes. I'd better get going. I pushed the chair back and walked across the perfectly laid oak floor to close the large bi-fold door.

The air was cool with a warm promise and held the fresh smell of spring, even though it was early June. As I reached to pull at the handle of the door, something caught my eye. A leaf, bright green with serrated edges, was turning in circles, slowly round and round on the slate grey paving. I stared at it. A small wind caught it and spun it off the ground like a miniature cyclone. It lifted as the wind carried it upwards, swirling it in a circle towards me. I stood perfectly still, caught up in the wonder of it. The wind came closer, swishing past my face and with it came a scent that I missed every day and hadn't smelt in eight years. Tears choked my throat and eyes. The leaf hovered in front of me as the wind subsided, and instinctively I held out my hand to catch it.

A hazel leaf from the hazel tree, a tree I was named after.

All the hairs on my body rippled in a tidal wave from head to toe as each one goose-bumped. The smell that filled my senses was real: her essence, clothing, hair, and perfume —my mum.

I stood, rooted to the spot.

"Mum?"

My eyes darted around searching for her, looking for any sign, expecting her to appear. There was nothing. I took some deep breaths and sat down, forcing myself to think rationally. It must have been a combination of scents coming from the garden. I instantly countered myself. I knew all those scents. Confused, my mind spinning, I checked the clock and brought myself back to reality, fanning my eyes with my hands and taking a few deep breaths. I had to go. Now.

If I cut through the woods, it would be quicker. I grabbed my bag, stuffing in my phone and herb bundles from the table. The leaf was still in my hand, and I pushed that in too. I swiped my jacket from the chair back, slammed the door shut on my way out, and stumbled down the path with my trainers half on, hopping to pull each one over my heels as I went. I ran past the flower and herb borders, polytunnels and allotment, down the worn garden path and through the robust wooden gate in the brick wall. Calm descended on me as I leant for a moment on the back of the gate, feeling the grain of the wood flat on my palms. Nature wrapped her comforting cloak around my shoulders, and I breathed in the cool fresh scent of the trees and the earthy mulch of the forest floor. I began to walk down the narrow path that led to the village, and my thoughts turned to my mum.

Althea, known as Thea to everyone who knew her, had died eight years ago. She was a well-revered doctor in neuroscience and microbiology and had published numerous papers on her work concerning autism and higher emotion. Most of her drive to study was for my son, Jay, due to his autism. Apparently, over one hundred areas of the cortex are still undiscovered, and we have no idea what they do. She had been on the brink of making a breakthrough discovery just before she died.

My heart twisted at the memory, forever holding on to the pain. A sudden freak accident had caused an explosion in the lab she was working in. It was late at night, and the chemicals exacerbated the fire in the lab, the heat incinerated everything, and I never got to say goodbye. I immersed myself in nature and study and vowed to stay as healthy as possible to be there for my children.

A waft of pine and rich, organic earth brought me out of my thoughts, and I allowed the wood to infuse its healing essence deep into my soul.

The woodland path was narrow, and you had to look closely to follow it. The creatures of the wood had walked this way many times before me, away from the wide man-made gravel paths that were for humans. I knew where they were, though. Years spent in this wood had brought me more in sync with nature.

A vibrating flurry suddenly shot out of the dense shrubs and whizzed past my eyes with a flash of blue. I reeled back, searching to follow it, but it had disappeared entirely. A feeling I was not alone crept over my skin and compelled me to look to my right, where I gazed directly into large, watchful brown eyes. They stared directly back at me from the undergrowth, no more than five metres away. I froze on the spot and took in the majestic strength and beauty of the creature staring back at me: a fully grown red stag, whose deep russet coat blended perfectly with the bracken and earthy brown hues of his surroundings. His antlers were fully grown, fanned outwards and upwards wider than his body, each one ending in a sharp lethal point. He breathed out a billowing cloud of mist from soft, flared nostrils and took a step forwards, each foot thumping firmly on the ground one after the other. I tried to keep my heart from racing as he paused, reaching his nose forward to sniff the air, then walked straight to me. He brushed aside the branches and shrubs with little effort from his powerful antlers. As humans are creatures with binocular vision, I was aware I was viewed as a hunter and, therefore, a threat, so I lowered my gaze and turned my head slightly to the side to show I meant no harm.

His body quivered as he came to stand beside me. Then lowering his head to my neck, he breathed in my scent in a way that told him everything about me. I could smell his musty scent and feel the damp heat from his body. Moving my head slowly, I looked straight into an eye that was wise, dignified, and calm. He rubbed the side of his face up and down, once against my shoulder in acknowledgement, then turned slowly and walked back into the wood, quickly blending and becoming more camouflaged with every step.

Feeling lightheaded and realising that I must have been holding my breath, I exhaled loudly and took several large breaths in and out. Well, that had never happened before. I couldn't stop the grin from escaping as I brimmed with the excitement and sheer privilege of being that close to such a powerful animal. I marvelled at the encounter. He wasn't scared of me at all, and I felt I had passed a test of some kind and been accepted.

Hurrying through the wood, I emerged from the trees, still grinning, and walked the plank across the ditch - the one I had placed there after realising I couldn't jump it - that ran alongside the western edge of the wood. On the other side was protected meadow land that I, along with other local council members, had been proactive in securing for the sanctuary of many insect species, including bees, that were in rapidly declining numbers.

Many villagers had come together to plant native plant species and sow wildflowers, and now, in the summer months, the colourful display was a sight to behold as you turned the corner and drove into the village. I made my way up to the road, sticking close to the fence that denoted the meadow's boundary.

Skipping up the bank onto the pavement, I turned left, passing the estate agents, hairdressers, card shop and post office. I was late. I scanned ahead and could see a familiar figure peering into my shop window.

Rosa Fielding was impressive. She had been the first customer through my door when I opened the shop ten years ago. At 96 years old, she was fit and active with good eyesight. Her hunched over upper back, seemed out of place with her energy and enthusiasm for life, but her mind was as sharp as a needle, she didn't miss a trick.

My shop was nestled between the florist and the newsagent. 'Herbalist Store,' it said, in white scripted writing against the bottle green-painted wood background of the shop frontage. Underneath, smaller writing read 'natural teas, tinctures & salves.' All the village shops were labelled the same way with the shop type as the main heading, with owner and description underneath if required. It meant you could easily spot the kind of shop you were looking for, and I liked the format. I broke into a run so as not to keep her waiting any longer.

2

Arriving in a flourish of disturbed air and heavy breath, I fumbled for my keys. "Morning Rosa, sorry I'm late. How are you?"

"Yes, good dear, same same," she replied with a slight impatient nod.

I opened the shop door, which triggered the small tinkling brass bell that hung over it, and Rosa followed me in, the smell of all the herbs, teas, and spices instantly comforting.

"Can I take your coat? It's quite warm today."

Rosa always wore a heavy, brown woollen coat all year round that buttoned securely and came to her calves.

"What? No, thank you, dear."

She reached to grab hold of it around her neck, pulling it tighter for security and fiddled with the blue chiffon scarf tucked there. A flash of blue light shone out as she did so, and my eyes widened as I focused on the area. Then instantly dismissed it. The scarf material was slightly glittery, and it must have caught the light.

"I tend to feel the cold these days."

Being of small stature, she peered up at me with clear, bright, piercing blue eyes that captured the colour of her scarf and seemed to twinkle with a light from within.

"Something hold you up this morning?" She enquired.

The question caught me off guard.

"Err, yes. Sort of." I thought of the mornings events. There was no way I could explain all that, Rosa would think I was nuts. "I had more herbs to get ready than I thought," I said, thinking quickly. I smiled at her, but she remained where she was, searching my face for a few seconds, then gave a small nod.

"Mmm, it's started."

"What has?" I asked. Rosa looked back at me quizzically,

"What dear?"

"You said, 'It's started,' and I was just asking you what had started?" I prompted.

"Oh." She shook her head. "Yes, yes, quite so, don't mind me. Lots of things happening. It will all come about. You carry on, dear," she muttered in a quick ramble.

I walked around the counter and smiled fondly. "So, what will it be today?"

"Well, I would like some more of that Brain Food Tea, as you call it, please, Haesel. That's worked wonders. A very good mix of herbs you have in there. Yes, good results."

"Oh, that's good to hear," I said, retrieving the packet of tea from the glass-fronted cabinet behind me and placing it on the wooden counter.

'Yes, yes," she said, "that's it, quite so. I think the ashwagandha made all the difference. That was missing before." She looked up and to the side, her forefinger tapping her lips.

"Oh, well, I'm glad you liked it." My brow knitted. "Although it's always been an ingredient in my Brain Food Tea?"

"Mmm," she muttered absently.

"Anything else?"

"Yes, and rosemary oil, please. The two together really sharpen the senses." She winked at me, eyes sparkling.

I grinned. "I'm intrigued. What are you using these sharp senses for then?"

"Oh, this and that, just getting ready, nothing much," she mumbled, flicking her hand in the air to make light of my question.

"Well, if you have any secrets on their abilities, be sure to share them with me," I said. "It all helps my knowledge." I collected the rosemary oil from a drawer and placed the small brown glass bottle on the counter.

Rosa looked at me intently for a moment. "You have all the knowledge already, my dear," she said. "You'll see."

I was about to ask what she meant but then thought better of it. I would probably get another cryptic answer that didn't make much sense.

"That's kind of you to say," I said instead.

"Mmm," she replied again, "quite so, what do I owe you?"

I put the money in the till and placed the bagged items in her carrier bag.

"I'll get the door for you, Rosa," I said, skipping in front of her.

The bell tinkled gently as I opened the door, and a cool breeze blew in, blowing my hair away from my face.

"Oh, the wind's getting up a bit," I said, and as I turned to look at Rosa, she reached out and grabbed hold of my hand, covering it with her other. I jolted, surprised, but kept it there.

"You can feel it on the wind," she said, looking straight at me. Her blue eyes were now sparkling with the most amazing iridescent light as the sun broke through the clouds and streamed through the open door. "It will tell you all you need to know. Listen for the songs." She pulled me closer, moving towards my ear, and I bent lower to oblige her. "Listen and feel it, Haesel."

A chill ran through me that lifted the hairs on my arms. Before I could reply, she released my hand and was out of the door, calling behind her, "Thank you, yes, it will all come about. See you soon."

"Have a good day," I called after her, rubbing my arms briskly. I gave a quick shake of my head, rolled my eyes, and smiled. Rosa was a funny one, I thought fondly.

Closing the shop door, I picked up my bag and went through the door to my workroom at the back of the shop. This was where the packaging took place. I did the main work of drying herbs and making salves and oils at home, where I had more room. After making a drink, I sat down, getting out the herbs I had brought to top up supplies. The hazel leaf fell onto the bench, and I sighed.

I felt a bit weird and on edge. Then I breathed in sharply as I thought about what Rosa had just said and remembered the wind that brought the leaf straight to me. The tinkling doorbell broke my thoughts as the next customer entered the shop.

The day passed quickly, my mind occupied with people popping in and out enquiring after things to help one ailment or another. I loved my job, helping people and making them feel better.

Mrs Sanders called in to thank me for the salve I had made for her daughter Emma, whose sore, itchy skin had been driving her crazy. A simple concoction of castor, olive, jojoba, and coconut oils with sea buckthorn, lavender, cinnamon, and clove had provided the skin with all the support it needed to calm and heal itself.

"You have a natural talent, Haesel. I can hardly see a mark

on her, and all the itching has gone," she said beaming. "I'll take some more, please."

"Oh, I'm really sorry, I don't have any more. I made it just for Emma. However, now that I know it helped, I will make more and stock it as a regular product line," I said, giving her a broad smile. Being Friday, I said I would have it ready for her in the shop to collect the following week. "I'll call you when it's ready," I assured her as she left.

Closing the door behind the last customer of the day, I tidied up quickly, grabbed my things, and locking the door behind me, headed for home. The wind had increased, and it was now feeling chilly, unusually cold for early June. I decided to go back along the road, and I set off at a good pace. As I passed the meadow field, I looked at the flowers and thought it a shame that it wasn't looking so good this year. Although too early for it to be in full bloom, the very late spring frosts we had been having had halted the plants in their tracks and killed many of the newly sown seeds.

As I approached the lane that led down to my house, the wind strengthened further, and I put my head down and stepped up my pace. It was the end of the village, and the trees gave way to open fields and gently rolling hills that meant the wind had free rein to run with no obstacles in its path. Windy Corner my children and I had named it, and I remembered many a morning on the way to school shouting, 'hold your hood, put your head down, and squint your eyes,' to my children, especially in winter when we would battle against it, tears streaming down our faces. The strongest gusts would stop us dead in our tracks for a second before we turned the corner, and the tree line broke the onslaught.

The wind started howling, wrapping all around me, pulling and pushing like being jostled in a crowd. I turned the corner and braced myself. The strength took my breath away, and I leaned in, surprised at the sudden increase and ferocity. I glanced over the fields and saw the blackening clouds. There must be a storm brewing, I thought. I reasoned the wind would ease as soon as I reached the next tree line down the lane, but I didn't get that far.

The wind was angry now, and I found it impossible to walk. Something in my senses told me this wasn't right. Bracing against it, I got nowhere. My ears started to ache as my bag was ripped from my hand. I let out a cry as my hair lashed and whipped my face as I turned around, trying to look for it. Then, as I turned back, the mother of all gusts hit me with colossal force. I was lifted off my feet into the air. I gasped, flailing my arms. Then everything froze.

It completely froze, like time had stopped still. There was no sound, leaves hung in the air, and the trees bent, stationary, facing the same direction. A couple of birds that had been battling the wind hung in the grey, frothy sky. Nothing moved.

I was stuck, held by some invisible force, a yard off the ground. The only thing I could hear was the sound of my heavy breathing, which was at intense panic level. My heart thudded like I was running on a treadmill. Every sense was on high alert, and I buzzed with a strange force of energy I had never experienced before.

I felt it coming before I saw it, and my eyes homed in. A delicate wisp of wind, almost a mist, was swirling its way in circles towards me down the lane. It came closer and grew larger, pockets of denser mist shooting out all around like something was fighting to get out. I wasn't afraid. Instead, I felt a hot strength, as though my body was protecting me. The mist undulated and twisted like it was trying to form a shape, and then for a split second, I thought I saw a face. My eyes widened as the dense mist shot out an ethereal hand, reaching for me, before retracting quickly back into the larger mass.

Then it dissolved slowly, blowing past my face, and as it passed, a faraway voice called out, "Haesel." My mum's voice.

3

Suddenly, I was released from my suspended state and hit the ground, landing in a crumpled heap. I was stunned and sat there on the pavement, processing what had just happened. The wind had returned to normal, and large billowing clouds in dramatic shades created intense dark and bright alternating moments as the sun was briefly hidden, then exposed again.

I asked myself how I felt, and the answer was primarily curious excitement. My mum was trying to make contact. I was sure this time. For two years after she had died, I had visited numerous mediums and spiritualist churches, searching for any sign from her that she was somewhere and was okay. She had always said that when that day came, she would fight as hard as she could to send me a sign. After two years, I gave up, sought counselling for my loss, and made myself move on.

Now, at last, I was sure. I had heard her voice and smelt her familiar, comforting smell, and I was positive she was trying to make contact. I looked up, tears of emotion brimming, threatening to spill and said, "I heard you, Mum, try again." I waited. Nothing happened. I searched, but still nothing, and the loss took over. The sobs came, uncontrollably, in heaving breaths that I was powerless to stop.

A car turned into the lane and broke my thoughts. It came to an abrupt halt in front of me, and I instantly recognised the metallic, turquoise-blue vehicle through my blurry, tear-filled eyes. There had to be only one car that colour, and it belonged to Eve.

The door was flung open, and my lifelong friend dashed to my side. "Haesel, are you okay? What happened? Are you hurt?"

I sucked in a juddering breath. "I'm okay, really," I said, gathering myself together. "I'm so glad you're here." I got to my feet, my eyes searching around. "I lost my bag," I said, and then, "I'll explain at home," when I glanced at her and saw her confused expression.

The bag was in the field across the road. I collected it, along with my scattered belongings, then hopped into her car for the two hundred yards to my house. Her patchouli perfume permeated through the air, and my shoulders dropped as I breathed in the relaxing, familiar scent. Turning to her, I noticed her hair colour had changed again. Over the years, it had been almost every colour imaginable and was now a beautiful strawberry blonde that complemented her dark eyes.

"Oh, I love your hair. It really suits you."

Eve reached over and squeezed my hand. "Thanks." Then she glanced at my bag, her eyebrows rising. "Is that leather?" she asked, wrinkling her nose as though the bag was giving off a bad smell.

"Yes." I gave a definite nod.

Eve's mouth fell open, and her eyes grew wide, as she drew in a deep breath that was loaded with words of disappointment and heart wrenching facts. I held up my hands against the forthcoming verbal onslaught. No matter what tragedy had befallen me, it wouldn't have been as bad as Eve's wrath if I had used an animal for its skin.

"Don't worry Eve," I said, laughing and rolling my eyes, "It's vegan leather, and get ready to be very impressed with me, because this bag is eco friendly, biodegradable, and made from a prickly pear cactus." I threw the bag onto her lap.

"Whoa, you got one!" Eve grinned, "I'm definitely impressed Haesel, I've not seen one of these yet," she said, examining the bag in detail. "I can't believe it looks so real."

The simple conversation centred and calmed my thoughts. Eve was the best tonic in the world to make everything feel normal again.

Once inside with the kettle boiling, scoffing the doughnuts Eve had brought, I told her all that had happened. Eve had been my best friend since primary school, and we shared everything. I could trust her one hundred per cent. She was a free spirit, never marrying, preferring instead to have intense short flings with guys that she felt were good for her soul or who she connected with on some cause or another. A true eco-warrior, she was involved in all sorts of charities regarding pollution and animal species survival. If anyone could save the planet, the whales, the orangutans etc., she could.

"I can't believe it, Haesel," she said once I had finished explaining. Her eyes stared, unfocused, at the dining table where we now sat. "What are you going to do now?"

"I don't know, nothing, I suppose. I don't really know what to do." I dabbed my finger around my plate, collecting dropped sugar grains. "I'm sure she will try and make contact again, though," I said, nodding intensely at her to confirm the thought while sucking the sugar from my finger.

We chatted about all the what-ifs while we drank our tea, and then I remembered that I hadn't been expecting her.

"So…anyway," I said, frowning, "why are you here? You didn't say you were coming."

"Ooh, yes," she said excitedly. "I've got to show you this." She scrambled in her bag, bringing out a handful of crumpled papers.

"So," she paused, holding up a hand. "You know all these goings-on in the news about this killer virus?"

"Yes," I said slowly, dragging out the word, my suspicions raised.

"Well, something's going on that's not right," she said earnestly.

"Really?" I replied, with more than a hint of sarcasm in my voice. She sighed and tilted her head to the side, fixing me with a stare.

"I know, I know, but just hear me out." Her eyes flicked quickly to the side. "Actually," she continued, "come on, put the news on, then you'll see." She grabbed hold of my hand and pulled me through into the living room.

With a very grave expression on his face, the BBC newsreader warned that the following images were upsetting. The screen flashed with still scenes of people dying everywhere. They were lying in the streets, hospitals, or even in someone's house, where all the family members were strewn across the floor, laying in unnatural angles. The images were flashed up on the screen for a split second only. Large, bold writing on a yellow background scrolled across the bottom of the screen and read: LATEST UPDATE: KILLER SACL VIRUS SPREADS TO HUMANS. WORLDWIDE EMERGENCY DECLARED.

Eve grabbed the remote and paused the TV on an image of several men and women lying in the street. A woman in a blue blouse cradled the head of a man in her lap, her face frozen in an anguished scream. I stood with my hand covering my mouth and turned to Eve.

"Oh my god, I was only listening to the news this morning, and this wasn't mentioned. I didn't realise it had suddenly gotten this bad."

Eve laid the papers she was still holding on the coffee table and began shuffling through them.

"It hasn't," she said. "Look." She handed me a printout of people lying dead on a street.

"What's this?" I asked, my furrowed brow showing my confusion.

"Look at the building," she said, pointing to an area on the page. "This one here is the same building as this one here." And she walked over to the TV and pointed to the building on the screen. "It's from a different angle, see? Look at the sign here and here." She pointed them out. "And, this lady over here is the same one holding the man in her lap. It's just taken from further up the street on the other side."

"Oh yes," I said, "but I'm sure there must have been other photographers there?"

Eve took the paper from my hand. "There were...but this," she said, holding the page up to me at eye level and jabbing at it with her finger, "is from the disaster that happened five years ago when the earthquake hit northern Japan. It's fake, Haesel, and so are all these." She gestured with her hand at the papers on the table.

"What? Why?"

"I don't know." She shrugged, looking back and forth at the images. "But like I said before, something's not right. We are being lied to for a reason, and it doesn't feel like a good reason," she said, biting her bottom lip.

Eve showed me the rest of the fake photos and told me her friend Richard had found them. He had remembered the earthquake as his relatives were there at the time. It had rung a bell and made him look it up. Now curious and geeky with computers, he was currently running further searches.

I reached for the remote and pressed play. The screen returned to the newsreader who announced: "We are now heading live to London and the CEO of VialCorp, Dr Julius Malicen, for an update on the Severe Acute Clotting Virus or SACL as its now known."

A thin, tall man with light brown hair that had mostly turned to silver-grey, and small, sharp, mean eyes that peered over rimless glasses, was standing outside on the steps of the enormous glass-fronted pharmaceutical building. The mainstream media jostled for the best spot, cameras running and microphones thrust forwards in outstretched arms. Silence descended as Dr Malicen, dressed in an immaculate bespoke suit, approached the podium and prepared to speak. Leaning close to the microphone, he tapped it a couple of times and cleared his throat.

"Thank you all for coming. I would like to inform and reassure everyone, first and foremost, that there is no need for panic." He held up his hands, palms facing the crowd and took a minute to look around at everyone. Flashbulbs exploded. Each photographer determined to get the best shot to give their newspaper the front page edge over all the others.

"We have been studying this type of disease for some time," he continued, "and there are plenty of other diseases that cause clotting, so we had a good head start." He gave a little wink, one side of his mouth twisting upwards. I shuddered involuntarily.

"I am pleased to announce as head of VialCorp," he continued, "that we expect a solution to the SACL Virus to be available within the next five to seven days." He paused for dramatic effect and leaned forwards, gripping the edges of the podium with both hands, and his tone became more serious.

"Due to the virus causing clotting, speed was paramount, and we have pulled out all the stops to make this happen. The treatment will be a series of tablets, definitely two at the moment, maybe more, designed to thin the blood and strengthen the immune system, increasing white blood cell count. It contains a powerful antiviral agent that we have developed here at VialCorp, to surround and protect the blood cells, weakening the virus should a person become infected. This tablet will be a stop-gap until a way is found to neutralise the virus. We at VialCorp advise everyone to take this medication, young and old alike, to protect yourself and your children. The tablets will be rolled out from your local doctor's surgery or health centre." He straightened up and clapped his hands together in front of him.

"OK, folks, we're pretty busy here, as I'm sure you can all imagine, so I'll update as soon as we have a closer timeframe for release. Thank you, and don't worry." He pointed his finger at the cameras, swept his hand in a semi-circle, and looked at each one in turn. The cameras set off like a lightning storm. "VialCorp has your back," he said, grinning. The press surged forward shouting questions, but he turned on his heel and walked swiftly back through the large glass doors into the building. Police and security were left battling the press.

"Wow, always the showman," I said. "I swear I can actually see that man's ego surrounding him."

"He's a complete two-faced, lying arsehole," said Eve. "I wouldn't trust him as far as I could throw him. The whole company is corrupt and untouchable."

She did have a point, I conceded. VialCorp was the largest of all the big pharma companies and was responsible for developing the majority of the world's vaccinations and medical treatment products. A monster corporation, they were also known to not be wholly ethical in their product manufacture and testing protocols, having paid out billions in the past in damage lawsuits and, more recently, one of the largest health care fraud settlements in history. A liability exemption clause was now put in place and meant they had free rein to manufacture products without repercussion. We now had to rely on trust alone that their aim to prevent all manner of illness worldwide was true. Airtight confidentiality agreements ensured that anyone who left the company would not talk.

Many individuals and families of people suffering permanent damage, and even death, from their drugs now had no chance of any compensation. Many had tried to bring about legal cases, only to be squashed flat when they eventually reached court. Everyone could be bought when you had that much money, and Dr Malicen associated with the elite, the top of the rich lists, billionaire bankers, and business moguls. He had his fingers in many pies and owned many people. He could get away with murder if he wanted. As the payouts would indicate, he already had.

I felt a knot of apprehension in my stomach. "I don't like the feel of it," I said.

"You're not kidding," Eve replied, and we both stood there, quietly, lost in our thoughts. Eve came out of the trance first.

"Hey," she said suddenly, pointing her finger at me, "don't you know someone who works at VialCorp?" I looked at her and shook my head, my chin wrinkling. "Yes, you do," Eve pushed on urgently. "He used to work with Thea. Ooh, what was his name?" She pressed her fingertips to her forehead and squeezed her eyes shut."

"If you're talking about Mick, I haven't spoken to him in years. I needed the clean break."

"Yes, yes, Mick, that was it. You could go and see him. He would still talk to you. He's been there years and was good friends with your mum, wasn't he? You could see if he knows anything?" She fired these points at me, her hands becoming more animated by the minute.

"Eve, I don't even know if he works there anymore, and we have no idea what's going on, if anything. Besides, it would be weird me just turning up on him after all this time."

Eve was always straight in, feet first, before thinking, although her proactive enthusiasm was inspiring, she could convince a non-swimmer to jump in at the deep end with her 'you can do it' exuberant attitude.

"Well, let's see if he does still work there," she said, dashing off into the kitchen.

I followed her, curious myself.

"Right," she said, grabbing her phone. "What's his surname?"

"Jenkins," I replied, and she googled 'Mick Jenkins, Vial-Corp.' Within seconds the internet had provided the answer.

"Yep, he's still there," she said triumphantly. "Right, call him tomorrow morning and see if he'll talk to you." She stretched her neck towards me, her eyes wide and insisting.

"OK," I said.

"Wait, really?" Her eyebrows shot up, and an almost lunatic grin spread across her face.

"Yes, really, I agree. This just doesn't sit right, and there's no harm in asking," I said with a shrug. My usual stance of overthinking everything was now thrown out of the window. I couldn't explain the feeling I had about this. It was unnerving with all the strange things that had been happening to me today, hearing my mum's voice, being suspended in the air, the flashes of light, the deer... And Rosa had definitely been acting strange. Now that I thought about it, there had been more weird things going on than I'd realised, and that made me want to find out more.

Eve and I chatted for the next half an hour. At the door, we hugged each other, and I promised I would call her in the morning with any news.

4

My dreams were troubled. Full of people and places I didn't know. Sinister beings and shadows lurked—snapshots of time. My daughter was lost. I caught glimpses of her and tried to get to her. She turned and saw me, reached out, then fell off the edge and disappeared. I was choking. I couldn't breathe.

I woke suddenly, sweating and gasping for air. I had been crying in my dream, and my nose and throat had blocked. My face was wet with tears; it was so real. I flung off the covers and grabbed my phone, throwing on my dressing gown. Dialing Rowan's number, I blew my nose and listened to the rings. She picked up, sounding groggy. "Hello? Mum?"

"Rowan, are you okay?" I asked, fresh tears spilling.

"Yes, why? It's 4:20 a.m. Mum. Has something happened? Are you okay?"

Relief flooded my body, making me shaky, and I sat down on the landing. "Yes, I'm fine, don't worry. Sorry to call so early. It's really silly, I know, but I had some terrible nightmares. They were so real, and I just wanted to check that you were okay. Sorry, sweetheart."

"Aww, that's awful. I'm fine, Mum, don't worry. Are you sure you're okay? Shall I call you later?" she asked.

"No, no need. I'm fine now, honestly. I've got lots to do today, so that will keep me busy. Just have a good day."

"Okay, you can call me whenever you want Mum, you know that," Rowan said, and I knew she meant it.

"Sorry I woke you," I said, feeling better. "I love you."

"Love you more," she replied before hanging up.

4:30 a.m. on a Saturday, and now wide awake, wasn't how I planned to start the day.

By 9 a.m. most of the chores that needed doing were ticked off, including collecting fresh herbs, which I had tied in bundles and hung up to dry. I made some tea and sat down to call Mick, googling the number on my phone. The main VialCorp number answered with an automated message, giving me several options to press for various departments. I didn't need any of them, so I let them run through again and decided just to wait. Silence usually meant you got connected to a person. Sure enough, a female voice answered in an authoritative voice.

"Good morning, you're through to VialCorp, Brenda speaking. How may I direct your call?"

"Oh, hello, err, yes, could you put me through to Mick Jenkins, please?"

"Do you have an appointment?" came the reply.

"No, I'm his niece," I lied, not knowing why I did that. I didn't even know if he had siblings. I felt the heat rise in my face at the thought of being caught out.

"Dr Jenkins is only seeing people by appointment, including telephone calls. Would you like me to check his diary?" Brenda said efficiently but in a monotone voice that suggested she had said that line many times before.

"Yes, please."

I could hear her tapping the keyboard for longer than I

would have expected for her just to check a diary. I waited, listening to her breathing heavily down the phone, her headset microphone was too close to her nose and magnified the sound.

"Dr Jenkins' diary is full for the next three weeks. He has a telephone slot available on July second at 11 a.m. Would you like me to schedule that in for you?" she asked.

"Oh," I said again, "couldn't I just have a quick word with him. I only need a minute." My voice had an exasperated edge to it that I tried, and failed, to hide.

"I'm afraid not. Dr Jenkins has meetings all day, so would you like me to schedule the second in for you?" she tried again, in a brisk fashion that had me imagining her pursing her lips.

"No," I sighed, "that's okay, thank you."

Brenda ended the call, and the recorded message played.

"Have a good day, and thank you for calling VialCorp, where we take care of you." The line went dead.

Bugger, I thought, leaning back in the chair and looking up at the ceiling with a loud sigh. Then I remembered the notebook. I ran through the house, rummaging through drawers and cupboards. I checked in the office and sideboard cupboards in the living room. Where was it? Exasperated after being sure I would find it in the top drawer of my bedroom dresser, I fell back, outstretched on the bed and closed my eyes. After a few moments, I'd located it right underneath where I lay. Rummaging at the back of the drawer in the divan bed base, I pulled out the small, blue, leather-covered book with gold-edged pages, my mum's notebook. I stood, turning straight to the back page.

Tracing the lines of her handwriting, my throat tightened, and a drawing sensation ran along my collar bone as I thought how strange it was to be touching her words when she was no longer here. My fingers ran down the list of names and numbers and stopped at Mick Jenkins. Suddenly the pages ruffled wildly, and a strong blast of air blew up into my face.

I gasped and staggered back, dropping the notebook and sitting down hard on the bed as the gust brought with it a familiar smell of my childhood—the smell of the VialCorp office room for children, where I would often sit and wait for my mum to finish her work.

I was meant to go. I could feel it pulling me.

I dashed back downstairs for my phone and dialled the number, sure that he would have changed it by now. He had, but a voicemail message gave the new one, and within two rings, Mick answered.

"Mick Jenkins speaking," he said.

His voice brought memories flooding back of happy times, and my voice caught in my throat.

"Hello?" He tried again.

"Hi Mick, this is Haesel, Thea's daughter."

"Haesel? Well, I never… hang on." I could hear doors opening and shutting as Mick went somewhere more private. "Haesel," he said again, and I could hear the smile in his voice. "Well, what a lovely surprise. I'm so pleased to hear from you."

"I'm sorry I didn't keep in touch, Mick. I couldn't handle what had happened and just needed a clean break."

"I can understand that, but I was worried about you. I had no idea where to find you."

"Yes, sorry," I said again, "I should have gotten in touch with you."

Mick had been a good friend and colleague of Mum's. He used to be at our house regularly, often staying for dinner as he and Mum discussed their research findings.

"Well, let's not dwell on it" he said, "it's so good to hear from you now, and my goodness, you sound like your mum. What do I owe this wonderful pleasure to?" he asked.

Sighing, I sat down on the arm of the sofa. "Well, this is going to sound strange for sure, but I think something is going on that's quite worrying, and I would really like to run it by you if that's okay?" I asked. Now I had voiced it; I felt more sure of myself. "It's pretty urgent," I continued, "and I was hoping to catch you tomorrow if you have time; only Brenda said you were in meetings all day today."

"Is everything okay?" he asked, and I could hear the worry in his voice.

"Yes, it's fine, really, more of an instinctive thing, I suppose."

He laughed a warm, genuine laugh and said, "Ah, well, if it's an instinct, then of course I'll take a look. Thea always had plenty of those, and it was uncanny how many times she was right. I will always love to see you, Haesel, whatever the reason. Please know I would have contacted you before now, but I didn't know how to reach you."

"Thank you," I said, "the memories were just too raw to face."

"Of course," Mick said, and the line went silent for a few seconds as our memories flicked briefly over the disaster. "So," he cleared his throat. "I'm actually not in meetings all day as it happens. Sorry, that was a little white lie I'm afraid, otherwise I get bombarded with all sorts of things that take me away from my work. However, I am busy tomorrow, and I'm not able to change that. I'm really sorry," he finished.

"Oh, well, that's actually better for me because I'm free today, too," I said, brightening. I swapped hands to hold the phone to my right ear. "Could I see you today?" I suddenly felt like I was being quite pushy. "Sorry," I added before Mick could answer. "This is coming across pretty weird."

"No, not at all," he said with a small laugh. "Again, I'm

always glad to see you, Haesel, and if I can help you with anything, then it will be my pleasure." We arranged to meet in his office at 2 p.m. Then, just before hanging up, I remembered.

"Oh, Mick? By the way, I told Brenda at reception that I was your niece, sorry. I thought maybe she would put me through if we were related."

"Nice try," his laugh was deep and genuine, and his voice warm in his reply.

"Haesel, your mum meant a great deal to me, as I know you are aware. I would be honoured to think of you as my niece and keep up the ruse for Brenda. It wouldn't have mattered, you know, if you had said my house was on fire, she would not have put you through. Brenda is the rottweiler of first contact with VialCorp."

I laughed this time, saying, "She did seem to take her job very seriously." I gave Mick my number, and we said goodbye. I got straight back on the phone to Eve.

"Oh, bloody hell, I can't make it today. I've got a meeting with EcoForce to discuss our campaign. It's brilliant you got to see him so quickly. I'm gutted," she said in an up and down yo-yo of emotion.

"I know, I was really hoping you would be able to come, but I'll call you and fill you in once I'm in the car on the way back."

Eve said she would leave all the evidence she had collected for me, in a bag by her back door. As she only lived ten minutes away, I could collect it on my way past.

After a quick shower, I threw on my favourite comfy, black skinny jeans and a sage green shirt, and it wasn't long before I was on my way.

The drive to London was easy going. I enjoyed the change of scenery and listening to the radio, watching the changes in the clouds as the stormy showers built up, releasing their swathes of five-minute downpours, then giving way to blinding sunshine. I stopped once to grab a coffee and arrived at VialCorp Head Office twenty minutes early. The vast, green glass, hexagonal frontage of the building was imposing. The one-way mirrored glass was made up of interlocking hexagons, which linked its relevance to the shapes of DNA nucleobases. It was repeated for the dot of the 'i' in the Vial-Corp logo, the main body of the 'i' being the spiralling double helix of the DNA strand. Clever, I thought.

Mick had said I could park in the underground car park for the employees. I just had to give his name at the intercom. Once parked, I followed his instructions to take the elevator to the third floor and follow the signs for Immunology Reception. The receptionist would escort me to Mick's office.

Stepping out of the elevator, I followed the wide, pristine white corridors, my trainers making no noise as they sunk into the plush grey-flecked carpet. I passed numerous doorways made of heavy grey glass, all numbered with the initial 'I' followed by a number. I couldn't see into any of them, and I heard no voices. Large, grey stone urns housed various leafy house plants of areca palms, birds of paradise, and Madagascar dragon trees, which were strategically placed near the doors and made the surroundings look softer and a little less sterile.

A sign hanging from the ceiling ahead pointed to the door I was looking for. I was greeted by a well-practised smile from a small, slim woman in her mid-thirties, wearing a grey skirt suit and stiff white blouse. Small bi-focal glasses sat on her nose, making her look both intelligent and efficient, and her strawberry blonde hair was tied back in a low ponytail, adding the only splash of colour to the room. She stood up and reached over the curved, white acrylic desk, holding out her hand.

"Hello," she said warmly, "you must be Haesel Greenwood. I'm Kirsty."

I shook her hand, smiling.

"Yes, hello," I said. "I'm here to meet Dr Jenkins."

"Please have a seat," Kirsty said. "I'll take you through shortly."

I declined a coffee and settled down on the luxurious, white leather sofa, picking up a magazine from under the large glass coffee table. Being lower to the floor, I noticed that the carpet wasn't flecked but was covered in tiny white lines that connected to make a uniform hexagon pattern. I liked that detail and wondered how much that must have cost to be made bespoke for the whole building.

Medicine Today magazine advertised an article on the front cover that caught my eye, 'The use of plants in modern medicine.' I turned to page forty-two, amazed to read that advances had been made with bilberries improving the micro-circulation of the eye, and they were now being used to treat glaucoma and cataracts. Bilberries also stimulated retinal purple, which improved night vision. I was so absorbed in the article that the sudden sound of the phone ringing made me jump. I glanced up, my heart upping its pace as Kirsty said, "Of course, Dr Jenkins," before hanging up.

"Haesel, I'll take you through now." I must have looked disappointed, and Kirsty read my mind.

"Take a picture of it with your phone, then you can read it later," she winked.

"Oh, that's a good idea, thank you," I said, flashing her a smile.

"No problem, it happens a lot," she said, stepping out from behind the desk. "The articles in there are so interesting that they suck you in."

Placing my phone back in my bag, I walked towards the door.

"Oh, just a minute," Kirsty called out to me. "I just need to create a visitor pass for you. It won't take long." She directed me to a table at the end of the desk, picking up a long white tube from a small vase. "It's just a cheek swab," she said, opening the sterile wrapping. "Once we've swabbed, it goes into this machine that reads your DNA and prints out a unique code on your pass here," she said smiling, pointing to another machine.

"Oh, I don't know," I said. Kirsty's eyebrows shot up. My hesitation made me feel silly, but at the same time, something felt wrong about this and, if I'm honest, didn't entirely make sense as to why that level of detail was required. Kirsty recovered from her surprise.

"Oh, there's nothing to worry about. Here," she said, handing me the swab, "You can do it yourself if you like. The data analyser gets automatically rinsed with a chemical that completely sterilises it in between swabs, and the used swabs are immediately incinerated in that machine over there afterwards," she said, pointing to another larger, grey machine not far away. "The codes are shredded when you return the lanyard. Nothing is kept," she added, giving a small shrug and an over-wide grin. She interlaced her fingers together in front of her, but I noticed the skin on her thumbs turning white as she pressed them into her hands.

"Oh," I said, still hesitating, my frown showing my unease. "Do I really need to have a pass? I mean, I'll be with Dr Jenkins."

She flattened her lips and gave a slight nod. "Company policy, I'm afraid. Technology's gone mad, hasn't it?" She laughed. "It was much easier when you just wrote your name on a sticker and stuck it on your jumper."

I laughed a little reluctantly, my feeling of unease

remaining as a tightness in my chest. I had to see Mick, and it looked like this was the only way. Picking up the swab, I silently reasoned with myself. *This is technology, Haesel. You have to get with the times at some point, like it or not.* One minute later, my pass had been printed and slipped into the plastic housing on the lanyard. I looped it over my head.

"I'll just get rid of this," Kirsty announced, holding up the swab. She swept her other hand towards the door. "After you."

As I headed towards the door, a feeling of extreme cold trickled through my body. I shuddered as my skin started to prickle. Adrenalin surged, and then a sudden flash behind my eyes produced an image of Kirsty handing a swab to Dr Malicen. It was a second at the most, and then it was gone.

My breathing became laboured, and I stood rooted to the spot, wondering what the hell had just happened and how? Kirsty appeared beside me. "Are you okay?" she asked, reaching out to take hold of my arm. As soon as her fingers touched me, she recoiled, jumping back with a loud cry, covering her hand tightly. She shook it and made a fist, breathing in sharply through her teeth.

"Whoa," she said, looking at me wide-eyed, her mouth agape. "That was a massive shock I just got off you. My whole arm is pins and needles."

I couldn't make sense of it, but I was annoyed at myself for not following my instincts, and I knew I didn't want Kirsty anywhere near me. "I'm so sorry," I said, quickly hiding my unease, thinking fast I looked down at my feet. "Maybe it's my trainers on this carpet. They must have generated some static electricity." I looked at her, feigning concern. "Maybe that's why I felt a bit light-headed?"

Recovering, Kirsty breathed out loudly. "Well, just don't touch anything metal," she said. "You'll go bang," and gave a small laugh.

Haesel

"Yes, good point. I'll definitely watch out for that." I smiled awkwardly.

Kirsty's phone beeped twice in a high pitched tone, and she took it out of her jacket pocket, glancing down at it quickly. "Oh, sorry, Haesel," she said, looking back up at me, "I've been called away, I'm afraid."

"That's okay," I said. "Just tell me where to go, and I'll find it."

We said goodbye and headed in opposite directions. Kirsty called after me. "It was nice to meet you, Haesel." She waved as she turned on her heel and hurried off.

"Yes, you, too," I called after her, which it had been initially, but now I wasn't so sure. I turned left at the end of the corridor and followed it around the next corner to the end. The door opened before I could knock, and Mick welcomed me in with a beaming smile.

"Haesel," he said. "It's been much too long." He pulled me into a warm embrace.

5

We sat in oversized, expensive, c-shaped chairs that were much comfier than they first looked, a small coffee table separating us, and reminisced for the next fifteen minutes before Mick turned to me, his eyes warm.

"So, what actually brought you here to see me out of the blue?"

I reached into my bag for the printed pages that Eve had left for me. There were more than she had shown me at my house. Some of them proof that the cattle shown on the news, strewn dead over the fields, were also fake and were actually from a severe drought that had happened eleven years previously.

"Okay," I began. Laying them on the table, I explained the whole thing to Mick. "What do you think?" I asked, suddenly feeling a bit crackpot. He took a deep breath and let out a long sigh.

"I think it looks like there is something going on," he said, nodding and frowning, his lips pressed together.

"I know," I said. "I feel it. I can't explain. It just feels different."

"Wow, Thea used to say the exact same thing. It's like going back in time," he shook his head half smiling, his fondness for my mum clearly showing.

I smiled back. "I miss her," I said, my voice breaking, allowing the pain to momentarily break through. Breathing deeply, I quickly shelved the feelings of loss. I couldn't let myself think about it too much, it was too painful, and I blinked rapidly to clear the tears that had started to fill my eyes.

Mick reached forward and held out his hand. I offered my own, and he grasped it warmly, knowing my pain. "I miss her too," he said. "Anytime you want to talk, I'll be glad to listen."

I looked back into his eyes, sincere and genuine, and smiled weakly. "Thank you. I'll take you up on that one day." Now was not the time, and clearing my throat, I made myself focus on what I was here for.

"So, what's happening? Do you know anything? Dr Malicen is talking of developing an antidote in the next couple of days and saying every single person should take it. That's pretty scary if all this is fake?" I said, indicating all the papers lying on the table between us with a sweep of my hand. Mick put his head in his hands and rubbed his eyes. He looked up with one hand over his mouth, sighing deeply. When he spoke, his voice was quiet.

"Yes, I think something has been going on for a while. I don't know what, but all this you have shown me confirms my suspicions." He looked down and rubbed the back of one hand firmly with the other. The silence stretched out between us, and I remained quiet, not wanting to interrupt his train of thought as he pondered on past events.

When he looked up, his eyes flicked back and forth between mine, and he nodded a small, almost imperceivable nod to himself before speaking.

"Malicen has been acting very strange lately. He has been spending a lot of time on the lower second floor. Now, this has happened in the past when we have been very close to discovering a way to cure, or counter, a particular virus or disease, but usually all relevant departments and employees are involved." Mick lowered his voice and leaned closer to me, whispering. "It's known as the money room because once it's gone in there, the company is in for a sizeable windfall." He straightened up again, pointing his finger at me. "But this time," he continued, "we have all been kept out of the loop except three of his very trusted, close-knit colleagues who are appointed to advise the government."

"Is it possible to get in?" I asked, biting my lower lip.

"Well, it would be difficult. Access is only permitted via a DNA pass…"

"Ooh," I interrupted loudly, jumping out of my chair, my eyes wide. "I forgot to tell you. I had a sort of vision while I was in reception. It was only a second two, but it was of Kirsty handing a swab to Dr Malicen. You don't think it was mine, do you? He would have my DNA. What would he want with that?" I finished in a rush, breathing heavy. Mick stared at me. "I've lost the plot, haven't I?" I said, suddenly feeling like an idiot and collapsing back into the chair.

Mick continued to stare at me, open-mouthed, processing what I had just said. Then, pressing his lips together in a thin line, he looked at me determinedly and said,

"No, you definitely haven't." He stood and walked around the table to stand in front of me, and putting both his hands gently on my shoulders, he looked me straight in the eyes. His face softened.

"There are a lot of things I need to tell you about your mum, Haesel." He shook his head gently, and a smile touched the corners of his mouth. "You have the same traits and abilities, and I want you to know that I will always take seriously the things you say. You'll never look silly to me." He sighed and checked his watch. "Anyway, that's a long conversation for another day. Right now, I think we have to figure out how to get in that room."

"Really?" My skin prickled. "What, break in?" My breathing became fast and shallow. I didn't know if I was up for that. I would have to think about it first, work out all the scenarios, overthink it like I always did.

Mick smiled, "Don't worry," he said, seeing the panic on my face, "you won't be on your own, and I do work here, you know, so I'll find a way in."

We agreed to meet in a café down the street when Mick finished work in a couple of hours. I left the VialCorp building and walked the ten minutes down traffic-laden streets to the park. The green space renewed me. I could feel the oxygen emanating from the trees in the warm air and breathed in deeply. My thoughts turned to the events of the day, and I wondered what Malicen could be up to. Whatever it was, it felt sinister, and it left me with a wary, uneasy feeling that clung tightly in my chest.

Ahead I could see a weathered, wooden bench beneath the gently undulating leaves of a giant, ancient oak tree. I made my way over to it. The dappled shade was calming, and sitting down; I reached into my bag for my phone to call Eve.

"Ooh, are you going to break in?" she asked excitedly after I filled her in on what had happened. "God, I miss all the fun. Make sure you cover your face. Do be careful, Haesel. You might set the alarms off. Don't get arrested."

"Oh, Eve, you do make me laugh. I bet you're imagining some kind of mystery spy movie."

"Well, it sounds more exciting than - meanwhile, back at Eve's house," she said. I laughed, imagining her exaggerated eye roll. "I did find something out, though," she went on. "I was searching the internet for recent medical advances to see if there was any more information on the tablet Dr Malicen was talking about for the SACL virus. There wasn't, but last month VialCorp filed a patent on a new technology they call MagnanogenR4. Maybe you could ask Mick if he knows anything about that?"

"Okay, I'll ask him," I said, scrabbling in my bag for anything I could write the name on. I settled for a crumpled supermarket receipt. "I'll let you know if we find out anything later," I promised.

"You'd better. I'm not moving from this phone," Eve said.

After hanging up, I checked my messages. My spirits lifted when I saw Jay had messaged me. I clicked on his name and smiled as an image opened of him sitting cross-legged with his eyes closed, his hands turned upwards while resting on each knee. The message read, 'Hi Mum, I know you will be thinking of me. Just thought I'd let you know I'm fine, it's hard work here as you can see.' An animated smiley emoji did repeated grins at me. 'I'm thinking of you. Just remember, whatever happens later you'll be ok.' He finished with a kiss.

Whatever happens later? I questioned in my head, then reminded myself not to overthink this message. It will have been some spiritual teaching he was learning or one of his cryptic messages, I thought, and I found myself remembering earlier times. As a child, he would express what he had to say in an entirely different way to most children. Most of his sentences were born from emotion and feeling. Over the years, I had learnt how to decipher it...most of the time.

It was once he had embarked into the real world, from the cushioned school years, breathing exercises, and calming techniques, that he fell apart. This modern world just didn't seem to suit him. It was too fast, too angry, too anxious, and he couldn't compete with it. The autistic elements that made him the wonderful, extremely kind, gentle, almost naive person he was, backfired on him, along with his sensitivity to his own and others' emotions. He just couldn't process it, and he would quit the job he was in at the time and shut down.

Work colleagues and employers would see him as a person with 'problems,' not very PC I know, but that's the thing with political correctness. Being told to think of something in a certain way didn't necessarily mean you actually thought it was that way. However, he had surprised people a hundred times over with his intellect. Jay was extremely bright. His brain could work at lightning speed. He had easily worked his way through A Level Maths at thirteen. Then calculus and honours degrees, including degrees in psychology, all within half the time it should have taken, but it was the emotional pressure in the jobs he went for that stopped him. Having read the studies Thea had published, he then read a study by a Harvard neuroscientist who had found that meditation can actually change the structure and thicken the cortex of your brain to help with emotion. Completely out of the blue, he drew out some of the money left to him by Thea and took himself off to India to study and research meditation and yoga practices.

I sent him a reply. 'Lovely to see you relaxing. All good here, and yes, of course I was thinking of you. (Heart emoji) Love and miss you, Mum x'

I checked the time, 4.30 p.m. As much as I would like to sit here all day, I thought, enjoying the gentle whispering of the leaves wafting the sweet, fresh smell of the long grass in my direction, I'd better get going.

Corner Café was fresh, bright, and practical. Pale yellow tablecloths were placed on the diagonal over the simple wooden tables, each one displaying a small glass vase of fresh white carnations and gypsophila. The matching chairs had padded seat covers in the same material and made the place look cosy and homely. I suddenly realised how hungry I was and ordered a panini with my skinny latte. Mick walked in just as I was getting seated at a sunny table tucked in the corner by the window. He waved, went to grab his coffee, then sat down opposite.

'Right," he said, "we haven't got long. I persuaded Chris, the security guard on the car park doors, to go home early. I've known him for years and told him I would be there working late, so I would check out with the next guy when he comes in at 7 p.m. So," he checked his watch, "we'd better drink up and go, I think."

A few minutes later, we were on our way, walking the longer way around to approach the VialCorp building from the back. The car park was almost empty, and we hurried into the elevator. Once inside, I had a thought. "What about the cameras?" I asked, remembering the monitor in the reception.

"I can turn them off from the tech room, next floor up," said Mick, swiping his pass in front of the elevator sensor and pushing the button for Ground Floor. "I have a pass to get us everywhere except the 'Money Room,' so, just before closing, I nipped into the canteen kitchen and told Audrey I had a craving for some more of those nice biscuits they put out for guests. I think she has a soft spot for me," he said, grinning and nudging my arm with his elbow. I grinned back. "While she was off getting me a new packet from the cupboard," he continued, "I grabbed Julius' coffee mug out of the dishwasher, swabbed it and made a pass." I stood gawping at him while he grinned smugly back at me.

"Ooh, nice, you really thought it through, didn't you? I'm impressed, but how did you know what mug was his?"

Mick threw his head back and laughed. "Well, that was easy. Julius' ego is pretty big, so his is the mug with the cartoon caricature of himself, and the words 'Trust me, I'm a Doctor' written on it." We both fell about laughing.

The elevator stopped with a small jolt, and a mechanical female voice said, "Ground floor, doors opening." Mick beckoned me closer to him and put one finger on his lips, miming for me to be quiet. We peered out of the sliding doors and dashed to a set of double doors across the hall. Once inside the room, Mick flicked the switches to turn off the cameras, then we hopped quickly back into the elevator. The mechanical female voice announced, "Lower second floor," and then said, "Security clearance required." Mick scanned Malicen's pass, and the lift replied, "Clearance denied."

I took a sharp breath in. "Oh no, it didn't work!" My heart started racing, expecting alarms to sound any minute. Mick looked at the pass and rolled his eyes at me, taking out another pass from his pocket and holding it up.

"Wrong one," he said, tutting and giving a little shake of his head.

"For God's sake, Mick, I'm sweating here!" He shrugged and pulled a wry expression.

"Sorry."

The lower second floor was not decorated as nicely with plain white walls and polished concrete floors. We walked down the corridor until Mick indicated a room on the right. The doors were solid grey metal with no windows, making it impossible to sneak a look in. Once Mick swiped the pass, the door made heavy clunking sounds as a series of bolts slid back into their housing. We looked at each other nervously, then pushed the doors open.

The room was huge, more like a warehouse, and I marvelled at the size of it. A third of the way in sat an immense twelve seat conference table, looking out of place in the stark surroundings. Workbenches lined both sides and were adorned with various pieces of technical and very expensive looking equipment. Behind those were large filing cabinets.

"Mick?" He turned to look at me as I pulled my phone from my bag and looked on my notes for the name of the product Eve had told me about. "Do you know anything about MagnanogenR4?"

The corners of Mick's mouth turned down, and he shook his head, frowning. "No, it doesn't mean anything to me. What is it? How do you know about it?"

"Oh, a friend has been digging around on the internet and found VialCorp had filed a patent for it last month."

"Really?" Mick said, rubbing his jaw. "Which friend is this?"

"Oh, just my friend Anna," I lied. I didn't want to bring Eve into this and risk her getting into any trouble. Briefly, I wondered why he needed to know which friend, then discarded the thought. Heading across the room towards the far cabinets, I quickly added, "Shall we take a look in these and see what we can find?"

The cabinet drawers were conveniently labelled, and I pulled out a drawer with '*MAG4*' written on it and hauled out a handful of papers. "Here," I said. My eyes scanned over them quickly, and I stuffed them into the waistband of my jeans to read later. I glanced over at Mick, who was opening drawers further up, and as I did so, I noticed a red light flash behind him towards the door. I gasped loudly,

"Mick, there's a camera still on. You can't have turned them all off?"

I had hardly spoken the words when the door opened, and in walked Dr Malicen with a burly security guard. The guard closed and locked the doors then placed himself squarely in front of them. I stood rooted to the spot, my heart racing. Malicen gave a thin-lipped smile that tried and failed to look friendly.

"Well, well, and what might you be doing in here? Haesel, isn't it? Thea's daughter, if I'm not mistaken?" His eyes narrowed and pinned me with a look that sent a chill racing through every cell in my body.

His eyes flicked to look at Mick, and he gave a quick nod. Mick glanced at me, hesitating. His expression looked torn, and his eyes said sorry. Then with a small shake of his head, he walked over to the wall next to the cabinets, where there were four large levers. Mick pulled the first two swiftly downward into their locked position.

"Mick", I called out.

He paused briefly, but he didn't answer. My ears started to ring, and I grimaced. The third lever went down, and a sharp pain shot through my head as a loud crackling and buzzing sound came from behind me. I put my hands to my head and turned, gaping, open-mouthed at the sight before me.

Two thick, ceiling-high poles were placed ten yards apart with hundreds of wires attached to them, leading to huge computers stations on either side. The computer lights were flashing erratically, and an LCD screen displayed a series of shaky lines that reminded me of a heart monitor. Between the poles, the air undulated and shimmered, making the wall behind it blur and giving it a liquid quality while a loud electrical buzzing sound resonated around the room.

How did I not see this when I came in? I thought, turning towards Mick. He held up a hand and started to walk towards me. I was about to run to him when he said.

"Haesel, just stay calm and let me explain. Nothing bad is going to happen."

I stopped dead. "What? What's going on?"

"The last switch, now Jenkins!" shouted Malicen through gritted teeth.

"No. Mick!" I cried out, backing slowly away as Malicen turned and walked towards me.

"Quickly Jenkins," growled Malicen, quickening his pace. His mean eyes were fixed on mine, his fists clenched in determination. I glanced at Mick, who hesitated, and I could see the conflict play out on his face, then he turned and pulled the lever.

Several things happened at once. A searing pain shot through my body, and the undulating, humming wall thickened and swam in and out like a stormy sea. Malicen shouted to me, "Just stay calm, Haesel. We need to talk about this… I just want to talk, that's all," and he quickened his pace across the room towards me, his white coat billowing behind him.

The buzzing was getting louder, and I backed away from him. To my horror, he drew a syringe from his pocket and adrenalin coursed through my blood as my body got ready to run.

Mick was edging towards me. His eyes looked pleadingly at me while he beckoned me with his hand. The undulating wall of air behind me shot out an almost invisible bolt of energy, which tore across the room at lightning speed straight at him. It hit with a loud crack and lifted him off his feet as he flew backwards, landing in a crumpled heap.

I screamed, "Mick!" He was crunched over in a ball on the floor, groaning. He lifted his head slowly towards me, then looking at Malicen, he summoned the last of his energy and shouted, "Grab her Julius!" before collapsing.

I gasped in shock, my mind racing, confused. What did he mean?

'Mick!" I yelled again. Was he dead? Turning to Malicen, I saw his face was fixed on mine with a look of fear, awe, and something else that I knew instinctively was sinister. It was the something else that scared me the most, and my intuition screamed at me to get out. I gritted my teeth and felt a surge of something unfamiliar take over my body. I put out my hands to shield myself from Malicen, who was now running straight at me, and the energy from the forcefield behind me tore through me and out through my hands. The invisible shield spread out, the thickened air blurring my view of him, and crackles of gold flashed erratically across the space. Malicen stopped dead in his tracks. I could see him, slightly blurry and distorted through the forcefield, sweat running down his face, fighting to get to me. His face contorted with rage and effort, but somehow, I was keeping him where he was.

I can't hold him for long, I thought, shaking with the effort. I felt like I was being squeezed by invisible arms. The pressure around me was immense. Then everything in the room started moving away from me. It took me a few seconds to realise that it was actually me that was moving backwards. I was getting pulled into the energy field. I screamed out and tried to resist. A voice that seemed to come from behind but also inside my head whispered, *Haesel, let go.*

A calm fell like a veil over my entire body as I let out all the air in my lungs, then gave in. I could see the room get smaller and smaller. I was being crushed and couldn't breathe. My last image was of Malicen leaping forward in one final effort to grab me. Then it all disappeared, and everything went black.

6

I opened my eyes. I didn't recognise my surroundings. The room I found myself in was small and dimly lit by a single candle. All the furniture was wooden and rustic. A wall of shelves housed glass bottles and jars of different coloured liquids and powders, all neat and precisely labelled. Lifting my head slowly, I turned to see that I was lying on a bed in one corner of the room. Next to me on a low stool was a cup of orange coloured liquid. A slight movement across the room caught my eye, and I made out the shadowed outline of a figure. Panic overtook me. A flashback of what had happened at VialCorp played out in my head at lightning speed, as I realised at the same time that I was not alone. I tried to get up, and pain shot through my head and ricocheted through my body. The room began to tremor and shake, and the figure stood up. I tried again to rise, the panic increasing. Items in the room fell over, and jars crashed to the floor from the shelves as the ground shook like an earthquake.

"You must stay calm, Haesel," said the figure rushing towards me. "Don't be afraid, sweetheart."

Haesel

All my breath left my body in a rush as I gaped open-mouthed in shock, recognising the voice at the same time as she knelt down in front of me. Lifting my hand in hers, she removed the hood from her head. The light from the candle illuminated her face and her now long silver-grey hair. The room stopped shaking as my eyes filled with tears and spilt over, rolling in symmetrical rivers down my cheeks.

"Mum," I croaked as my voice broke. Ignoring the pain, I threw my arms around her and clung on for dear life, my body shaking from the heaving, erratic sobs.

"I'm so sorry, Haesel," she said, squeezing me tight. "I've missed you so much." Tears streamed down her face to match mine, and my chest jerked in heaving, stuttering sobs. When she tried to release her arms to let go, I grabbed her even harder.

"No, don't let go, not yet. I don't want to wake up," I cried, and we held on to each other until our tears ran out.

"Haesel, it's ok. I'm not going anywhere. I promise. I'm really here." She drew back to look at me, but I kept my hold on her all the same, gripping the material of her cloak. It felt real in my hand. My head wouldn't work this out. All I knew was that I didn't want to disrupt it and cause it to stop. "Drink this," she said, reaching out with one arm and picking up the cup from the stool. "It will heal the pain of coming through and help stop your emotions from escalating too much. You need to be able to take in what I'm going to tell you."

I drank the sweet liquid and felt myself relax. The pain in my head and body disappeared almost immediately. I put the cup down and wiped my mouth with my hand. My other hand relaxed a little on her clothing but still maintained contact.

"Wow," I stammered, "you should sell that."

Thea smiled and leaned over to kiss me on the forehead.

My mind had lost some of its fogginess, and I now had a million questions.

"You said coming through?" I moved my head to look at her sideways, then looked around the room. "Where are we? The accident? You died. Mum? And wh—"

"Shhhh," she soothed gently, holding up her hand, cutting me off. She took a big breath in, letting it out in a long sigh. "Okay, get ready. What I'm about to tell you is going to be hard for you to take in, but it's true and real, and I'm going to be here to help you."

Pressing her lips together in a thin line, her subconscious not wanting to let the words out, she looked up pensively and took hold of both my hands, gripping them firmly. "You're in another world, Haesel, on a different plane to the one we know, in another realm that exists alongside."

I stared at her with a slack jaw. I'm definitely dreaming this, I thought, and I sat back, releasing the tension in my shoulders, happy to let the dream play out.

"You came through a portal," she continued, "or rather, I pulled you through. This world is called Alchemia. It's a world of magic, and you can only come through if you have magical abilities." She looked at me, holding her breath, waiting for me to respond.

The serious expression on her face made it worse, and I burst into peals of laughter. "Oh my god, now I know I'm dreaming. I couldn't make that up if I tried." I said, in between fits of giggles. "Go on then, do some magic..." I was suddenly brought up sharp as a pain shot through my arm. "Ow,' I cried out, "What was that?"

"I pinched you," Thea said. "Sorry, but you would have woken up if this was a dream. As hard as it is for you to believe this right now, it's absolutely true." She moved to sit beside me as she continued.

"Your powers are in your emotions, your intuition, and in all of nature. You are a herbalist for a reason, and you have the ability to draw to you the elements you need, down to the smallest pollen grains and molecules, extracting the most potent ingredients from the trees and plants and magnifying their powers. You simply have to learn to train your mind to focus." This time I was listening, open-mouthed.

"You're serious?" I stated and questioned at the same time.

"Yes, I am, and I'm going to teach you. Now that you have come through to this world, it has unlocked key parts of your brain that cannot function in our Earthly realm. There are over one hundred parts of the cortex that are inactive, and scientists are still continuously trying to find out what they do. Well…," she paused, "I now know what a few more of them do, as I was using myself as a test subject. This is what I was working on for a new study when…" She broke off and looked down, biting her lip.

"When the accident happened," I said.

She shook her head gently, and when she looked up, there was pain in her eyes. "When I faked my death," she said quietly, dropping her gaze. I gasped, and fresh tears spilled down my cheeks once again.

"What?" I stammered. Jumping up I spun round to face her, my eyes wide with shock. "You did it deliberately?" My voice rose to a higher pitch. "How could you do that?" The liquid I had drank earlier was no match for the strength of this emotion.

"It wasn't like that, I…"

"Oh no," I cut in, holding out my hand, my heart rate increasing as my anger quickly escalated. "There's no excuse with this one," I shook my head continuously as I spoke and paced back and forth across the room. "You could definitely have told me, warned me somehow." I clenched my fists and shot her a look. She flinched and looked away.

"I was devastated," I continued, "the kids were devastated, they cried for weeks, and Rowan stopped eating with the shock. I re-lived the accident over and over in my head and thought of nothing else for months on end. Did you even think of me at all?"

Thea seemed to shrink as her whole body drooped, and I watched a tear roll down her cheek. "You were all I was thinking about," she said in a quiet voice.

I scoffed in reply, and an ache grew in my chest. "I sat for hours at the church, wishing I could see you, staring at the flowers in front of your…," my chin wobbled, and I sucked in a ragged breath as hot tears burned my eyes and my face crumpled. The memory quenched my anger, immediately replacing it with renewed sadness.

She rushed to fold me in her arms, and I gave in and let her. Maintaining her hold on me, she spoke over my shoulder, "It was the hardest decision I have ever had to make to leave you." I could feel her pain merging with mine and let my tears fall, too exhausted to think. When they abated, she drew back, lifting a wet strand of hair from my face where it had stuck to my tear-stained cheek. Her eyes searched mine for understanding.

"I had to act fast, I was called here, and there wasn't time to prepare. Malicen was on to me, and I was putting this world at great risk to stay on Earth."

The candle sputtered, and the flame fought to continue its struggle for life as the waxy, molten sea closed in around it.

Thea walked to retrieve another from a drawer, lighting it quickly before the light died. Turning back to me, she continued. "I came here to protect you. I'm certain that he would have killed me had I stayed, and then you would have been in grave danger. He is a devious, powerful man Haesel. His greed is out of control and it has taken hold of him. He will stop at nothing to get what he wants. This is why you are being called on now. It's known as waking, and it's your fate."

That worried me. My mind, in its battered state, switched back and forth and turned to overthinking. Cautious and considered, that was me, doubt crept in along with denial… but there it was, an underlying feeling that countered it all. I just knew what she was saying was right because deep in the centre of my being, I felt it.

But that didn't mean I welcomed it. It always seemed to be that in the past, people had just, well…presented things to me to sort out, and if that thing happened to contain an injustice, then there was a part of me that took over that was stronger than I realised. I had an uncontrollable need to correct an injustice, and in those circumstances, I seemed to become another person, and I did whatever it took. That was the part that fired my strength, gave me courage and dispelled my fears. But this? No.

I looked straight into her eyes and shook my head firmly. "No, that's not for me, you can do it, you're already here and have loads more experience than me, plus you know Malicen better and…" I stopped talking as she looked back at me shaking her head, her lips drawn into a thin line.

"I can't, it's not my purpose." She held out open hands, her shoulders hunched. "Our paths are set, and my abilities are now hampered by my experiences. I was meant to use my knowledge to help and heal others, to discover the full potential of our brains. This could help humans in years to come in so many ways, and the portal to another world can bring its own learning and healing but…where there is good, there is also bad. Malicen will bring unprecedented harm for his own gain…" she reached to hold my shoulders firmly, "but you will stop him."

"No, I said matter-of-factly. "No, I can't, I just can't.

That's too much. I'm not magic. I don't know what to do. It's ridiculous!" My voice rose, and I shook my head in continual confirmation of my statements.

Thea reached out and cupped my face in her hands.

"All the signs were there already, Haesel. You heard my voice when I was trying to contact you. You felt my presence. When I tried to reach you the third time, you were afraid, and your fear slowed time itself, and that's why I couldn't reach you. That's an immensely strong power for someone to have who hadn't come through yet, and your full potential is yet to be unlocked. You are a very powerful witch already, and you are needed."

"Witch!" I exclaimed. "Oh, this is too much. No." The plethora of emotions I had just gone through was taking its toll. I still wasn't entirely sure this was real, and now I was wishing this really was a dream and thinking how much I really wanted to wake up. "No." There was a sick feeling in my stomach, and I felt light-headed, and my breathing was coming in shallow bursts. A pain shot through my head at the back of my eyes, and I could feel a force ignite within and tear through my body.

"Haesel, you're panicking. It's the shock, it's a lot to take in. Look at me. You're safe, it's okay," Thea said, grabbing my arms.

The feeling intensified. I couldn't breathe. All the items in the room started to move away from me and were forced against the wall. Everything shook, and the shelves rejected their neatly labelled jars onto the floor. Adrenalin surged. A crack appeared, snaking its way across the floor. I couldn't stop it.

Thea was pinned to the wall along with everything else. She held out her hands and shouted to me, but I couldn't hear what she was saying as my ears filled with a high-pitched ringing. A crackling yellow light formed between her palms, and she brought them together with a deafening boom. Light flashed as bright as the sun as she sent forth the crackling, spitting magic in my direction. I held up my hand automatically against it and gasped to see a glowing white light emanating from its centre. Pins and needles tingled through my fingers as Thea's light ran around me in a circle and I realised in that instant, that I was shielded from it. I had protected myself with some kind of forcefield. I looked to Thea, who was grimacing, teeth gritted, with the effort.

I watched, stunned, as the scene played out before me. Frozen with shock, my eyes returned to Thea. Her face was red, straining with the effort to reach me, her mouth was moving and after a few seconds I made out the words *let go*. I let out a long breath and concentrated on clearing my mind of all thoughts. The crackling golden light slowly tore small holes in my protection and ate its way in. With it came calm and a feeling of safety. My wall of fear melted around me, and I slumped to the floor. *It's true,* I thought as realisation dawned. *All of this is true. I am a witch.*

I felt drained, the panic of before now gone. My mind was so overwhelmed with all that was happening I couldn't even hold a thought. Thea came to sit beside me and pulled me close.

"It's okay.' she said, and I knew that it was, even though I had no idea how. I looked at her face—serene, strong, and steady. "You will get stronger," she continued, "and everything will fall into place. I'll be here to do this with you."

A shard of dawn sunlight found its way through a gap in the window shutters, and lit the flecks of green that now sparkled in her brown eyes. I had no voice. No words came.

"Always remember that you were destined for this," Thea continued. "If you think back, there were signs, little things that showed themselves in your intuition. Things that pointed to it that you discounted with logic and reason. This is what humans do, and it keeps our senses dull and suppressed." She shrugged her shoulders in a dismissive manner. "The fact you were never sick and always healed extremely quickly for one."

My mind flashed back to a moment in time when I was around nine years old. It was a hot day in July, and I had climbed up high into the aged horse chestnut tree in our garden to catch the small breeze amongst the shady, gently fluttering leaves. I leaned out over a branch, shouting for Mum to look how high I had climbed. Then I lost my balance and fell, smashing my shin on the branch below before hitting the hard, dry earth with a definite thud. The pain had been extreme, but only for a few minutes. Mum had covered the area with her hands, reassuring me that it would be okay. When the pain stopped I dared to look, and could see blood and torn fabric, but when I rolled up my trouser leg, there was only a livid red line and the remnants of bruising. I rubbed my shin, remembering and turned to look at Thea, my brow furrowed with the understanding of all the things that now made sense.

Thea stood and brushed herself off. Holding out her hand, she pulled me up next to her. A small smile tugged at the corners of her mouth as she glanced down at my leg then back up at me. "Not that I let you see at the time, but your shin bone had completely snapped and was sticking through the skin." My jaw slackened, and I gawped at her. "You got stronger as you grew older," she said, walking over to pick up any jars and other items that hadn't broken, and put them back in their rightful places. "Any sickness only lasted a day, or overnight at most, and all colds and illness stopped having any effect on you once you turned thirteen, as your body countered it before it took hold." I went to join her and bent to collect the broken glass of the jars that didn't make it.

"Sorry," I muttered, breathing in the heady aroma of their contents that permeated from the floor.

She waved my apology away, shaking her head. "It's nothing. I have plenty and don't be sorry for your powers, ever. They are an amazing gift to be nurtured and honoured." Her eyes twinkled with knowing as she added, "It's not all bad, you know. Most of it is amazing and very rewarding."

"What did I just do?" I asked, still feeling dazed.

She shrugged like it was nothing. "Protected yourself. Your emotions are strong, but you'll learn to control them."

Had I known? I thought, skipping through memories like a series of photographs. Yes, there had been signs, many signs, and many more once Mum had gone, but I had found a way to counter them every time. The pain of loss an inhibiting protective shroud on my senses.

"Are you hungry?" Thea asked, and I suddenly realised that I was starving.

"Yes, very."

She walked to the window behind me and opened the shutters letting warm sunlight stream in, instantly banishing every dark corner and shadow.

"What time is it?" I asked suddenly. Thea glanced at a small clock that was sat on a shelf at the end of a stack of books.

"A little before 6 a.m."

"Oh no! I've got to get back. Eve will be calling the police. I was supposed to call her!"

"It's okay," Thea said. "Time in this world runs faster than back on Earth. It doesn't feel like it when you're here, but I've worked out that a day here only takes between one or two hours back home." She shrugged. "Sometimes there's a surge which increases it a bit. I guess it's not an exact science."

I exhaled loudly, and Thea grinned at me. "That's why it

hit you so hard, coming through this first time, your powers weren't strong yet, and the journey through time and planes is not for the faint-hearted. You can't do it as an adolescent witch unless originating from here, and a normal human wouldn't survive it."

I took a deep breath, relieved that I didn't have to cope with leaving here so soon. As crazy and mind-blowing as this all was, a part of me was also curious and itching to find out more. I looked around the room and saw that the bed I had been on was actually a large sofa. All the furniture was wooden, and the floor was laid with small grey tiles. Some had lifted and scattered where my energy from earlier had driven through them. The walls were plain and greyish-green in colour. They looked like clay that had been rubbed smooth, and every so often, there was a wooden beam that divided it into smaller sections. The ceiling was vaulted and beamed also. A table and chair sat across from the sofa, and a series of papers and scribbled notes were neatly piled up next to labelled bottles whose contents I couldn't make out.

"Is this where you live all the time?" I asked.

"Yes, this is it." Thea pointed to a door. "There's another small bedroom through there. It's very simple, but I like it. Come on, let's go into the kitchen, and I'll get us some food." I followed her through a narrow corridor into a very simple kitchen. A wooden worktop and cupboards lined the back wall and to my right was a tall clay chimney that disappeared through the roof. Beneath it a flat grate on legs stood over an open fire. A table and chair fitted perfectly to the left-hand side of the room.

"Grab the chair by the desk from the other room, would you? Sorry, I'm not used to visitors, but, having said that, you are definitely the best visitor I have ever had." Her smile stretched wide across her face, and her eyes were soft with unspoken affection. She walked over to fold me in a tight, warm embrace. "I'm so glad you're here," she whispered into my hair.

"Me too, so much," I replied, and swallowed the lump in my throat as I went to retrieve the chair. As I walked, I felt something scratching my waist and pulled out the documents I had taken from the lab. I placed them on the desk, making a mental note to discuss them with her later.

Back in the kitchen, I sat down and looked at her properly for the first time. This is my mum, I thought, *but not the mum I remember.* She looked different, surprisingly younger, and she had a relaxed, sure confidence about her.

"You look really good, Mum," I said. "Actually, you look about the same age as me, even with the grey hair…" I hesitated, feeling awkward. "I don't know why, but it feels a little weird calling you Mum. I mean, you look so different, and being here, and I said goodbye to you…" My words trailed off, and I lowered my head, looking at the table. "I know you're still my mum, and I still love you the same and everything," I added hastily. 'It's just… I need some time to adjust to all this."

She turned to look at me, nodding. "It's okay, I understand," she said, walking over to me and kissing me on the forehead. "This world renews you, and all the healing and regenerating powers are absorbed into our bodies, so I do look very different. Just call me Thea if you like. We both know how much we love each other. That will never change, so it's fine."

"Okay. Thanks…sorry, this is all just so weird for me." I closed my eyes and rubbed my face with my hands. "I'm just trying to get my head around it."

"I know," she said quietly. "I've missed you so much, the kids too. I hope I can see them again one day…but I can't go into that right now." She took a shuddering breath and looked up to the ceiling blinking away the tears that were trying to surface. Then, going to retrieve the plates from the side, she placed some salad and bread on the table in front of me and sat down. "Right," she said, having gathered her thoughts. "We're here now, and that's got to be a good thing, so eat up. Then I'll take you outside and show you around this world."

7

I stepped through the door and looked at the world that would be my new second home. It was breathtaking.

"Wow, it's absolutely beautiful." My eyes slowly absorbed my surroundings, drinking in the vibrant array of colour and the voluptuous freshness of a truly healthy world. I could feel the serenity and peacefulness of it work its way into every fibre of my being, and I couldn't stop the smile that spread widely across my face. I took a deep breath. The air smelt amazing, pure and clean. The blue sky was such an intense colour it gave off an indigo hue.

My eyes swept across the land that rolled gently with small hills and dips, filled with lush flora and fauna. Pockets of woodland interspersed the terrain and grew in its density, until it turned into a forest on the other side of the valley. I picked out a couple of structures some distance away that looked like dwellings and turned to Thea, pointing them out to her.

"Are they houses? Are there other people here?"

"Yes, some, but not many, sadly. Most generations have died out. Our line is the strongest, and it needed protecting, so our name was changed to Greenwood by our ancestors in the fifteenth century."

"What was it before?" I asked.

"Wiccan." Thea smiled at me. "We are direct descendants from the original Wiccan witches." Her face beamed, "come on, let's walk, and I'll tell you as we go."

We set off walking together when Thea reached out and got hold of my arm to stop me. "Oh, you'll need to take your shoes off," she said.

"What? Why? I'll hurt my feet," I protested, shaking my head a little in irritation.

"Haesel," Thea came to stand in front of me and looked me in the eye. "The first thing you have to do from this moment on is to trust me when I tell you something. You are in a magic realm now. Everything in this world is interlinked. The trees and plants feed the soil and give it an immensely powerful cocktail of very potent, active ingredients. As a witch, you have the ability to connect to this energy through your feet. This is what activates your powers and connects you. It's known as grounding, like an initiation."

I stared at her as she spoke, my eyes growing wider by the second. "Will it hurt?" I asked.

She laughed, then stopped abruptly. "Sorry, I forget just how innocent you are to all this, and no, it doesn't hurt," she stated sincerely, but her eyes still held an excited sparkle of anticipation.

I sat down on the ground and took off my trainers and socks. Placing both feet on the soil, I stood up quickly, bracing myself. The soles of my feet tingled and felt warm, but that was it. I must have looked disappointed because Thea laughed again.

"It's gradual, not like a thunderbolt out of the blue."

"Oh," I replied, feeling as disheartened as I obviously looked. If my destiny is to be a witch, I thought, then I hope it gets a bit more exciting than this. I took a few steps. "Ooh, that feels weird. I can't actually feel the ground. It sort of feels soft?" I questioned, looking to Thea for answers.

"Yes," she said, squeezing her hands together excitedly. "The energy flows between you and the ground, giving a cushioning effect. That said, you can't go bouncing off things without feeling it, and sharp items will still push through if done with force. Let's walk for a while, and you should start to feel the transformation take effect."

We set off through the lush, vivid landscape, and Thea talked of our heritage.

"Wiccan is the ancient art of witchcraft," she began, "and witchcraft was always the art of taking what nature has given us and using it to heal whether grinding seeds or boiling leaves, nuts, bark, and flowers together to make teas or a poultice, or in order to heal wounds, cure coughs and illness, ease stomach upsets or headaches, etc. To do good and harmonise all living things."

I looked at her, my mouth falling open as I took in what she said. "So, the fact I went into herbalism fits perfectly then?"

"Yes," she said, nodding thoughtfully, looking at the ground ahead of her as we walked.

"It will have been intuitive and instinctive. Genetic even?" She glanced across at me then gave a small shrug. "You just didn't realise it was in your subconscious at the time."

Thea continued to tell of what had happened as we walked through the widest range of plant species I had ever seen in one place, most of which I recognised, but some, I had never seen before. Her shoulders drooped a little as the conversation took a sombre turn. "As you probably touched on in school, witches were persecuted heavily during the fifteenth to the late seventeenth century, throughout the period of the Reformation. Individuals turned on their fellow human beings resulting in the greatest slaughter outside of war. Up to 100,000 witches burned, drowned, or hung...all for trying to help or heal others."

"Yes, I do remember learning about that," I said. There was a silence as we walked. The horrors of what I remembered played out in my mind. Now that I was a witch, the sad realisation of it appeared even more sickeningly abhorrent.

"People fear what they do not understand," Thea said with a deep sigh. "All witches hold a special ability to harness and increase what nature provides, which is not easily explained or understood, especially not in the fifteenth century. Genetically we are different, and humans tend to create division when faced with differences." She shrugged again and looked at me with raised eyebrows and a small sideways smile.

"Yes," I said. "Although I can understand that in those times, it must have appeared frightening for some."

"How do you feel?" Thea asked, glancing down at my feet. I hadn't been paying attention to how I felt, but now I looked at her, my eyes wide with excitement.

"Great," I said, smiling. "No, really, really great, actually. I feel strong, and I don't ache at all." I bent my knees and straightened up again a few times, and clenched my fists. The feeling was weird, like energy was flowing within me, a connection to the world and all that was in it. I felt more able, and there was something else. *What was it? I thought... Yes, that was it. More powerful.*

Thea turned to me. "Good," she said. "Now, let's test it. Imagine that you need to heal a wound. Close your eyes and think of the herbs you would need." I did as she asked, biting my lip nervously at not knowing what to expect.

"Now," she continued. "Hold out one hand, palm up, and concentrate on those ingredients." I followed her instructions again and focused. I could pick out a wide variety of individual scents, and they were sharp and defined.

My hand felt warm, and there was a strange, pulling sensation. It tingled like a million tiny needles were prickling all over. I opened my eyes and gasped. My hand was glowing with an iridescent white light. It was extremely bright, spreading out in a circle above my hand, white sparks crackling and jumping in all directions. In the centre of my palm, minuscule grains were forming a small pile of greenish-brown dust. The light subsided, and I stood staring at my hand. Thea bent forwards and, lifting her trouser leg, took out a knife from a holder strapped to her leg. Before I knew what was happening, she had cut a large gash across the back of her forearm. Blood gushed forth and spilled into the fertile ground, where it was instantly absorbed and disappeared.

I stepped back as my mouth falling open in shock. "What are you doing?"

She held up her hand to silence me. "Control your emotions. Your energy will be clouded by them. You can learn to use them later in order to increase the power of your actions, but for now, you have to think of healing. Sprinkle the powder over the wound and place both your hands, palm down, over the top. Leave a small gap between the wound and your hands, and then think of the action you require. Imagine the cells mending and knitting together."

I followed exactly. My hands felt extremely hot and the light crackled and sparked beneath my palms, reminding me of popping candy, before slowly fading. When I removed them, there was no sign of the livid red gash. It had completely healed, not even a scar.

"Oh my god," I exclaimed, "it's gone. That's amazing." I stared at her open-mouthed.

"It feels good, right?" she asked, grinning back at me.

"Oh, it's way better than good. I love this!" I said with a

squeal, grinning from ear to ear, "although I think I may get hung myself, albeit in modern terms, if I offered this treatment in my shop."

"Watch out," said Thea suddenly, grabbing my arm and pulling me closer to her. I heard it before I saw it—a series of clicking, tutting noises. Wind rushed past me and knocked my arm. It circled me, then rushed back and forth with great speed. The creature shimmered and undulated, blending into the background of everything it passed. My eyes focused and followed it, but I couldn't keep up. I was only able to make out a rough outline as it jumped and dashed about. Suddenly a pair of playful black eyes appeared right in front of me, blinking and looking straight into mine. I cried out and stepped back in surprise, hovering behind Thea, who, to add to my confusion, started laughing.

"Come on, that's not fair," she chided, a smile dancing on her lips. "Show yourself and say hello."

The creature clicked and tutted again and did another round of dashing about before coming to a stop a couple of yards in front of us. A thin, stick-like creature around a yard tall slowly materialised into view. It could well have been a small shrub or tree at first glance, but as it walked towards us, I could see that the illusion was just the clever pigment colouring of its skin. Its lithe form moved with effortless ease and suppleness towards us, hardly making a sound. It eyed me cautiously, keeping its eyes fixed on mine as it moved to hide behind Thea, grabbing the bottom of her shirt in its hand and holding it up to its nose. It rubbed it comfortingly between its palm and thumb while peering out at me from behind the safety of her body.

Thea put one arm around the creature, drawing it close. "This is Noi," she said, smiling at me. "He's a Stiknean, and he's a young one, known as a Stikling. Noi, this is Haesel.

She's my daughter, my child." Thea patted her chest and held out her hand lower to the floor when she said, 'My child.'

Noi looked at me, his eyes twinkling with curiosity. He tilted his head to the side like he was trying to work out if I was anything to be worried about or not.

Now over my initial unease, I knelt down to be less threatening. "Hello Noi, I'm Haesel, and I'm very pleased to meet you. Do you think you can show me that amazing thing you do when you blend with your surroundings? I would love to do that. If you show me, do you think I could do it?"

Noi looked up at Thea and made a series of clicks and tutting sounds. To my utter amazement, Thea responded the same way.

"Wow, can you speak their language?" I asked, my eyes wide. "That's brilliant."

"Well," she said, "only very basically, and it's taken me a long time to learn. It's a bit like morse code but more dots and dashes." She grinned.

Noi said something to Thea, and she gave a couple of clicks and nodded to him, grinning.

She turned to me. "Noi thinks that would be a great game, and he wants to see if you can tell where he is," she said. "Young Stiklings are very playful, and this will be a good test of your intuition. Try and feel where he is. Everything has its own energy that moves the energy around it, so try and home in on that feeling."

Noi dropped Thea's shirt and took a step towards me. He had the most mischievous little grin on his face. A few sprouting leaves on his head started twitching this way and that, and the patches of tiny leaves that covered the outside of his arms, legs, and torso rippled up and down. He was clearly excited to be playing a game. Then he disappeared.

I strained my eyes for the smallest movement, but he was

gone. Then a couple of clicks and a poke in my side told me where he was. I gasped, surprised.

"Right," I said, laughing. "I'll find you next time." Again and again, he won the game.

"You're using your eyes," Thea said. "Close them and feel."

I did as she said, and my senses focused. It was as though I could see better without looking. I felt where the distorted energy was and followed it as it circled around me, closing in, bit by bit, until... "Got you!" I shouted, diving to my right. My hands encircled his little body, and we fell to the floor. He gave a small high-pitched shriek and instantly appeared.

"I win!" I shouted triumphantly and tickled his tummy, resulting in a musical array of purring noises that was just the sweetest of sounds.

"He's laughing," Thea said grinning, and came over to join us. "That was brilliant," she said, smiling down at me. "You got that on your first try." Her face lit up with pride. I smiled back.

"I could see it quite clearly when I wasn't looking," I said, laughing back, shaking my head in wonder and more than a little disbelief. I sat up in a squat and turned to Noi smiling, holding out my hands. "Come, I'll pull you up, little one." Noi sprang to his feet, then looked at my outstretched hands as I stood. He looked at his own hands, then looked up at my face intently and reeled off a few clicks and low whispers.

"Sorry, I don't understand," I said, giving a small shake of my head and shrugging my shoulders. I turned to Thea, who looked puzzled, her eyebrows pinched into a frown.

"I didn't quite understand that either, sorry," she said, giving a small shrug back at me. Noi turned and looked up to his left. He spoke again, gazing intently into an enormous ancient cedar tree whose horizontal branches swept fronds of grey-green needles downwards in majestic waves, the lowest of which hovered just above the ground, like nurturing arms offering comfort and shelter.

The branches shook and shivered, sending wafts of the most heavenly, fresh aromatic scent towards us on the breeze it generated. Then part of the tree seemed to separate from the rest and stepped forwards, materialising into a much larger version of Noi, around twenty feet tall. I gasped open-mouthed and stared up into the grey-brown weathered face that looked down at me.

Large, deep brown, kind eyes wrinkled at the corners and narrowed slightly as a small smile appeared on the bark-like skin.

"Ah, there you are," said Thea, shielding her eyes against the glare of the sun and gazing up at the Stiknean. "I knew you wouldn't be far away."

Thea turned to me. "This is Loai," she said, gesturing with her hand towards the tall statuesque figure, "and I think you can guess who she is," she said laughing as Noi ran off towards the giant creature. He launched himself upwards, landing effortlessly just under her knee. Then using his tail to support himself, he shinnied up her body in a lizard-like motion and came to rest in the crook of his mother's arm. He purred and clicked musically, and his whole body vibrated visibly as the leaves ran like a Mexican wave up and down the length of him. Loai responded in kind, the tone deeper and the vibration making the outline of her body blur.

Noi looked up at his mother, and they shared a quick conversation. She looked down at me from her regal viewpoint. Then, turning to Noi, she rubbed her face against his with affection and purred before giving him a small nudge. Noi scurried down his mother's body, and in a blink of an eye, he was standing in front of me. He held out his hands, palm up, and it struck me how different he was. His hands were essentially just a thumb and one large finger. He gave a few low tuts and whistles.

Thea turned towards us. She had walked over to Loai, who was bent low to listen to her.

"Oh, I don't think that will work, Noi," Thea said, giving a couple of clicks in Noi's direction. Her mouth downturned, she shook her head.

Noi turned back to me, ignoring her and grabbed my left hand, placing it palm down onto the palm of his right hand. He indicated with a series of tuts for me to do the same with the other one. I glanced at Thea, who shrugged and nodded back at me.

It was the strangest of sensations. His palms were rough, but tiny scales moved independently and settled into every crevice of my hand, gripping them tightly. I couldn't pull away. Noi closed his eyes and disappeared, then reappeared but only partially. His whole body was an opaque pale blue colour that glowed, and the glow started to creep into my hands. I instinctively tried to pull away, but I was held tight. The glowing light was now surrounding my arms, and I cried out in alarm at the cold prickling sensation. My concern deepened as I watched my skin become transparent, and I could clearly see the blue glow spreading through my veins.

8

Whatever this is, it will be okay, I told myself, taking some deep calming breaths as the light reached my shoulders and started to crawl coldly up my neck. My whole body shuddered as it filled my head, and I closed my eyes as images of Stikneans appeared in my thoughts.

Then the image changed, and I was sitting with Noi and his mother. They were telling me about their home and how they lived. More images flashed, faster and faster, too fast for me to know what they were about. Then my hands felt warm. I opened my eyes to Noi smiling cheekily at me. His hands pulled away from mine and released me with a slow sucking sensation, which made me shudder involuntarily.

He tilted his head to one side, fixing me with a curious, self-assured gaze. Then he spoke in quick tuts and clicks.

My mind instantly translated the language, and his voice resounded in my head. *"Did it work?"*

My jaw dropped open. "How did you do that?"

A wide smile spread across his face. His leaves shimmered and flushed upwards, where they hovered for a few seconds before falling back down. "It worked, it worked, I said it would," he cried, bounding off, racing in circles around Loai and Thea, his colours changing erratically.

Thea ran over to me and hugged me close. When she pulled away, her eyes were wide with excitement.

"I can't believe it. You're now connected to Noi telepathically. That's so amazing. I've tried and tried to link to them, but it's never worked." She gasped and jumped slightly as a thought occurred to her. "You'll be able to help me with the translations now." She grinned.

We walked to sit down on the grass beneath the cooling shade of the cedar. Its large branches were fanning the breeze in our direction now and then. Quietly looking around at the beautiful surroundings I now found myself in, I could feel the connection to all the living things growing stronger. I could hear the call of birds I was unfamiliar with, noises that were not known to my normal senses.

Thea turned to me. She had a soft light in her eyes that made her whole face look serene. She looked more peaceful than I had ever seen her.

"To bond with a Stiknean so soon is a great honour, Haesel," she said. "You have powerful abilities by virtue of the fact that you could accept the bonding, and your intentions must have shown to be true."

I leaned to the side to look at her, propping myself up on one arm. "What do you mean by that?"

Thea smiled with a sigh. "All beings give off an energy that our instincts can pick up on. We respond to those around us and place protective barriers in front of our true selves when we are let down, made to feel embarrassed, or, sometimes, when we experience greed and hurt, etc. All these things accumulate and close down our feelings, bit by bit, as time goes on. I think that's why I can't bond with the

Stikneans. I am too closed off and untrusting due to my experiences."

"Oh, that's a shame," I said, lowering my gaze, "but understandable considering the circumstances."

"Well, it does have a good side. My perception of the bad elements in beings is increased, so I can spot anything before others can, and that makes me a greater protector of this world."

I nodded in agreement, slowly looking around me. "Yes, this place is so amazing. I can see why you would want to do that."

"Once you fine-tune your skills," she continued, "you'll see the energy so clearly that everyone may as well wear a sandwich board announcing what type of person they are."

I smiled back at her and sat up, shuffling closer to lean my head on her shoulder. I felt so happy and contented to once again be in her company. The weight of uncertainty and loss had almost dissolved, and it was as though the past eight years had never happened.

The day continued with Thea teaching me how to summon all the elemental molecules from nature, ready for 'as and when' I needed them. She taught me about all the most powerful leaves, barks, berries, and roots and how to increase their potency. Which ones were poisonous and which would calm. We ate fruits and nuts from the large variety of trees and shrubs and drank pure, mineralised water from the crystal-clear streams that wound their way, gurgling through the landscape. Loai and Noi stayed with us for a while, Noi chattering away playfully while Thea took down notes on a small notepad in her pocket. I was collecting the bright orange berries of the sea buckthorn, known as the miracle berry due to its many uses when Noi ran over.

"We going now to join others," he chirped and clicked

happily, reaching out to touch my face, his black eyes shining. "I see you again, Haesel, many times."

"Yes, I hope so, Noi," I replied, walking my fingers along the underside of his arm. He purred musically in response, then dashed off. "Oh, wait!" I called after him, suddenly thinking that I didn't know where the others were. "How will I know where to find you?"

He was beside me in seconds. "You will know here," he said, reaching out a hand and touching the front of my head.

It was early evening when we arrived back at the house. The sound of the evening chorus was breathtaking. So many songs all mixed together that I didn't recognise, and yet they all seemed to harmonise as one. I stopped in front of the door and turned to look over the valley as the sun spread its orange glow across the land, lighting up gold the tips of everything it touched. *I could really get used to living here*, I thought. It's like Earth, but pure, before humanity left its scars.

Thea went to sort out the herbs we had collected during the day, and I lit the fire and put a pot of water on the grate.

I had gathered some food for us to eat from the store and turned around to see Thea standing in the doorway. Her face had taken on an ashen sheen that stopped me in my tracks. Her eyes were wide and fearful as they locked onto mine, and she held out a shaking hand containing the papers from the Lab.

"Haesel, when did you get these?"

My eyes flicked down to the papers and back up again. "Just before I came here," I said, slowly placing the food I was carrying on the table. "I stole them from the VialCorp Lab. Mick and I broke in to find out what was going on. Malicen has built a portal. He came in and found us, told Mick to turn on the portal, and—"

"Mick?" Thea interrupted her mouth agape. "Mick Jenkins?"

"Yes," I said, "He was helping me, at least I thought he was. Now I think maybe he was using me the whole time." I shook my head and looked down at the floor, trying to decide what I thought.

Thea took a deep breath in, pressed her lips together, and exhaled loudly through her nose. She walked over to the table, pulled out the chair and sat down, laying the papers on the table front of her.

"He's *made* a portal?" she asked, staring at me intensely. I nodded. "Oh, this is really bad, Haesel," she said, pulling on her bottom lip. "I could feel your presence, and I thought I had somehow opened the portal from here when you came through. You had better tell me what's been happening."

For the next hour, I explained all that had been going on with the virus and that I had gone to VialCorp to see if I could find out anything.

"It's been a day to remember for sure. I certainly didn't expect to find a portal into another world, I can tell you that, and I definitely didn't see it coming that you would be alive in that world," I finished.

I flipped through the documents on the table, scanning the pages. They gave details of the portal and how it was made. Details that could only have come from Thea's notes.

"I knew he would do it," Thea said, her shoulders slumping. "He must have been tracking me for ages. I did this. I led him here." Her head dropped.

"It wasn't your fault." I stood and reached across the table so she would look at me. "You left everything and everyone you loved to stop this very thing. You couldn't have done more than that."

The corners of her mouth twitched but never made it to a smile. "Malicen and I go back a long way, we used to get on and had the same objectives, but when my intuitions developed and I started working secretly on studying them, I saw a change in him." She shrugged. "Maybe he was just sore that I didn't share it with him. I didn't know he was watching me at the time, but gradually he became closed off and bitter." I nodded and sat back down as she continued.

"Towards the end, I could feel the threat, and one day I found a tiny camera on the hem of my coat and knew he had seen me go through the portal. I had to work on putting some protection in place for you, so I erased everything and faked my death, but I was too late. He already had everything by then. Being my daughter, he would have suspected you might know how to work the portal in some way." She looked up and sighed, then wrapped one hand over the other, and leaned forwards on her forearms.

"Do you think Mick was in on it?"

I shrugged, raising my eyebrows. "It's hard to say, but if I had to guess, I think I would have to say yes. I don't want it to be true, he was so nice, and he spoke so highly and fondly of you…but he did do as Malicen asked…and he did shout to him to grab me." I stopped and leaned back in my chair, closing my eyes, my hands interlinked on top of my head. Then looking up at Thea, I said, "Now he could be dead."

"Poor Mick," Thea said, hanging her head. "He was a good friend. Genuinely a kind, decent man, but he always wanted to be noticed more than he was. I guess Malicen's manipulative ways had to sway him at some point."

"That makes sense, I suppose," I said.

Thea straightened suddenly. "Malicen has no powers of his own, so he can't come through the portal," she said, her mind back on track. "It would kill an ordinary human, but he will be hell-bent on finding a way."

"Oh god," I gasped, clamping a hand over my mouth. "He has my DNA. Would that work?"

"What? How?" Thea's expression was incredulous, with just an inkling of intense fear.

I proceeded to tell her about Kirsty and the swab.

"He knows," she stated blankly, tapping her middle finger rapidly on the table while her other hand lightly rubbed over her mouth as she thought aloud. "He would also need the blood from a magical being to be able to pass through, and even then, it's never been done. All human immune systems are very clever at recognising an imposter and would kill or reject it....and it wouldn't be the same blood type." She glanced in my direction. "What?"

"You don't look one hundred per cent sure to me," I said, raising my eyebrows.

"Well then, let's sieve through this lot," she said, tapping the pile of papers. "Then we can work out what he's really up to and have a head start on stopping him."

We poured over the papers until nearly midnight. There were details of the portal and mathematical equations but nothing regarding his intentions. The last page made a brief mention of the SACL Pill and its important ingredients.

"I don't understand the point of this," Thea said, throwing her hands up in the air in exasperation. "It seems the main ingredient of the pill Malicen has developed is graphene oxide, but that's not going to stop anyone from clotting. It's not an anticoagulant. If anything, it's the opposite, and I don't see how that is going to protect people from the Virus."

I nodded. "He made no mention of these other ingredients in his TV announcement either," I said.

Thea sat back giving small shakes of her head and, ticking off points on her fingers, before finally voicing her thoughts. "Graphene is extremely light and thin," she said. "It can be made so small it can only be seen under a microscope. It conducts heat very well. In fact, it's the best conducting material ever discovered, and I had begun to study its uses in bionanotechnology." She pressed her fingers momentarily to her lips.

"By putting it into the SACL Pill, it would infiltrate every cell in the body, including our DNA. But why?" Thea looked up at the ceiling, holding her hands out, palms upwards as though hoping answers would drop from the sky. "Maybe it will be heated somehow, killing the virus, but that would kill all other cells too." Exasperated she leaned back heavily in the chair.

"Wow, you can use something that small?" I said.

"Yes, we can now make nanobots, tiny microscopic robots that can sit on the tip of a needle, and they can be injected into the body to carry out certain functions." I shuddered as goosebumps rippled down my body. I really didn't like the thought of that.

Thea leaned forward and put her head in her hands, then looked up and fixed me with her intense brown eyes. "You have to go back, Haesel. Some information is missing, and you have to find it."

"I can't," I said automatically, then explained when her eyes widened. "I can't get in without Mick. He had the pass."

"You have to try," she said. "I know you will think of a way."

"Come back with me."

"I think that would be foolish," she said as her shoulders fell. "The portal will create a signature unique to me when I pass through. I didn't have time to study it before I left, but I'm sure the energy trails it leaves behind will be traceable, and Malicen probably already knows how."

I sighed deeply and nodded, knowing she was right. I was asking for selfish reasons, but the last thing I wanted was for all this to have been a waste of time, and I too, did not want to endanger this beautiful place.

Thea stood and walked around the table to rub the back of my hand. "He'll be on the lookout for me for sure, and I don't want to give him any ammunition.

I yawned loudly, "Come on, it's late," she said, "let's get some sleep, and in the morning, we can do more training."

9

I went to bed exhausted and woke early to the same beautiful world. I felt completely refreshed and better than I had for a long time. We were just finishing breakfast when Thea froze on the spot. She tilted her head like she was listening and held up her hand for me to be still, then her eyes widened, and her lips parted slightly as she inhaled sharply.

"Come on," she said, jumping up and grabbing my hand. "She's coming." She quickly snatched a bottle of something off a nearby shelf as she dragged me outside.

I stood squinting in the bright light. The air was warm already, and the vibrancy of the plants and flowers were sharply defined as the sun created intense dark shadows against their vivid colours.

"What am I looking for?" I asked, my eyes scanning the surrounding countryside.

"Oh, you'll know when you see her," she said, grinning at me, her eyes dancing with sparkling light. "Just don't freak out," she added, her voice taking on a serious tone. "Well, you might freak a bit…but you don't need to…so try not to."

"Err, okay, if you say so." My hands were already growing clammy. "Can't you just tell me? You're making me a little nervous."

"It's probably best if you don't have time to think about it," she said. "Sorry, but trust me, it will be fine."

A distant buzzing, humming sound reached my ears, and a warm breeze blew towards us from the west. Thea started walking in that direction and motioned for me to follow. I could see a large area in the scrubland ahead that was different to the rest of the surrounding land. The small meadow was worn in patches, and it had fewer plants that were smaller and dotted here and there. I stood before it in the warm wind, my hair lifting away from my neck and flapping against my shoulders behind me. The buzzing sound merged with a gentle humming, whispering that rose and fell as the wind carried the sound in rhythms of air in our direction.

Ahead, my eyes settled on an oval form that appeared in the distance. It was growing steadily larger as it made its way towards us. The colour of the moving object constantly changed, flushing from white through shades of grey, up and down, left to right as it moved through the air, following the peaks and dips of the land. Like a giant pliable bubble, it rose and fell, altering direction sharply and suddenly, as though bouncing off walls inside a box.

The sound got louder and louder as it approached, and then I saw it. It wasn't one object but hundreds of separate entities flying in unison together. At first, I thought they were insects of some kind, and then my eyes grew wide as I inhaled slowly. I could feel my heart beating harder as my excitement increased.

I glanced at Thea, who was grinning at me, her clothes buffeting in the wind.

A broad smile spread across my face as I realised that

what I was looking at were miniature beings with beautiful full iridescent wings. A brilliant blue light drew my attention to one of them. She hovered, maintaining her position while her eyes searched me intently. The others swarmed around me with great curiosity, tilting their heads from side to side. I turned around in a slow circle, my eyes darting in all directions as I tried to focus properly on the tiny creatures, and I breathed the word, "Faeries."

They were too quick to be able to focus on for more than a split second. Instead, they formed an almost transparent kaleidoscope of swirling rainbow light. Thousands of voices blended seamlessly together creating a sound that took hold of my senses and filled me with a serene peacefulness, it was unlike any feeling I had ever known. I had no concept of danger, no thoughts of anything bad. I felt light and floaty, drifting in the air.

Suddenly, via a signal known only to each other, the whole collective moved as one and swarmed into a nearby thicket, disappearing completely. The noise stopped.

I turned to Thea, my eyes half closed and a lazy smile on my lips.

"That was amazing. I can't believe it," I said dreamily, then yawned loudly. Thea walked over to me and placed her hands on either side of my head, turning my face towards her. I grinned a silly lopsided grin, my vision hazy, as though I was looking through sheer organza. I was euphorically happy, and my body felt weightless and free.

Thea rubbed her hands together, and a red glow slowly appeared, growing steadily in its brightness. I watched the colour spreading, swirling, making patterns around her hands. It was mesmerising. *I could stay here and watch that all day long,* I thought.

"That's so pretty. Can I try that?" I slurred. Thea opened

her hands and held them both in front of my face. Pain shot up my nose into the centre of my head. I staggered backwards, lost my footing, and met the ground hard.

"Ow," I cried out, pressing my hand to my forehead to try and control the sharpness of the pain. "What the hell was that?"

"Hartshorn," Thea said. "I brought it with me just in case. It's made from deer antlers and has the same effect as smelling salts. Although, I think it's actually much stronger when its potency is increased with magic." She looked upwards while she considered this and gave a little shrug. "So, are you back with me now?" she asked, peering down at me, a bemused expression on her face. "I really didn't think the faeries would affect you, but it appears your sensory powers still need some time to develop."

My eyes were watering, and I pinched the bridge of my nose to relieve the burning sensation.

"What did they do to me?" I asked, getting to my feet and brushing myself off. "I can't believe there are faeries here. They were so beautiful. I wish I could have seen them for longer."

"Oh, you'll see them again, don't worry. Their song created a sort of relaxed hypnotic stupor. It put you in a trance and rendered you incapable of causing any harm. When they've checked you out and are sure you are not a threat, they release you, but the effects can take a while to wear off."

"Wow, passive defence, that's brilliant," I said. "I suppose they need that, being so fragile and tiny."

Thea threw her head back and laughed a rich, rolling laugh at my comment. "Don't be fooled," she said, pointing her finger at me but still smiling. "It's their first line of defence against a being they don't know, but they have many tricks up their sleeves and many different hypnotic powers with quite different effects. They are also not as tiny as you think," she said with a bemused smile. "As a collective, the Fae are very powerful."

"Well, I didn't freak out," I said, lifting my chin with a touch of pride.

The atmosphere suddenly changed, and the air grew rapidly cooler. I turned to look in the same direction the faeries had come from. Large, billowing clouds had quickly formed and filled the sky. Shades of metal and snow mixed and rolled in the previously pristine blue, looking all the more ominous lit up by the sun that was warming my back. A large black shape could be seen drifting through them.

"The faeries are not what I had in mind when I said not to freak out," said Thea. "On the first visit, faeries always pave the way for Nithele."

As the wind picked up its intensity, I heard a loud guttural rumbling high overhead and then a deafening ear-splitting scream. It was raw and powerful and left you in no doubt that it was deadly.

I shuddered as the hairs rose on my neck, and I instinctively moved closer to Thea, who put her hand between my shoulder blades. She turned to look at me, her eyes fixed with assured determination.

"Hold your ground," she said. "Keep your head up and be proud, and don't show her any weakness."

I nodded, not at all certain that I would succeed, but I made a conscious effort to stand straighter and squared my shoulders all the same.

Above, the shape circled, then disappeared. I scanned the clouds for any movement, but all was unnervingly quiet. Then it came. A green, scaled head burst through the clouds, followed by a long serpentine neck and a huge, fully scaled body with enormous, webbed wings.

The dragon made a beeline for us and let out another scream. For a moment, I didn't think she was going to stop. I stood steady, trusting that Thea knew it would be fine, and I had nothing to fear. At the last minute, she pulled up, rearing almost upright, beating her colossal wings backwards and forwards to maintain the gravity-defying stance. Her long spiny tail that ended in a flat, leaf-shaped appendage, swished back and forth to aid her airborne suspension. She locked her sharp yellow eyes on mine with a confidence that came of such power.

The wind created from her wings made it hard for me to keep my footing, and I leaned forward to remain upright. Squinting my eyes now at the dust and grit that stung my face, I looked straight back through narrowed slits and concentrated hard on not gawping open-mouthed like a child. Her razor-sharp teeth flashed white in the rays of sunlight as her monstrous mouth opened wide. I braced myself for the roar that would follow but instead, a blisteringly hot blast of air swept towards us and hit like a solid wall. It was accompanied by a low rumble that I could feel the vibrations of inside my body. I gritted my teeth against the burning heat, aware in my peripheral vision that Thea was doing the same.

The dragon raised her wings outstretched and high and hung momentarily in the air, while blade-like talons three feet long spread out, emphasising their lethal sharp points. With her chest high, she landed with a solid connection on the earth, sending out a ripple that shook all the trees like a tidal wave moving across the valley.

The dust settled, and I stared in awe at such a magnificent creature, so immensely powerful in her enormity alone. Large, overlapping green scales covered her body and shone like gemstones, catching the sunlight. With her neck stretched high, she tilted her head to stare down at me with a regal presence. A horn of ridged bone protruded from halfway down the front of her face and petered out just over the tip of her nose. It rose, curving inwards to form a sharp serrated edge that could slice you in two with a swift butt of her head. Two smaller ridges followed the angle of her brow bones, above her gleaming eyes, creating sharp-crested points that extended outwards and ended in lethal sharp points. More bony protrusions lined the sides of her face making her look semi prehistoric.

Thea bowed her head in respect, and I quickly followed suit. Then standing tall, Thea called out, "Nithele, this is my daughter Haesel. We are honoured you came."

The dragon took a step forwards, her claws scraping over the earth like rotavator blades. Her wings bent halfway as they folded and tilted downwards. Scythe-like claws on the bony joint bedded into the earth on either side of her, adding width and menace to her stature. She dipped her head, keeping her eyes fixed on mine, and her long serpentine neck swooped low until her thick, scaled nose was close to my own. Beads of sweat started to run in rivulets down my back.

"I'm immensely honoured to meet you," I croaked, my voice sounding small and pathetic. I attempted a smile then stopped myself, remembering what Thea had said about showing weakness. I lifted my chin. Then wondered if that looked defiant.

Oh, crap, I thought, trying not to waver, *I'm not doing very well at this.*

Nithele inhaled a deep breath, taking in my scent, then her nostrils flared as she blew out a hot blast of air into my face. I felt like I heated up another thirty degrees as more sweat ran down my forehead and my hair stuck to my neck. I concentrated on my breathing. She turned her head slowly to the side and drew closer until, just inches away, her large yellow eye the size of a dinner plate was staring directly into mine. It darted in small jerky movements back and forth, crawling through my mind, searching my soul, all volumes of my archived thoughts scanned, every crevice picked out. The essence of me was completely exposed as I was laid bare before her. Golden flecks merged with shades of orange and yellow, and the elliptical pupil pulsed with deep darkness that held the secrets of centuries.

She drew back, still fixing me with her eyes that flicked quickly to Thea, then re-fixed on mine. A low rumbling murmur came from deep in her throat, and she spoke in a low voice that held a disparaging edge as it vibrated through her body.

"I know who you are, witch. The prophecy tells of you. Protector." She spat the last word, jerking her head towards me.

My jaw dropped, and I openly gawped. I glanced at Thea, who shot a quick look at me with raised eyebrows, her eyes wide, and gave a small, quick shake of her head.

I turned back to Nithele, whose terrifying mouth was upturned in one corner, giving the strange impression of a bemused smile. It snapped back immediately as my gaze rested on her, and her eyes narrowed and hardened. She walked around me in a slow circle keeping her eyes on me, her immense tail swinging just inches from my body. I closed my mouth and swallowed my shock that she could speak, let alone that she knew of me.

Nithele snorted another hot breath out of flared nostrils, and drew her powerful neck up, lifting her head higher and turning away a little, for the first time taking her eyes off me.

"Not at all what I was expecting." The words rumbled with slow menace, and she remained very still. Then she tilted her head slightly towards me as her eye snapped back to fix me with a disdainful glare. "Quite disappointing, in fact."

That did it. My fiery temper came to the surface at the

indignation, along with the injustice of being judged so quickly. "Oh, nice," I replied, glaring up at her and taking a couple of paces forward, my hands firm on my hips. "Well, I can't say you're inspiring me either. You haven't got a clue wh—"

The screaming roar was sudden and terrifying. I staggered backwards. Nithele lifted her head high, her mouth wide as white-hot flames thirty meters long escaped past her razor-sharp teeth. The heat made the air shimmer and distort, and I shielded my scorching face with my hands. Turning, I looked for Thea, who had started to run towards me. Flames seared the earth between us, and I cried out, unprepared, falling backwards in my haste to retreat.

The flat side of Nithele's tail whipped towards Thea in a sudden movement, knocking her hard to the floor. With a speed that belied her huge size, her head descended in a swift, smooth motion straight towards her target, nostrils wide, leaving a trail of black curling plumes of smoke.

"No!" I screamed with all of my breath as my adrenalin surged. I lunged forwards, placing myself in front of Thea and holding out my hands to the approaching jaws that were slowly opening, revealing a white-hot glow, and I screamed each word with all my might. "You will not harm her!"

The flames surged, and I cried out a long, loud roar of my own as they were ejected forcibly towards me. Green flames shot from my hands and spread out in a slowly increasing circle, deflecting and shielding the searing heat that came towards us. I gritted my teeth, and stealing every ounce of strength and determination I could dredge, I stepped forwards, braced myself, and leant in.

All the while, in my mind, I kept repeating to myself, *I won't let you kill her; I am stronger,* and just as I reached the point where my strength was ebbing, the flames stopped as her breath ran out.

Haesel

My arms dropped and hung limply by my sides. Visibly shaking and breathing heavily, I stared defiantly into Nithele's eyes and held her gaze. I felt Thea approach behind me and, without averting my eyes, held out one hand to the side to stop her. Nithele flared her nostrils and snorted a large black cloud of dense, smoke which enveloped us completely. I couldn't see. Closing my eyes, I concentrated on feeling her presence.

"Thea, get down," I said as Nithele circled me, and I turned to follow her. I raised my hand, directing my energy towards a slight change in temperature. The blast hit, followed by a menacing growling rumble. The smoke cleared as Nithele stretched out her powerful wings.

Thea ran quickly to stand beside me as Nithele, keeping one eye fixed on me, bent her head to her chest. A long, black, snaking tongue appeared, and she licked away, in one smooth motion, the soot where my blast had hit her. There was no damage, each scale an impenetrable shield in her defence.

"Mmm." The sound was deep, reverberating up her long neck. She curled her upper lip in a sneer that revealed rows of deadly, pointed teeth, a reminder to beware. Crouching low she swept one powerful wing around in an arc so that the hooked claw at the joint came to rest under my chin, and she lifted my head higher. I didn't flinch and held her gaze. She narrowed her intense yellow eyes.

"Not completely useless," she said, with slow deliberation, eyeing me sideways. "Maybe there is some potential after all." Her eyes flicked to Thea and she stepped back, withdrawing her claw from my chin. Her eyes slid away dismissing me as insignificant against all she knew of events now past. "Prophecies are so often exaggerated," she said, in a hardened, growling rumble.

Then with a final snort of intense heat from her nostrils,

she arched her neck up and back, stretched her wings wide, and with two powerful beats that left us squinting through the dust storm, she launched herself upwards on heavily muscled legs and rose slowly into the air. She let out another deafening screaming roar as she headed off across the sky—a reminder to all of the power she held.

10

My legs buckled, and I sat down right where I was. Thea joined me, and for a while, we said nothing, my head using all its remaining energy to cope with what had just happened. Then I turned on her. My breath became loud and erratic as heat rose to the surface of my skin.

I fixed her with a glare. "You couldn't have warned me about that? Don't freak out? That was all you could think of?"

"I'm sorry," she said, shaking her head but looking firmly back at me. "I thought if I told you, your fear would give a completely different outcome. You had to prove yourself in front of her."

"Huh." I turned away, dismissing her with my eyes, anger and disappointment now boiling to the surface. "Well, I should have expected it. You couldn't tell me you were going to fake your death either, and that you would really still be alive." My mouth clamped into a thin line, and my breathing became loud as my nostrils flared. "It seems to me that you can't trust me with any information. Certainly, nothing that would help prepare me for a major fucking incident in my life."

"Haesel, look where we are," she said, staying calm and indicating our surroundings with a sweep of her hand. "It's just not like that. This is important, and I can't mess around with your fate, warning you could change things, and there are more important things at play here. Nithele had to see you as you are."

"Great, good to know," I spat through gritted teeth, "and completely useless to know now. Same as your death… Oh no, hang on a minute…not death." I shot my anger towards her with a sharp glance. "Seriously, I thought a fucking great dragon was going to kill you just now, and then I would lose you all over again!"

I dropped my head forwards, rubbing my forehead with the palms of my hands. *I can't believe I just said that sentence. This is so surreal,* I thought, as my mind struggled to keep up.

Thea looked down, her shoulders slumping. "I missed you every second of every day," she said quietly. I glanced at her, and her eyes sought mine. "But I knew it wouldn't be forever."

I stared at her incredulous, my eyes brimming with tears that I was powerless to prevent. Then my face hardened.

"Well, I didn't! It was forever for me!"

She reached out to me, but I moved away, brushing the tear roughly from my cheek as I did so.

"She wouldn't have hurt you. She would have seen all that you are when she searched your eyes. She just needed to test your inner strength."

I sniffed, standing up, fists clenched by my sides. I looked at her and shook my head, then turned and strode swiftly towards the house. I didn't trust my emotions not to say something I couldn't take back. I felt hurt, drained, sad, angry, confused, and very, very tired.

Haesel

I walked through the kitchen to the sofa I had found myself on when I arrived and lay down. I must have gone out like a light.

When I woke, the sun had shifted in the sky, the air was hot, and there was little shadow to define the shapes of the landscape. Thea appeared beside me and placed a steaming cup on the table nearby.

"Good timing. I made you some herbal tea. This will help you to regain your strength," she said.

Now rested, I regretted my outburst earlier. She had made difficult decisions and had sacrificed a lot, but had persevered to protect us.

As she went to go, I grabbed hold of her arm. She turned and smiled.

"I didn't mean to have a go at you."

"It's completely okay," she bent forwards to kiss my forehead. "I'd say in the grand scheme of things you've had more to deal with than most people."

I looked down and pulled at a loose thread on the cover. "Not as much as you."

I glanced up at her flattening my lips, my mouth turning down at the corners.

She shrugged her shoulders, opening her hands wide, palms up. "It would be difficult to judge in a competition, but it sure is one hell of a ride."

One side of my mouth made it to a smile. "And...," she continued, "you've got to admit that even though she is pretty daunting, you must be secretly thrilled inside to meet an actual dragon. I know how much you always loved them and wanted to see one when you were little."

"Oh sure, I was thrilled all right," I said, raising my eyebrows high. "Although I think it would have been more enjoyable with more warning, and less of the imminent threat of death."

Thea threw her head back as she laughed out loud.

Then a thought struck me, and I looked up at her, seeing her differently for the first time. "How did you know what to do when you came through?" I asked. "You had no one to help you. How did you learn about our powers and all the things you know now?"

Thea sighed deeply, and the next word out of her mouth took me completely by surprise.

"Nithele."

My mouth dropped open. "What?"

Thea moved to sit down beside me.

"Well, it was mostly Nithele...and time, and the faeries, and figuring it out with a couple of other witches." She shrugged.

I made a rolling gesture with my hands for her to expand, and she turned to retrieve the chair by the table. Placing it in front of me, she sat down, crossing her legs and linking her fingers together around her knee.

"Nithele is from the Archaician Clan of dragons. They are Ancients and have existed here for millions of years. They are overseers and are here to serve one purpose, to keep order and protect the Alchemia Realm at all costs. Every new dragon born comes into the world with the knowledge of ages past. Anything they learn in their lifetime is passed on to the next generation, and so it accumulates."

"So, you know all their history?"

"No," she laughed. "I don't think our brains would be able to hold that amount. Nithele connected to me telepathically after I'd been here a few days. It was like a download, but I only got the essential information I needed. She's not really a big talker."

"Pff, I can imagine."

Thea continued, and I nodded along, taking it all in. "How did she know you could be trusted?" I asked.

"Dragons know everything. They sense you when you arrive and know your purpose...although I had a thorough brain check out too," she winked.

"Oh, isn't that the weirdest feeling, being searched on the inside? Like a gentle tingling that scurries about, but you can't break away. I could literally feel my mind releasing everything."

"Yes, and a tug on your heart when she searches your true intentions."

"Oh yes, I did feel that," I said, now understanding what that had been.

"Nithele knew of our ancestry, and apparently, I have a purpose that I am yet to discover."

"She didn't tell you what it was?"

"No." Thea looked at me, shaking her head. *In time,* was all she would say. All events have their place in time, so I'll know when I need to. The fact that she came to meet you so soon says a lot, though."

I hung my head and sighed. "Well, no pressure then. If she knows more about me than I know about myself, it would have been nice for her to share that because I haven't got a clue, what I'm meant to do." I looked at Thea, suddenly feeling out of my depth. "And," I added, "she certainly didn't seem impressed with me."

She stifled a laugh. "Yes, I can see how you would think that. She was testing you for sure," she said, moving from the chair to sit beside me.

"I have heard many stories of her," she continued. "She is kind with her power. All her actions have a purpose and are considered, and, although I wasn't aware of what she would do with you, and I couldn't intervene, I was never worried about you." Thea placed her hand over mine firmly and looked into my eyes. "I imagine a witch of prophecy doesn't come along very often, and she had to be sure."

I could see her pride in me, and I relaxed a bit. I understood at that moment that I was obviously important in some way, but I was new on this journey and had to follow the path. Thea nodded, reading the silence between us.

I leaned in to hug her, then pulled away, looking at her intently, analysing her face, ready for any changes that would alert me if she wasn't being honest. "Do you know anything of my prophecy?"

"No," she said without hesitation. "That's the strange thing about fate. It's written in invisible ink. The Fae are the keepers of fate, and knowledge of certain things along your fate line can be suppressed to prevent it from being changed. That's why it's so difficult to alter or predict."

I threw my hands up, exasperated. "So, if it's all a surprise," I said, "and I can't change it, then what's the point?"

"Well," she said, "Because what happens is usually meant to be." Reaching across me, she picked up my tea. "Drink this while I talk, or it will be freezing." I took it from her, wrapping my hands around the still warm drink, taking comfort from the sweet, aromatic liquid.

Thea moved her position to face me more. "Humans have a weak instinctive premonition. It's that feeling you get when you know something isn't quite right, or you feel something is going to happen. As a witch, our senses are not only stronger, but we can tap into more of them, and this means we get snapshots of events that are going to happen before they do, like dreams, but you're awake."

I watched her, listening intently. After finishing the tea, I placed the cup on the table, leant back, drew up my legs, and thought back to the lab. "So that's what I had when I saw Kirsty give my swab to Malicen?"

"Yes," Thea nodded. "Your powers were awakening, being close to the portal."

"When you have more practice," she went on, "you will be able to concentrate on something you are worried about and activate a premonition concerning that event or person. The responsibility of that is great, though, and it can be hard to decipher it accurately as you may feel the need to change something in order to affect the long-term outcome."

'Okay," I said. "At least that's something. I might get some clues that would help."

"It's unpredictable. You cannot always see everything that's ahead, which leaves you open to getting it wrong. It takes skill, caution and patience, and even if you see the full outcome, it's not always possible to change it." Thea's expression grew serious, and she leaned forwards to connect with my eyes. "Sometimes, you may wish you hadn't seen it." She paused and sighed deeply. "There's one thing you have to remember," she continued, "and this is very important to consider before you try and change an event. It can be dangerous. If you manage to change something that you have seen, seemingly for the good, then the whole fate line has been altered. Your fates line interconnects with others, and it could have a consequence that's bad, either immediately, or further on in time that you do not get a premonition about."

I nodded, frowning, and looked away, my eyes moving over objects around the room without seeing them while my mind processed that information. "I understand," I said, changing position. "So, how did you know to come through the portal the first time?"

"Ah, that was easy," she said. "I had a premonition, well, a lot actually. I dreamt of Alchemia before I knew what it was. I was writing a paper on the possibilities of intuitions to future events, and the existence of other planes. The more Malicen watched me and learnt my work, the more premonitions I had. Then one morning, I was out on a walk, thinking intently of the place I always saw in my premonitions, and the portal opened in front of me. I could see the images from my dreams beyond. It felt completely natural, every part of me knew this was meant to be, and the urge to step in was overwhelming. That's when I started planning what to do."

She leaned forward, her elbows on her knees and absently rubbed her eyes. I reached out and stroked my hand over her back.

"What is it?"

She sighed and massaged the skin above her eyebrows before clasping her hands together and turning to me.

"I knew that if I didn't do something, Malicen would study my findings then use me to get through. My premonitions showed him copying my work, so I got rid of everything and faked my death to protect both, then came through. I had to change the fate line to stop him."

"That all makes perfect sense. You did what you had to."

"Yes, but that's what I'm trying to say. What I know now is that the premonitions I had weren't of the future, they were of the past, and Malicen had already copied my work. I got them wrong. It was too late."

I felt the tension build in the back of my neck and rolled my shoulders back. "So, you didn't change the fate line? He still built the portal."

Thea nodded. "Yes, it appears so. I removed myself, so the path did alter... Maybe my changing it involved you? Or maybe that was your fate all along."

I nodded along while she was talking. "Ah, yes. I get it now," I said, stretching my arms back to pull on my neck. "It is complicated. Well, what's done is done. We just have to go from here and see what happens. Hopefully, one of us will get another premonition that shows more." I smiled at her, and her face relaxed a little. "Don't worry. It will go how it goes. It brought us together again, and that's got to be a good thing," I said, giving her a squeeze. I stood up to stretch my legs and walked around the room.

"So, regarding the portal? You just think of the place where you want to be, and that takes you back?" I asked.

"Yes, once your powers are strong enough to activate it and to withstand the return with little effect…and don't worry," she added, seeing the panic start to spread across my face. "We have time for that, two to three weeks should do it, and you will only have lost a day or so when you go back."

"Okay," I said, "how will I know when I am strong enough?"

"We'll check at the end of each week. It's okay, I know this, hands down," she grinned, then gave a small intake of breath.

I picked up on the energy change, and my eyes met hers. "How many times did you come back?"

She lowered her gaze before lifting her head with a sigh. "A few, when I couldn't hold out from seeing you any longer, to check you were okay. It took me a while to understand the portal, and I didn't know where you were as you had moved, so I searched your name on the internet and found your shop."

I looked away, finding all the times shelved in my memories of when I suddenly thought of her and felt her near. A feeling that had crept over the back of my shoulders, sometimes making me say her name out loud and other times making me turn around expecting to see her. It had made me sad and given me comfort at the same time. Somehow, I felt our bond had not been broken, and she was still looking out for me.

"Yes," I drew a deep breath and met her eyes once more. "I definitely felt you sometimes, and I liked to think you were there, but then I would reason it down to how much I wanted it. Why didn't you show yourself sooner? Let me know?"

"I couldn't," she interjected, shaking her head. "It would have changed things."

"Oh yes, of course."

She walked to stand in front of me, her eyes intense.

"I never expected all this to happen either, but the right time is now, and it's crucial that you are ready for whatever lies ahead."

I met her eyes and smiled. All the puzzle pieces were slowly coming together and for the first time, things were starting to fall into place.

Thea linked her arm through mine. "Right, come on, I'm starving, then we'd better get on with training."

I spent the next week devising spells and honing my skills, drawing out particles from plants, earth, and air. I learned how my emotions could enhance ingredients and how those powers were actioned. I felt more at home on Alchemia and more like the true version of myself than at any other time in my life.

My confidence and ability grew day by day, as did my strength, and I felt more prepared for the role destined for me.

After one long afternoon of training, we were walking over a hilly area of land filled with a large variety of moss and heather. I turned to Thea, pointing ahead. "Shall we rest by the stream?" She nodded, and we headed in that direction.

I had smelt the stream from quite a way off. The fresh earthy smell known as petrichor was filling the air. It was caused by the damp earth on the banks releasing the oils from nearby and overhanging trees, plants, and grass. Along with the soil releasing actinomycetes bacteria, the aerosols of scent infiltrated and infused all the air molecules nearby. It was one of my favourite smells just after heavy rain.

The stream was crystal clear and pure from the rock minerals the water had gurgled its way through and over as it meandered across the landscape. I leaned over and scooped handfuls of the pure, clear liquid. It tasted amazing, just as nature intended, unlike the processed chemical taste of tap water at home.

We sat on the bank and paddled our feet in the cool, fresh water. Thea turned to me, "So, no premonitions yet?"

"No," I said, hanging my head with a sigh, "still none."

Thea nodded. "It's early. They will come. The one you had was to warn you that Malicen, and probably most people at the lab, weren't to be trusted. Warnings of imminent danger are the strongest."

"Maybe I'm trying too hard," I said.

"No, I don't think it's that. It's either that you don't need any just yet, or that it is being clouded with all you are learning. Everything is for a reason, and right now, you have to learn as much as you can before you go back."

Thea leaned back on her elbows and smiled up at me. "Deciphering premonitions is not easy. They can be the tiniest glimpse in time, and you don't know how close or how far ahead they are. Try and look around in the premonition to give you more clues."

"Okay, that's a good tip," I said, jumping up and feeling refreshed. "Shall we head back?"

"Yes," she said, then quickly scrambled to her feet. "Oh, actually, now we're here, let me show you something. This way," and she pointed to a group of hills that lay not far ahead on the landscape.

We made our way over. The terrain thick with vegetation was challenging to get through with no path to follow. Creatures darted through the undergrowth but never exposed themselves to our eyes. Reaching the top of the highest hill, I looked out for miles across the land. Thea pointed to a far-off mountain range. Clouds partly covered its tops, and they were only just visible in the distance. "They are the Aaronly Mountains, the home of the dragons," she said.

"Oh wow," I turned to her. "Where Nithele lives?"

Thea nodded.

I turned back to stare at the mountains. Even from this distance, I could see bright flashes of orange light appearing sporadically for a few seconds, the flames igniting the air before going out.

"How many dragons are there?" I asked, not taking my eyes off the mountains, mesmerised, watching for the bursts of flame.

"Nine, I think, or maybe eleven. Some of them are young. Nithele is the Elder, the Matriarch. She is around 1300 years old."

My mouth dropped open, and I was about to speak, but Thea cut across me.

"And to answer your next question," she said laughing, "they live to around 1500 years old."

"Oh my god, that's so long," I exclaimed. "She doesn't seem old." We turned and headed for home.

"Nithele is the most powerful of the dragons and gets stronger with age," Thea explained. "A dragon's death is more to do with time, with their knowledge banks being full and being ready to relinquish it to a younger dragon to take over the reins, rather than their bodies wearing out."

As we walked, Nithele filled my thoughts and I considered all the things she must know. If there was a prophecy about me and she knew it, then I didn't see why I shouldn't know the outline of that too. One day, not just yet, I thought, but one day, I was going to pay her a visit and request just that.

11

Shortly before the end of the third week, I had my first premonition since being on Alchemia. I had risen early, intent on investigating the forest region in the valley to the east. From Thea's house, you could see the vastness of it rising and falling; a green, heavy wool blanket draped over the land.

I packed what I needed and made my way in its direction, picking my way through the meadowland. The temperature dropped as I reached the cover of the trees, bringing welcome and instant relief from the heat of the sun.

The smell hit me first, and I inhaled deeply, the scent instantly relaxing—so many different trees. I could smell the pine, eucalyptus, redwoods, and oak, hundreds of species creating pure, scented oxygen. I stood a short way in, marvelling at such a huge array of different species, all together in one wood. I noticed that the temperature seemed to be constantly changing, pockets of air, cooler then warmer—a whole self-contained ecosystem managing itself and regulating as requirements dictated. The forest wasn't as dense as I expected. Shafts of sunlight beamed down from above between the leaves. Again, it was ensuring that the right amount of light was allowed in, looking after itself as a whole, not allowing greed to starve one or proliferate another.

I crouched down to scoop a handful of soil. It was soft and heavy with nutrients and had an earthy, profoundly organic smell. And it was really warm, keeping the temperature perfect, coddling, nurturing. The cycle of life, falling decayed leaves, breaking down to feed the trees once again.

I always found the smell of woodland and forests renewed my soul. A smile spread across my face that I couldn't prevent. The peacefulness took over me, and my senses focused on the smallest of things.

Small furry creatures scampered through the undergrowth, and faeries, smaller than the ones that preceded Nithele, flitted effortlessly thorough the leaves as they rode the delicate currents of air. Without my enhanced senses, my eyes would have overlooked them, their colours changed constantly through shades of green and brown, blending perfectly with their surroundings.

I continued further in, collecting ginkgo biloba and willow for their anticoagulant properties. Then a bright flash of blue caught the periphery of my eye. I froze but moved my eyes to look in that direction. *I had definitely seen it,* I thought when nothing further showed itself. My eyes scanned the surroundings, and I slowly stepped back, leaning my weight on my back leg. It flashed again, then was gone, but my eyes had pinpointed the spot. I moved forward slightly, and the blue light shone bright and clear. I could see now that it was something glinting in the sunlight as I moved.

Keeping my eyes locked on the area, I made my way over to a small clearing around three yards in diameter. There were no trees here, no leaf litter. Instead, thick green moss densely covered the floor. My feet sank, heavy, into the soft, spongy carpet, so I knelt, placing my splayed hands out in front of me to displace my weight and watched as they disappeared. My weight, still too heavy, broke the moss at the ends of my fingers, and blue light shone through. I gasped. It was the most beautiful blue and had an almost hypnotising intensity.

Mesmerised, I carefully peeled back the green moss. My eyes grew wide with surprise and maybe a little disappointment, as underneath, I saw a tiny patch of blue moss, only an inch across that glittered and shone with an iridescent light that seemed to be glowing from within. It was growing on a small white rock that had also been hidden beneath the thicker green covering. *Not enough to take,* I thought. I would ask Thea about it when I got back.

Suddenly Eve's face flashed in front of me. Her eyes were wide with shock and fear, her mouth open in a gasp. She was looking straight at me, or it could have been just behind me. Then it was gone, the whole thing lasting no more than two seconds. I closed my eyes, trying to retain the image. "Damn it," I exclaimed, "I wasn't ready. I didn't get to look around," My voice was instantly lost, muted by my green surroundings. I could only recall her face, but she definitely looked to be in trouble.

I hastily picked up my things, stuffing my collections into my bag. Taking one last look at the forest I longed to explore further, I turned and ran for home.

I could see Thea in the herb garden of the house as I approached, and she looked up as I ran over.

"I've had a premonition," I gasped, between breaths, bending forwards with my hands on my knees to steady myself. Thea waited for me to get my breath. "It was of Eve. Only a couple of seconds. She looked scared, terrified, in fact. What if she's in trouble? I have to go back now," I said in short statements, the length of my still heavy exhalations.

"Okay," Thea said, dropping her tools, "no time like the present. Let's go and try it and see if your powers are strong enough this time."

We walked over to the clearing Nithele had landed in, my breathing now almost back to normal. I felt excited to go back. I was ready.

"Now," Thea said, "as we've practised, picture the place in your mind that you know well, and remember, no one must see you arrive. Look at all the details and imagine the portal being there. Then keep repeating the place in your head."

"Okay," I said, my hands suddenly feeling clammy. I took a deep breath and closed my eyes, imagining my living room at home. Then I opened them again. "Oh, I forgot to ask this before. Can it be indoors?"

"Yes, anywhere. The size will adjust as it's a displacement of energy between planes, so not a solid structure."

"Okay, ready." I nodded and turned back, re-closing my eyes and concentrating on the details. A crackling, buzzing sound hit my ears, and my eyes shot open. Before me, the portal shimmered, visible only as undulating air. The trees and valley behind were blurred and wavering, like looking through gently rippling waves in a clear pond.

I inhaled sharply, turning my head quickly to look at Thea, my eyes wide. My skin was tingling all over, and I let out a squeal of excitement.

"I did it. It worked!"

Thea looked at me, unable to help the smile that spread across her face. She raised her eyebrows and nodded her head towards the portal, indicating with her eyes for me to look. My eyes followed hers just in time to see the centre of the portal shrink in on itself, and it was gone.

"Oh, no." My shoulders drooped along with my enthusiasm.

"First lesson," Thea said. "If you stop thinking of the

place it closes, or if you can't focus on it enough in the first place, it won't open. Secondly, as soon as you are through, it will begin to close behind you."

"Okay, got it," I said, determined to be more focused on the task now that my initial giddiness at getting it to open had worn off. "I'll go and get my things together."

Thea followed me into the house. I collected my bag and Malicen's documents and went back outside. We gave each other a long hug, and as I stepped back, she took hold of my shoulders. "Make sure you come back to me," she said, and her eyes glittered in the light with fearful tears that threatened to spill over.

"I'll come back as soon as I have some news," I said, trying hard to shelve my emotions. "Is there any way I can contact you?"

"I'm not sure your powers are strong enough to connect with me yet," she said. "When you get back, test the portal. If you need me but can't come yourself, picture this spot and send something through, and if I haven't heard from you in two months, Alchemia time, I'll come looking."

I gave a small nod. "Oh, that reminds me," I said, delving into my bag and handing her a piece of paper. "Here's the address of my house, just in case."

Straightening my stance, I looked around at the world I was in, taking mental snapshots of the surroundings so I would be able to return. I refused to feel, or I would go to pieces.

"Okay, I'm ready," I said.

Thea stepped back. "You'll be fine," she smiled.

I turned to look across the small meadow field. I thought of my home, and the portal slowly opened in front of me, spreading wider until it hovered humming and undulating in front of me, a gateway through time and dimensions to my other home.

Without looking back, I walked through.

The speed created a force that was all-encompassing, crushing me inwards. Light, shapes, and sounds flew past at a dizzying rate and then I was out, ejected unceremoniously onto the floor of my living room. It was darker than I expected, the evening light was still fading outside, but the curtains were closed. My head was spinning with a sickly dizzy feeling. I stood up, taking several deep breaths. My home smelt familiar, but there was something else. I could smell fear. Someone else was in my house. All my senses switched to high alert. I willed to see and opened my hand, drawing to me any light particles still left in the room. My hand glowed white, slowly illuminating the room. Pressed against the wall, fear and disbelief painted on her face like a frozen mask, was Eve. The picture before me merged in a déjà vu moment, like overlaying layers of acetate, and time caught up with my premonition, revealing the image I had seen before.

"Eve, it's ok. It's me, Haesel," I said. "I can explain. Put the light on, and I'll make a drink."

Nothing happened. I walked towards her to turn on the light. She let out a yell and shot towards the fireplace, grabbing the metal poker and holding it out in front of her. I don't know why but the whole scenario suddenly struck me as the funniest thing I had experienced in a long time, and I burst out laughing, switching the light on simultaneously.

"Fuck!" Eve said, placing her empty hand on her heart, breathing hard. "Fuck, Haesel, what the hell was that? Was that some kind of a trick or joke?" She bent forwards breathing hard. "Christ, that nearly finished me off."

I laughed even harder, "I can explain," I managed, holding up my now normal hand, as tears rolled down my cheeks, releasing everything I had been through in one giant rush.

"It's not funny," she said, "my heart's running a fucking

marathon here." Then the contagion of my laughter got to her, and she started too, although at a much higher pitch than usual, making me realise for the first time what was meant by hysterical laughter.

My tension now released, I gathered myself. This was a complication I hadn't anticipated, and I grew serious with the thought.

"I'll make a drink," I said again. "Come on," and I headed for the kitchen. Eve followed me in.

"Why are you here?" I asked. "You were definitely not supposed to be here."

"Oh, yeah, good subject. Let's talk about things that are not supposed to be, shall we? You go first."

I rolled my eyes. "I'll come to that, but really, why are you in my house? Something must have happened. Are you okay?"

"I couldn't reach you after you went to the lab, and I still couldn't contact you the next day either, so I came here to wait for you. I didn't know what else to do. I hoped you'd come back here if you could. I was honestly going to call the police in the morning. Then I fell asleep on the sofa."

Eve came to collect the tea I had made, but her hands were still shaking too much. I opened my mouth to speak, but she held up her trembling hand against any more questions. "Okay," she said, "over to you. Explain Haesel. I'm all ears."

I sighed and walked back into the living room, placing both our cups on the solid oak coffee table. Eve followed, and we sat at either end of my cream, three-seater sofa, facing one another.

"Bloody hell," I said, leaning forward and placing my head in my hands. "You really, really weren't meant to be here. I honestly don't know where to start," I said and turned to look her in the eye. "But everything I'm going to tell you is true. You know me, Eve. You're my best friend."

I really could have done without Eve being there. I loved her dearly, but I needed some time to process everything and come up with how the hell I was going to get back into VialCorp.

So, I dove straight in as we drank our tea, and I tried to keep it succinct to test the waters. Not every detail was needed just yet, and I decided to leave everything out regarding Noi and Nithele.

When I had finished, Eve just sat there, slack-jawed, staring at me. I glanced away, sighed, then looked back at her. "So, what do you think? I've lost it, right?"

"Oh. My. God! Haesel, are you really a witch?" she squealed, stamping her feet excitedly up and down on the floor. She accepted what I had said like it was an everyday occurrence, and my eyes misted that even after what I had said, she trusted me so much that she automatically took it on board. Eve proceeded to tell me how she had always wanted to be a witch and what she would do if she were. Memories flooded back from when we were nine or ten years old, sat on her bed in her ever-so-pink bedroom, discussing all things magical and what powers we would have. Then the questions came, one after the other until my eyes wouldn't hold themselves open of their own accord. Eventually, I checked the time and called quits. I swore her to secrecy, but I knew I didn't have to. She would never tell.

"Right," I said with a yawn, now exhausted with the added relief that she knew. It would have been excruciating hiding it. "I have to sleep. It's one a.m. Tomorrow we have to work out a way to get into VialCorp. I need to find further information on the SACL pill Malicen is working on before it's too late."

"Oh." Eve hung her head. Her face was filled with apprehension when she looked up. She bit her lower lip. I glared at her holding out my hands in a 'what, just say it' gesture.

"That's why I was so desperate to find you. It's already too late," she said. "Malicen is rolling it out in two days' time."

"What?!" I jumped up. "No! No, no, no, that can't happen," I said, panic causing my heart to pound. Then anger took over. "Aargh, what's the bloody point?!" I threw my hands out in frustration. A white bolt of energy shot out and sliced through the coffee table as though it was butter left out on a warm day. It lay in its respective halves smouldering and crackling, plumes of grey smoke filling the room with its acrid scent.

"Christ, Haesel, warn me, would you?" said Eve, from her crouched position behind the sofa where she had jumped. "I was not ready for that. Remember, I don't know what you can do yet okay?" She moved to sit on the arm of the sofa. "But, whoa, look what you just did!"

I sat down on the floor and leaned back on the sofa, blowing out a long breath through puffed out cheeks.

"I don't know what I can do yet either," I said. "Although that particular skill may come in handy." I stared at the burnt remnants. "I liked that table." Eve came to sit next to me on the floor, and I dropped my head in my hands. "I'm not ready for this."

My best friend came to my rescue, ever practical and positive in the face of adversity. She put her arm around my shoulder and squeezed me to her. "You're not on your own," she said. "In the morning, we can go to VialCorp, and once there, I'm sure we will find a way in."

I turned to her, so immensely grateful for her support. "Thanks, I needed that."

She gave a subtle twitch of her shoulders. "Sure, I may not be a witch, but I'm still here to back you up."

12

We set off mid-morning with a quick stop at the shop. I needed to collect some herbs I thought may be helpful in case we ran into trouble at VialCorp. I gathered up what I needed and turned to go, then hesitated. Returning to the back room, I felt for the key hidden at the back of the top shelf, and opened a small drawer in the cabinet against the wall. I picked out a small bag of extremely toxic herbs that my instincts told me to take. I placed them in my bag, just in case. I had no intention of causing serious harm, but they might buy us some time if we needed it. Eve was waiting by the door.

"Nearly ready," I called to her. Going over to the reception drawer and taking out a notepad, I scribbled a quick note.

'Closed this week for restocking.
Apologies for any inconvenience,
Haesel.'

Eve looked at me, confusion knotting her eyebrows.

"Just in case we get delayed," I shrugged. "We don't know what we are going to find, or what will happen."

It was comforting to have her with me this time and nice to have my mind taken away from everything that had happened so far. I now had a confidant I could talk to about anything, well, nearly anything—one thing at a time.

She chatted away as the miles sped by, telling me of a charity that had just received funding to build a sanctuary for three more species of Ape, that unfortunately, were next on the endangered list.

I forced my mind to relax, refusing to let the worry of what was coming rise to the surface, and settled into the driving.

We were almost at the M25 when Eve turned to me, a weird smile on her face that looked like it was trying not to escape but just couldn't be stopped. I knew that look.

"What?" I asked blankly. "Come on, out with it."

"Well, I was wondering if we could make a quick detour?" she wheedled. "I mean, like just an hour or so, only..."

"I know," I interrupted, glancing at her, my eyebrows raised high. "Tom, by any chance?"

Eve grinned, squeezing her shoulders up around her neck excitedly.

"Okay," I said, lifting my hands off the steering wheel for a moment. "What the hell. The chances of us getting into VialCorp are pretty slim, let alone anything else."

"Aww, c'mon, Haesel," Eve grinned. She leaned over to elbow me. "You have always wanted to iron out the details before you know the main points, but you can't possibly be on a downer now that you're a witch... with really awesome powers, I might add."

I glanced at her, letting go of some of my pent-up energy.

"Stop thinking the worst, you're way better than you think," she continued. "As long as I've known you, you have always had a determination to stick at things until you've found the solution, you never give up…and besides, it's fate, right? What is it you always say again?" Eve turned her head to look up to the right, twisting her mouth into an exaggerated thoughtful expression while tapping her cheek with her finger.

I laughed, my worries that only I created melting. I played along and quoted my line for her. "All our lives are fated. We just need to follow the path." Eve said each word in time with me, and we both laughed. "I love you, Eve," I said. "You're the yin to my yang."

"Yep," she said, gathering her hair and twisting it forward over one shoulder before settling back in her seat. "So now we just need to follow that path…to Tom's house."

I laughed again, and the smile stayed on my lips. Eve was right. I was a problem solver. Although I always considered all avenues before making a decision, I absolutely had to fix it once I decided.

If I wasn't able to sort the problem instantly I was left frustrated. This gave me time to reconsider my course of action, and then doubt would creep in, clouding my logical judgement. I made a mental note, again, to try not to overthink.

"This being a witch thing is weird," I said, staring at the road, half talking to Eve and half voicing my thoughts. "In a way, I feel like I've been preparing for it, for something, all my life. What you said before, about me always thinking the worst, I do that because I've always felt that I need to know what the worst thing is that could happen, then I'll be prepared for it." I shrugged and glanced over to her, adding, "You had better check if…"

"Already done," Eve interjected with a cheeky grin. "I messaged him when we set off. He's home."

I shook my head, giving her a rueful glance, as she

proceeded to alter the satnav's directions with the new postcode.

"What's with you and Tom anyway?" I asked as the car's tyres ate up the miles on the motorway. "You've been together on and off for years. I mean, it's a bit odd. How do you still keep hooking up if you don't want to commit to each other?"

Eve shrugged and smiled. "It's not odd to us. We are happy being independent souls. We don't own each other, and there are so many things that we both want to do in life, but not necessarily the same things. This way, there's no pressure to behave in a certain way, and we can just be ourselves. It's very free and easy, and I think we just know that we will always be in each other's life. We just gel, you know?" she said, reclining the seat and laying back, crossing her arms above her head. I nodded along as she spoke. "We have so many things in common, and both feel the same about the world." She looked at me and pulled a face that said, it didn't matter if I didn't understand it. "We're just connected," she finished.

A relaxed smile broke on my face. "Well, when you put it like that, it sounds like a very healthy, stress-free relationship. That's not so easy with kids, though," I added, pulling into the inside lane to come off at the next slip road.

"That's probably true," she relented.

At this present time, Tom lived in Croydon, in a two-bed terrace that he shared with a flatmate. He was several years younger than Eve and, like her, had flitted about, in and out of jobs in between charity work.

Eve had met him at the Hay-On-Wye Festival in Wales, which brought people together to celebrate their favourite musicians, actors, books and authors, and discover new ones. It was known as the ultimate festival for book lovers, focusing on sustainability, reducing waste and carbon footprint, and they even employed a renewable energy supplier. With learning and discussion on 'Green Topic' events throughout the festival, people could get involved to help the planet and learn ways to slow climate change.

I remembered how excited she was to tell me about it in every detail afterwards. She had gone over to the bins to dispose of some rubbish, and Tom was in front of her doing the same. She had watched him separate his rubbish into the appropriate bins, then put his cardboard cup in the general waste. Eve tapped him on the shoulder and advised him that he had put the cup in the wrong bin as it was wax-coated cardboard.

He had corrected her, saying that the coating was, in fact, polyethylene and couldn't be recycled; only the plastic lid and cardboard sleeve could. He then went on to advise her in earnest that only nine per cent of all plastic ever made had been recycled, that all plastic from kids' toys couldn't be recycled, and that we had, to date, since the mass production of plastic started in the 1950s, now accumulated over eight point five billion tons of disposable plastic that has ended up in landfill.

And that, he had finished, is why there has been leakage of global waste systems into the oceans because, it took 400 years to degrade.

Eve had looked into his eyes with awe and was smitten.

They had spent the rest of the day together, with Tom talking about conservation and various charity work he was involved in. They had laid under the stars at the festival and shared the same thoughts on their love of nature and a dedication to helping the planet heal.

Eve then joined him on various projects. Together, they had planted trees for the Woodland Trust and travelled the world for two years planting trees in Indonesia and the Borneo rainforests to help preserve the native habitat of the orangutans, which was severely threatened due to deforestation and degradation from logging.

We turned into Tom's road, and Eve sat up excitedly and checked herself over in the visor mirror. All the houses looked similar with white or cream rendered fronts, and some were slightly shabbier than others. Some people had replaced the windows and upgraded the straight, square design of the downstairs bay window with a gentler and prettier curved one, and some of the small brick walls that ran along the front of the path had been changed, either painted or replaced with various types of fencing. Essentially, the look was the same, with a small path leading to the front door and a square of garden in front of the bay window.

"Guess which one is Tom's?" Eve grinned as we made our way down the street. It was pretty obvious. While all the other houses had either laid flagstones, brick weave, or various shades of gravel with a few pot plants, Tom's small, square front of garden was filled to overflowing with flowers.

"Wow," I exclaimed as we pulled up outside, and I felt myself smiling as we got out of the car and stood looking at it together. It was amazing how this small area of nature could instantly relieve anxiety, and I felt the tension in my body melt away, and my shoulders relax.

Wildflowers of all shades were filling every last inch of space in a beautiful, frothy display that rose up and reached out over the small brick wall. All manner of insects, bees, and butterflies were making the most of the little oasis, and in the middle, a small, solar-powered water feature produced the relaxing sound of gurgling running water.

The door opened, and Tom came out to greet us. He was well built with thick, sandy coloured hair that looked slightly unruly, and he had a relaxed, casual demeanour that matched his outfit of a t-shirt and joggers.

"Here you are," he said, grinning. "It's so good to see you, and I'm so glad you could stop by." Eve kissed him excitedly and looped her arms around his waist. He pulled her close in return, and they looked completely natural and comfortable as though there had been no separation of time. I felt a pang of envy but shelved the thoughts as quickly as they appeared.

Tom pulled away from Eve and reached out towards me with one hand.

"Haesel, at last, I get to meet you," he said, shaking my hand, then pulling me into a quick but genuine embrace.

"It's good to finally meet you, too," I said. "I'm not sure why it's taken this long, other than life just gets in the way."

"That could be it," he said, "but I like to think the right time was meant to be now." I met his eyes with a broad smile.

I turned towards the garden. "This is amazing. It's so beautiful, and so many insects have found it."

"Yes, it's great what you can do with such a small space, isn't it? This was just a box of mixed native wildflower seed. It cost no more than five-pound. Just sprinkle on, rake, and wait for the magic." He grinned, reaching into his pocket to produce a notebook, his face animated with enthusiasm. "I'm logging all the different species of insect that manage to seek out and use this small space," he continued. "There's enough for four gardens in one box, so I aim to get most of the street joining in next year. So many people have commented on it and want to do the same."

"Oh, that would be amazing," I said.

"Yes, it's really important," he continued. "Did you know that between 1980 and 2013, we have lost a third of our wild pollinator species? Just this plant alone," he said, reaching forward and spreading apart the longer stems to reveal a shorter plant with bright yellow flowers, "is called Bird's-foot Trefoil, and supports over 160 different species." Tom glanced back at me from his bent position. "Sorry." He grinned, standing up again, his hands on his hips, and his face apologetic. "I get a bit carried away."

"No, not at all," I said. "You're speaking to the converted, and so many of these plants are medicinal. Lamb's Ears and yarrow help stop bleeding, and the latter is thought of as nature's styptic. It's astringent, antimicrobial, and anti-inflammatory, and both were extremely valuable and used during the war to pack wounds."

Eve poked her head between us. "Okay, okay, you two, that's enough now," she said, grinning. "I knew you would get on, but I'm desperate for a cuppa."

"Sorry, Eve," Tom said with a small laugh, giving her a hug. "Come in. I'll put the kettle on. I really do think I could talk to you all day though, Haesel," he said, glancing back at me. "Maybe you could talk at some of our wildlife seminars?"

"Yes," I nodded, "I don't see why not," and followed him and Eve through to the kitchen, whispering in Eve's ear on the way. "Okay, I know why you like him now."

She turned, beaming, and her smile said it all.

We chatted over tea and a bite to eat, Tom and Eve reminiscing and telling tales of their travels, and Tom asking about my shop and knowledge of herbs and plants.

Tom glanced down at his watch. "Well, I don't know how long you two were planning on staying. Eve mentioned that you were passing as you were going out for a meal in London tonight. Anywhere nice?"

I started to panic, being caught off guard. I hadn't had time to think of a reason as to why we were passing, but Eve interjected quickly.

"We're not sure yet. Haesel is meeting up with a couple of friends she met while studying and invited me along." I breathed out.

"Ah, that will be nice," Tom said smiling. "I can't be long myself, actually. Sorry, Eve, I'm off for a couple of days. I've got to meet up with other organisers and coordinators to discuss future projects for The World Land Trust. After that, maybe we could get together?"

"Yes, that would be good. Let me know what your projects involve at your meetings, and maybe I can do something with you?"

"That would be great. I'd like that…. Oh," he said suddenly, jumping up. "That reminds me," and he dashed off into the kitchen. A few seconds later he returned, and held out a key to Eve. "This is if you get stuck and need a place to crash," he said, bending over to give her a kiss. "Use it anytime."

"Ah, thank you," Eve said, jumping up to give him a hug. "We may use it tonight then, as hotels in London are not cheap."

"Yes, that's very true," Tom said, turning and pointing to the sofa. "Haesel, this is a sofa bed, so you're welcome to stay anytime, too, and there's bedding and pillows in the wardrobe in my bedroom."

"Thank you, that's very kind," I said with a broad smile.

We spent the next forty-five minutes catching up. Then Eve followed Tom out of the room to check out where everything was.

I stood and walked to the window. There wasn't much to see, but I watched a man walk past with his dog. He was lost in his own thoughts, staring at the pavement. The dog was small, white, and fluffy, and I made a bet that it wouldn't have been the man's first choice of dog breed. It stopped to cock its leg up the next wall it came to, and he waited patiently for it before continuing down the street. I felt someone watching me and turned to look directly at a woman four houses down who was leaning on her elbows at her upstairs window. She turned away immediately, surprised at being seen. My senses were much more active now, and I felt more in tune with them.

A quick check of my phone said it was nearing 3 p.m., and I was just thinking that we should get going soon, when a car pulled up outside.

13

A squat, burly looking guy with dark, short hair stepped out. From the passenger side, a slim woman with fine, light brown hair just past her shoulders walked around the front of the car to join him. She was wearing a smart white blouse and black skirt, with flat black shoes and carrying a large holdall-type bag. They both headed down the path to the house.

I looked at the woman, and a sharp intake of breath unconsciously caught me off guard as an image of her sitting, waiting in a reception area, flashed in front of my mind. My skin prickled, and my adrenalin started to surge. I knew that reception. It was the one I had sat in at VialCorp.

My breathing became erratic as my protective senses got ready to respond. What did she want? What if she knew about me? What if my picture was displayed in the office, and everyone there was on the lookout for me? My mind raced and mixed up rational with irrational possibilities. I looked down at my right hand, which had started to tingle and gasped to see it glowing with a white light that was jumping and crackling. I dashed to the small downstairs toilet, locking the door.

It's okay, I said, talking to myself in my head and taking some big, slow, deep breaths. I used the techniques Thea had taught me to calm my emotions, thinking of her words.

It had been a day on Alchemia set aside for me to explore my powers. Thea had told me it would be tough. We had walked to an open area of ground with large rocks lying sporadically among the long blades of meadow grass, they swayed and rippled in waves in the constantly shifting breeze. She sat me down on a rock and told me that Rowan would be in danger in the future. She had seen it. My panic attack had been induced. They were something that had started after I thought Thea had died in the fire. My breathing was heavy, erratic, and I felt lightheaded and sick. I felt like I was trapped and needed to escape. Bolts of energy had shot from my hands, exploding a nearby rock that had happened to be in the way. The fragments were instantly swallowed up in the long grass. Thea had come to stand behind me and had wrapped her hands around my waist, pressing her hands flat against the base of my ribcage. I thought of her voice.

"Breathe, Haesel, with me, deeply, contain it." Her hands glowed a warm amber and quelled the ball of acid that was growing like a cancer in my centre. "Repeat in your head. I am okay. If I am calm, I can protect her. I need to be calm to see it." I did as she said, and slowly my panic eased. She had turned to me explaining, "Your panic induces fear and leaves you open. It makes your powers erratic and less controlled." She then told me, that what she had said about Rowan wasn't true, it was part of the training and had been deliberate to initiate my emotions. At first, I had been angry with her, but then I had understood. I had to be able to control my powers, no matter what I was told.

I leaned against the bathroom door, my breathing slowing. Before I had left Alchemia she had said that the key to my strength was control. If I could think clearly of the effect I wanted my power to achieve, I could then direct it elsewhere.

I opened the bathroom door as Tom and Eve walked past into the hall.

"Lee's here," Tom called back over his shoulder, and as he opened the door to let him in, I remembered that he shared the flat with another guy.

"Hello," he said, "wow, we have a full house," and a warm, genuine smile lit up his face. Within seconds I had formed an impression of him. I could sense his honesty and that he was trustworthy. Tom introduced us. "Nice to meet you," he said, his eyes crinkling in the corners, then he turned towards the woman behind him.

"Eve, Haesel, this is Katherine." She held up a hand briefly. "Hi," then went back to fiddling with the thin, gold ring on her middle finger. We all moved into the living room, and Tom looked at her expectantly.

"So," he said, his hands outstretched, palms upwards, "how did you get on?"

Katherine beamed, "I got it," she announced, with a small shrug. Her eyes flicked briefly between us, then down at the floor. She was obviously not used to being the centre of attention.

"Ah fantastic, well done," Tom said, moving to give her a quick hug.

Lee encircled her waist and pulled her closer to him.

"You did great, I knew you would."

"Well done," Eve said. "What are we are we celebrating?"

Lee pulled a face. "Oh god, sorry. I didn't mean to be rude. Katherine went for a job interview today to keep in order some very prestigious offices." Katherine elbowed him sharply and widened her eyes at him.

"It's only a cleaning job," she said, her skin taking on a pink hue. "Nothing special."

"It's very special," I said, hoping to defuse her embarrassment. "You got a job today, and that's brilliant."

"Thank you." She smiled, and her shoulders relaxed a little. "I think Lee helped. He knew about it from work and said I should apply. It pays more money than my job at the coffee shop, so I thought I'd give it a go."

Lee pulled her to him with a little squeeze, planting a kiss on her hair at the same time. She looked at him, smiling, her eyes lingering on his for a few seconds, then bent to pick up the bag she had brought in with her.

"Sorry, you'll have to excuse me. I have to get rid of this bag and get ready. Lee is taking me out to celebrate, and we booked a hotel in Brighton for a couple of days." She looked down at the bag with a small shake of her head. "They gave me so many uniforms to try on, different sizes in case they didn't fit." She turned to Lee. "I'll leave them on the bed. My training doesn't start until Wednesday."

"Is the job local?" Eve asked.

"Not to here, not really. It's at VialCorp. Lee works security there, so when he's on an evening shift, he can stay with me, and I can go in with him. My flat's not too far from there."

"I think I'll be at yours more than here," Lee said with a laugh.

So that was it, I thought, letting out a breath that I hadn't realised I was holding, at the same time glancing at Eve, whose jaw had hit the floor as her brain processed what that might mean for us. She recovered quickly.

"That's amazing. Well done again," she said, her raised eyebrows and wide grin making her statement look genuine. "It was meant to be," she added, throwing me a quick glance.

I looked at the clock on the wall, and she took the hint.

"Well, it was very nice to briefly meet you both," she said, standing up, "but myself and Haesel are going to have to dash off, I'm afraid."

We said our goodbyes and I waited in the car while Eve finalised future plans with Tom. A few minutes later, she came running down the drive and threw herself into the car. "Go, quick before I pop," she said, drumming her hands on her knees. I set off, heading into Croydon.

"Let's find a café and discuss what just happened," I said flashing her a quick, wide smile. "We now have a way in."

"Are you kidding me? Haesel, oh my god, I know you say that everything is fated, but seriously, this *was* meant to be!"

"We're not in yet," I reminded her. "We have to get into Malicen's office. I'm sure all the information we are looking for will be in there."

We pulled in at The Royal Oak pub car park. The building sagged but looked inviting, and we chose a round table in the corner. The dark red upholstered furniture was thin and almost threadbare in places from years of being rubbed by legs and arms along the edges. The decor was old and could have done with freshening up and updating, but it had a friendly, well used, relaxed feel. We ordered a drink and a bite to eat and made a plan.

"We can go back once the house is clear and check out the uniforms," I said. "At least that will give us a plausible cover for entering the building. All the doors are opened with a DNA pass, and I'm pretty sure that Katherine would have been given one since my premonition saw her sitting in the reception at VialCorp."

Eve looked at me sideways. "Err, your what?" she asked.

"Oh, sorry, I must have forgot that bit. I have premonitions of events, things that may happen or have happened, like warnings. Thea said I will be able to control them more precisely when my powers get stronger. I saw Katherine through the window when she got out of the car and had a premonition of her at VialCorp."

"Oh, that's so cool," Eve stated. "Don't suppose you can see what happens when we get in there can you? Because that would be really useful."

"Yes, wouldn't it? But unfortunately, it doesn't seem to work that way."

We chatted over our meal and returned to Tom's around 7 p.m. Everyone had left, and we quickly opened the large holdall bag and checked out the uniforms, selecting our size. Eve got undressed to try one on while I went through the bag containing a manual and strict instructions on 'Do's and Don'ts.' One of the 'Do's' was to make sure hair was neatly tied back if long, the hairnet provided, which looked more like a bag than a net, should be worn over the top. Gloves and hair nets were to be worn at all times. *Good*, I thought. With our hair covered, we wouldn't be so easily recognisable.

"Ta-da! What do you think?" I looked up at Eve, who was displaying exaggerated model poses in the new uniform. The powder blue, straight leg trousers matched the longer length fitted top that had a collar and a full buttoned front. A contrasting grey front panel and sleeve cuffs gave it a nice shape.

"Wow, that's actually quite smart for cleaning."

"Err, hmm," Eve said, with a stern expression, picking up the pass and attaching it to the loop of material just under her left collarbone. She pointed to it, her eyebrows raised. "Sanitising Administrator, I'll have you know."

I laughed at her faked posh accent. "Right," I said, feeling more positive. "The manual states that staff are to enter and leave the building via the service entrance at the back. I'll get changed, and we can cover all of the scenarios on the way there."

"Okay, you take the ID," she said, throwing it over to me.

"She's paler than you, but if they hesitate, you'll just have to say you put some fake tan on when you saw how pale you were on the photo." She grinned at me, an exaggerated smile that showed all her teeth, and jumped her eyebrows up and down a couple of times.

I laughed. "That's actually a good idea."

We kept the uniforms on, stashing the gloves and hairnets in our pockets. I looked back to check everything was as we had found it before we headed to the car, chucking our clothes on the back seat.

The journey only took just under an hour, and as we pulled up to the car park barrier, we tucked our hair into the hairnets. Eve checked out her look in the mirror.

"Bloody hell, what on earth do I look like with this on?"

I grinned at her. "You look the part," I said, dropping the window and leaning out to hold the pass over the reader. The machine displayed the message, 'Access Denied.'

"Oh no, it's not working," I said, trying it again. The same message appeared. I tried it several different ways, but the message was still the same.

"Umm... Haesel," Eve said. I looked in the direction she was pointing to see a burly security guard heading towards us whose belly looked like he needed to cut back on the fast food, or maybe he just needed bigger trousers?

"It's okay, keep calm," I said, more to myself than Eve. "We've got this."

His face had a well-practised stern expression as he approached the car. His mouth set in a thin line, he placed his hands firmly over the car door and bent to look in the window.

"Evening ladies, what seems to be the problem?" His breath smelt like some kind of meat stew.

I smiled up at him. "Hello, can you help? This is our first day, and the pass doesn't seem to be working."

"Can I see your pass please?" he said, extending one hand into the car and refusing to smile back. I handed it over and he glanced at it, breathing out heavily through inflated cheeks with the effort of holding himself in position one handed. I wrinkled my nose and took tiny breaths, and Eve wound down her window. Placing one hand on his back, he grimaced and stood up, then reaching into his back pocket he produced an electronic device and scanned the pass. I held my breath. After a quick look, he handed it back and peered back into the car.

"Did you both attend on the same day?" he asked.

We both replied "Yes" in unison, and Eve made a show of scrabbling through her bag on the pretence of looking for her pass. He waved his hand at her, shaking his head. "That's okay. It's all good ladies. You are free to go," he said. Judging by the remnants around his mouth and fresh stain on his shirt, I guessed that he was keen to get back to his food. "I can see you're registered, but the details may not have been loaded onto the main database just yet in order to activate the pass. It should be active within the next 10 minutes." He turned and keyed a code into the number keypad and the barrier duly lifted.

"Thank you," I said, sighing with relief. "We don't want to get into trouble on our first day."

He nodded again, still without humour, and held out his arm, palm flat, indicating the way. "Go straight down to the bottom and take a right. You'll see the signs for the service car park."

"Aww, thank you so much," I called as I wound the window up and proceeded slowly past the barrier, giving him one of my best smiles and a little wave as I went.

"Eww, can I breathe now? His breath was rank." Eve stated, wafting her hand in the air. I shot her a look, eyebrows raised, "Try being where I was. You were lucky."

She gave a nervous laugh and jiggled her legs up and down as we made the right turn. "Ooh, I need a wee. This is getting me all jittery."

"It will be fine," I said with assurance, looking her straight in the eye and smiling. "We've passed."

I felt much more confident this time. Maybe it was because I had been in before, or maybe I was just getting a handle on my emotions. After all, I had faced a dragon, so I was feeling fairly confident that I could handle breaking into an office, and my powers should keep Malicen at bay if need be.

14

We found a parking bay and got out of the car. A short distance to the left, I could see an elevator with 'Service Entrance' signed above. Another security guard was at the door.

"Oh no, Haesel, there's more security, and I don't have a pass."

"It's okay," I said. "You've got this, Eve. Remember what we practised coming over here? If anyone can chat up a guy, it's you." She turned to me, feigning a wounded look, her hand resting lightly below her throat. "What's that supposed to mean?"

I rolled my eyes at her. "Come on, let's just do it."

As we approached the lift, a tall, slim built guard in his thirties with dark eyes and hair stood up from his seat nearby and smiled. His uniform was immaculate with sharp iron creases, and his hair, recently cut, was gelled so that it remained fixed neatly in place. My bravado wavered slightly. He's going to like everything done by the book, I thought.

"Evening, Ladies."

"Evening," we replied again in unison, which made Eve giggle. She flashed him a smile, and he grinned back at her.

"Are you on all night?" she asked, extending her hand at the same time. "I'm Ann, by the way."

He grinned back at her. "Derek," he said, shaking her hand. "I'll be here 'til eleven." His smile broadened at the same time as his eyes briefly gave her the once over .

"Ooh, you feel like you could protect me with those hands?" she giggled.

I let out a giggle at that and gave her a nudge. "Sorry about my friend," I said. "It's our first day, and I think she's a bit giddy."

Derek drew himself up, planting his feet and crossing his arms over his puffed-out chest, keen to look impressive in his pristine uniform. "That's quite alright, Miss," he said, although his eyes were having trouble looking anywhere other than Eve's unbuttoned cleavage that was on full display.

Eve followed his eyes and looked down. "Oops, sorry," she said, doing up a button. She looked back up at him, smirking and biting her bottom lip in full-on coy mode. She was actually turning pink, which added to the look, although I knew that she was genuinely feeling embarrassed.

Derek looked a little flustered at the attention.

"Come on," I said. "We don't want to be late," and I flashed Katherine's pass at the reader to allow lift access. The machine denied again. I looked at Derek, rolling my eyes. "So much for technology. This happened at the gate. Apparently, the system hasn't updated yet."

"That's fine, Miss," he said smiling, waving his hand in a blasé manner. "I can let you in."

He turned to Eve. "I'll have to see your pass though, Miss?"

Eve made a show of patting her pockets and checking round herself. "Oh no. I must have forgotten it," she said, genuinely panicking this time. "Oh no, no, no, I can't lose this job," she said, her eyes round and pleading. "I promise I won't forget it next time." Derek looked at us both, then turned to Eve, switching straight back into security mode. "I can't, I'm afraid, Miss, it's more than my job's worth." My heart rate increased.

"Oh, please," Eve pleaded, bringing her hands together in prayer, "my mum's sick, and I need this job to look after her. I'm on this shift tomorrow and I'll bring it then."

Derek sighed and looked between us both. "She really does need it," I said. "Could you ask us a question? Something that would prove she's meant to be here tonight?"

Derek rubbed his fingers over his chin and looked at Eve as he considered this, then gave a slight nod.

"Alright, can you tell me who interviewed you for the position?" he asked.

"Mrs Simmonds," Eve answered without hesitation. "Severe looking, very short brown hair, overdone eyeshadow and wonky lipstick, and...badly needing some deodorant. Not a good representative as head of the department for cleanliness at all," she said, wrinkling her nose and pulling a face.

Derek threw his head back and laughed loudly at her description before quickly gathering himself together, coughing.

"I'll accept that answer," he said with as much of a straight face as he could muster, then reached over to place his pass against the reader. He nodded his head towards the opening lift doors and flashed us a wry smile. "Go on, just this once."

"Ooh, thank you so much," Eve gushed as we stepped into the lift. "You're a lifesaver. Maybe we could catch up when I'm finished?" I pushed the button to the sixth floor. "Your uniform looks lovely, by the way," she called out as the lift doors started to close.

Derek looked a little flustered, but his face lit up with pride. "Sure, I'll be here," he said, as an electronic voice announced the doors were closing, and we jolted upwards.

"Oh my god, you were amazing!" I gushed. "How did you know about Mrs Simmonds?"

"I looked it up on the way down here and saw her profile picture," Eve giggled. "She looked like she would have B.O. so I just went with it. I figured it would sound authentic." She gave an involuntary shudder, "God, my heart's pounding, that was really cringy."

"It was brilliant. You were very convincing," I said, grinning, then suddenly grew serious as the lift got to the third floor. "Right," I said, turning to Eve. "Let's find Malicen's office, and remember, in and out as fast as we can. Look for, and grab, anything that may tell us something. There will probably be cameras so just keep your head down."

Eve looked at me with wide eyes that were nervous but determined. "Okay," she said, absently picking the side of her fingernail, "but couldn't you just disable the cameras?"

"Yes, I could, but I imagine there's a security room somewhere, and if the screens are being watched and suddenly go blank, then we are going to have security surround us in no time. I'm hoping these cleaning uniforms will buy us some time." Eve just nodded, wide-eyed.

"Stay behind me and hold the doors in case we are met with security when they open. If anyone's there, I can hold them back.

The lift came to a stop and announced, "Penthouse, doors opening."

We both glanced at each other briefly.

The doors slid smoothly apart, and I instinctively put my hand back to protect Eve. I listened intently for any noise, my senses sharpening as I glanced up at the corners, looking for cameras. I spotted one, but the light was off, and our movement into the large square room didn't seem to wake it up. Eve gasped.

A cream interlinking hexagon pattern ran a border around the plush deep blue carpet. In the centre of the room, separated by a thick glass table, with solid wooden blocks at each end, two large, cream leather sofas faced each other. The walls were encased with beautiful deep wood panelling and displayed various art in heavy guilt frames. My eyes took in a huge screen sunk into the left side of the far wall, and plants and ornaments added a further touch of comfort. Eve nodded her head towards a smaller table that housed a bottle of wine and a glass decanter of whisky, complete with crystal cut glasses that called invitingly for the guest to take a seat and relax.

I pursed my lips, frowning and gave a small, adamant shake of my head. She rolled her eyes and mouthed, "Joking."

I rolled my eyes back at her and pointed to the door on the far wall to the right.

The ornate silver plaque on the door read 'Malicen Suite' and underneath 'Dr Julius Malicen MD.' The door was protected with another pass reader, and I looked at Eve.

"Well, I reckon the chances of my pass working here are pretty much nil, even if it had been fully registered," I said in a low voice. "I'll have to break it. Stand back."

Eve retreated a couple of steps as I raised my hands to the reader. A white crackling glow spread slowly outwards as I concentrated on the door yielding and opening. I could feel the tingling energy flowing through my body as the glow became brighter, turning to pale orange as a lightning bolt of light shot towards the reader. There was a bang and the sound of locks springing open. Eve's hands shot over her mouth, and I held my breath, waiting for the alarms to sound. None did. They must think security would sound the alarm first, I thought.

I turned the handle, and the door opened easily as we quietly hurried inside. I could hear no sound as I closed it behind us. I looked at Eve, who was standing with her mouth open, staring at the room.

"Wow," she breathed, "this must cost a fortune."

I nodded, taking in the scene before us. "Well, here's proof. There's definitely a lot of money to be made in medicine," I said.

The room was enormous and followed the same theme from the waiting room outside, but with added opulence and indulgence. Beautiful high ceilings with ornate plasterwork allowed full-length cream drapes at the windows to fall in heavy abundance onto the powder blue carpet. The walls were made up of blue-grey marble panelling and again were adorned with tasteful abstract art paintings. Silver statues and ornaments picked up and complimented the silver borders on the coffee table in the centre of the room, the frames around the artwork, and the silver feet and detail of the tiny silver studs on the luxurious brown leather sofas. Over to the left was an enormous glass desk with huge blocks of the same deep brown wood at either end to support the glass. A band of marble edged with silver ran around the top third.

My eyes were drawn to the wall behind the desk, where an enormous twelve foot print, in an elaborate ornate frame, displayed two hands coming together to almost touch at the outstretched forefingers—Michelangelo's Creation of Adam. *Wow, Malicen really does think he's God*, I thought.

A shiver ran down my spine and mingled with a cold

touch of fear. I glanced towards the exit door, biting my lower lip and gathered myself to concentrate on the job at hand.

The sound of another door opening across the room made me jump more than usual, and I swung around, bracing myself, instantly ready to stop whoever it was from sounding the alarm. Eve's face appeared from behind the door. I must have been so wrapped up in my thoughts that I hadn't noticed she had disappeared. My jaw ached from clenching my teeth.

"Eve," I hissed, "stay with me. What if someone comes in?"

"Just checking no one is in here," she said in a low voice, hurrying over. "Plus, I really, really needed a wee," she added, bending slightly and squeezing her knees together in emphasis.

"The bathroom is that door I just came out of if you need to go," she said in a loud whisper, straightening up. "It's amazing, and on the other side is a spa room." Eve's eyes were large and unblinking, and I suppressed a giggle at her 'caught in the headlights' look. "I mean bloody hell, Haesel," she continued, opening her arms wide, "This whole floor is just one suite." She pointed across the room. "That's a full bar in the corner full of different whiskeys and champagnes, and through the door next to it is the most amazing bedroom I've ever seen." She turned to look me straight in the eye, her mouth slack, and gave a small shake of her head. "I mean, who stays over in their office?" she questioned incredulously.

The intense stare I gave her shook her out of her stunned state.

"Sorry, sorry. Okay, I'm back."

"Come on," I said, heading quickly over to the desk. "I know this is obvious, but let's check anyway." On the other side, the sturdy legs housed a series of drawers.

"You look through this side, and I'll take the other," I

whispered in a low voice, my eyes continuously checking, darting around the room.

We opened one drawer after the other, my worry and disappointment growing in equal measure, as no files or papers on anything to do with the SACL virus, the pill roll-out, or any info on the MagnanogenR4 patent that Eve had discovered were to be found.

"I'll go check in the bedroom," Eve said, darting off.

I sat back in the comfortable padded leather chair. Leaning forward, I rested my elbows on the desk, supporting my forehead in my hands. I closed my eyes and concentrated. Where would he hide important documents?

I imagined Malicen in the office sitting at the desk. I pictured him turning off the computer, and suddenly a close-up image of his hands flashed before my eyes. He was fiddling with the end of something silver; was it tubes? I couldn't quite make it out. The image was as though I was behind him, looking over his shoulder. I looked around the image quickly, but the background was blurred. I could make out a rectangular shape, colours of blue and brown, but that was all. The image disappeared, but I was sure it was in this room.

I sat up and looked around, starting with where I was sitting. My eyes landed on the drawers in the desk. The drawer was brown, and I could see the blue colour of the carpet and sofas beyond. A silver strip ran along the top of each drawer. I dropped to my knees for a closer inspection and saw that it was a tube. The end finished in a cap.

Eve came out of the bedroom. I waved my hand and hissed. "Over here." She came running over. "I can't find anything," she said. "I've literally looked everywhere, under and behind drawers, and at the back of the wardrobe in case there is a hidden compartment or something, but there's nothing anywhere."

"I think there may be something here. I had another premonition. Malicen was fiddling with something silver and tube-like. Maybe some information is rolled up inside."

"I'll check the others," Eve said, moving to start on the set of drawers at the other end of the desk.

After an hour, we had searched everything and still nothing.

15

My need to find more information forced my decision, and I pulled the heavy leather chair up to the desk and sat in front of the latest, pristine Apple Mac computer. Malicen would be careful, very careful. He was exact, calculating, and precise. Even if I could get in, I doubted he would leave anything on there that he didn't want to be found, but he would have a backup, or even several.

I expected that touching it would trip an alarm somehow, maybe send a message that someone was on the computer, but I needed to look all the same. The mouse sat neatly next to the silver keyboard, and as I reached for it, the small movement of my touch caused the computer to whir to life. My fingers started to tingle, and my heartbeat made an audible thumping in my ears. I was surprised that it had been left on, but not to find that it was password and fingerprint protected.

A small green light appeared in the centre above the screen. Someone was watching me. My ears picked up on a small click of an electric switch, and I looked up to my right into the corner of the room. The camera now had a red light glowing brightly from beneath it. I quickly shut the computer down.

Blood raced around my body, and my chest tightened. I jumped up, overturning the chair behind me.

"Eve, time's up. We've been spotted. The computer must have triggered the alarm. Let's go, now!"

Eve shot to her feet and ran to the door, mouth agape and eyes wide, waiting for me. "Haesel, what the hell are you doing?"

As much as we had to leave, I had to look. I knew that information was in here somewhere. I raised my hand holding up one finger. "One minute," I said, flashing her an intense stare.

My eyes scanned the room, flicking quickly from one thing to another. Nothing was standing out. My breathing became loud and urgent and I took a deep breath, conscious to remain calm. Time was up. I started towards the door, as I did so, my eyes passed over the huge ornate chandelier hanging in the centre of the room. All my senses seemed to draw me to it and I turned abruptly, my eyes scanning every detail. At first glance, it looked like a huge ball, but as I looked closer I could see it was made of silver interlocking tubes in hexagon shapes with tiny bright lights at the junction of every angle. My eyes rested on the base of the chandelier, where a short tube protruded from the bottom ending in a solid silver hexagon.

"That's it!" I yelled and dashed across the room. Leaping onto the thick glass coffee table, I stretched up, grabbing the short tube, and the image I now saw overlaid my premonition.

"Haesel! I can hear the elevator."

I glanced at the door. Eve's chest was heaving, and she was repeatedly tapping the sides of her thighs with her fists.

"I've nearly got it!" I twisted the hexagon, which

unscrewed, releasing the tube from the main light. I tipped it upside down and shook it into my hand. Out fell a memory stick. A quick burst of relief flooded through me, levelling my breath.

I shoved it quickly into the pocket of my padded bra, just as the door burst open.

Three guards rushed into the room, one made a grab for Eve, who screamed and pulled away, but not quick enough, he grabbed hold of her wrist, twisting her around. Energy fizzed through my veins, and every cell seemed to charge with increased ability. My hands glowed, and I aimed them at the guard. The white burst of light shot towards him, hitting him squarely in the stomach. He yelled out, releasing Eve, and dropped to the floor, unconscious.

"Look out!" Eve screamed, and I turned to see the remaining two guards holding tasers straight at me. The loud mechanical ticking of the tasers told me they were ready to fire. I lifted both hands and focused. Glowing light zig-zagged across the room, hitting one squarely in the chest. The taser released and hit the floor, as he flew backwards smashing his head on the wall before falling to the floor in a crumpled heap. The remaining guard released his taser towards me. I tried to shield it, sending a quick bolt of energy at the guard, but wasn't quick enough. The wall of pulsing gold air spread out in front of me, but not before one of the released metal probes clipped the edge. The electrical current drew my energy with it as it spun downwards at an angle, smashing into the coffee table I was standing on.

The thick glass cracked and separated into several large, razor sharp pieces. I yelled out as I lost my footing and fell heavily against the knife edge shard which sliced a deep crevice through the skin on my upper arm, from shoulder to elbow. I screamed out at the searing pain as blood spurted from the wound, spraying the glass, and dripping into the thick blue carpet, leaving a dark, sticky stain.

Eve ran to my side, her face ashen. "Oh my god Haesel, are you okay? Christ, there's so much blood," she whispered under her breath, her eyes staring at the pulsing wound.

The remaining guard recovered, and I turned to him as he got to his feet. His eyes were hard and fixed as he shouted, "Stay still and remain where you are."

It was Derek. I could see there was no way that his interaction with Eve earlier was going to make any difference now. He was in full-on security mode. If anything, he looked more determined than the others had been. Quite probably feeling foolish in front of her, I thought.

My head was swimming, and my vision blurred a little as the blood continued to seep from my arm. Fear automatically leapt to my defence as he ran towards us. I lifted my left hand, and a wall of pulsing energy spread out in front of him. His eyes opened wide in shock, and he took a step back, recovered and launched himself forwards, becoming ever more determined to push through. I kept him there, gritting my teeth in determination as time slowed on his side.

Eve hauled me to my feet, bracing her shoulder underneath mine. "C'mon Haesel, help me," she cried out as we staggered towards the elevator.

All the while, I kept my hand pointed at Derek, focusing only on him. We were almost there when pain and fatigue took over, and I couldn't hold it any longer. I fell heavily to the floor, and the forcefield disappeared. Through blurry eyes, I watched Eve dart to the elevator and push the button. The doors opened, and she ran back grabbing the clothes on my back, yelling out in determination, but she didn't have the strength to move me.

Pain sliced through my arm and ricocheted through my body. I lifted my head to see Derek running flat out across the reception room towards us. His face was twisted in anger, eyes bulging, and he was focused on Eve. He crossed the room in seconds, and the fear that ran like a cold trickle down my back boosted my cells into action.

I let out a cry and used whatever energy I had left. It wasn't much, but the shock wave that hit him spun him sideways, causing him to fall back into the table containing the whisky decanter and glasses. His head smashed into the glass, and he hit the ground with a thud. He made a deep noise as the air left his lungs and he lay, moaning and rolling around on the floor.

I grabbed hold of my arm and concentrated, imagining all the cells knitting together and the wound healing. A faint red glow escaped from under my palm, and the blood flow slowed as it started to clot.

"Derek, no, please!" Eve screamed.

He had staggered to his feet and had withdrawn a second taser from a belt around his waist. The taser ticked loudly as it fired up, and he pointed it directly at Eve.

She dropped to her knees, sobbing and holding out her hands to him.

"Please don't. Derek. Please." He hesitated for a split second. Enough time for me to reach back and grab the abstract gilt statue of a twisted DNA strand that was positioned near the elevator doors. I swung it with all my might towards him as he made his decision, and the metal probes released, shooting out on crackling wires.

The statue crossed paths with the taser and exploded into tiny pieces. My wound had now clotted, and I reached out for Eve. Wrapping my arms around her, I hauled her backwards into the metal box and pushed the button.

Derek made one last effort and launched himself towards the elevator. We fell against the back wall, and I surrounded us both with a protective crackling, golden arc of energy as the elevator doors slid closed along with my eyes. The last image of Derek's sweating, determined face just one step away, imprinted like a negative behind my eyelids. His roar rose in my ears.

I took a couple of deep breaths to slow my racing heart. Even though my wound was still fragile and weeping, my strength returned a little. Eve sat up and turned to me. Her face was white with shock, and her eyes were wide under the pinched frown as they flicked over the livid red gash on my arm.

"I'm okay," I said. "We're both okay." My mouth twitched into a small smile, and I squeezed her forearm. "You were so amazing." I staggered to my feet and pulled her up. She was shaking like a leaf from the adrenalin rush. With her mouth clamped shut, her breathing was loud and heavy.

"Eve, look at me. Slow your breathing, take some deep breaths in through your nose and blow them out slowly. We're almost to the car park, and we have to get to the car." She nodded and did what I said, still unable to speak.

The elevator bumped slightly as it came to a stop, announcing, "Ground floor, doors opening." I pulled Eve behind me as my hands started to glow. The small amount of anxiety I felt started to spread through my body. It felt like cold water seeping into and infiltrating every cell in its path. A chain reaction that once triggered, had only one outlet, and now I could intensify the feeling of my emotion as it started without waiting for it to become extreme and take over me.

The doors slid back to reveal a quiet car park. My senses searched all crevices, feeling for anyone hiding. Shouts came from the direction of the barrier, and I grabbed Eve's hand, dragging her over to the car.

Once inside, I reached for a bottle of Oasis that was lying the back seat. Opening it, I handed it to Eve. "Here, drink this. The sugar will help."

Haesel

She nodded urgently, grabbing it off me while twisting around to look out of the back and side windows. Her eyes darted all over the place. The knuckles and ends of her fingers on her right hand had turned white where she was gripping the edge of the seat.

She swung towards me. "Let's go, Haesel, now!"

As we headed up to the security gate, a guard ran towards us with his hand up. I wound down the window and aimed my hand towards the barrier. He staggered back, mouth agape, raising his arms to shield his face, as the mechanism exploded in a bright flash and shower of sparks. There was a splintering noise as the barrier broke off, and I hit the accelerator. The car jumped twice as the tyres rode over the broken pole, and then we were away down the road.

———

Neither of us spoke for ten minutes, both lost in our own thoughts, processing what had just happened.

Eve spoke first. "Pull over, I need a minute," she said, indicating a layby a short distance ahead. She wound down the window and took some deep breaths, then turned to me.

Her eyes widened as they scanned my uniform, and then she looked down at hers and gave herself the once over. I did the same, instantly reminding myself of our current state, and that I really needed to tend to my injury.

"I really don't think we're going to be able to return these," I said, checking out the torn fabric and deep red stains.

"No shit, Sherlock. That's a lot of blood," she said. The seriousness of her expression mixed with the ludicrous situation we had just been through, twisted in my head into something funny. A loud snort escaped through my nose, and

I clamped my hand over my mouth. Micro puffs of air escaped regardless.

Eve stared at me, deadpan, shaking her head. Then her eyes noticed something about the way I looked, and she burst into sudden peals of laughter.

"What?"

That set her off again, and I joined in, her laughter infectious. It was a good minute before she could breathe enough to speak. "Oh my god…you haven't noticed… " she wheezed through bursts of further laughter. Her cheeks were wet with tears, and her shoulders shook continuously.

"Tell me," I giggled back at her.

"We've still got…," *wheeze,* "…we've still got our hairnets on!"

I looked at her head. How had I not noticed?

"And yours…" Eve continued, pointing at my head, "…is at a really jaunty angle."

That did it. We both collapsed, holding our stomachs and rolling around in the car. The release of tension was euphoric as tears rolled freely.

"I mean, how the hell did they stay on through that?" Eve gasped through heaving breaths.

"I know…who knew hair nets were so robust? I'm gonna keep this with me at all times." And we set off laughing again until our energy drained.

My jaw ached as I started the engine, indicated, and turned the car back onto the main road, following it until it turned into a small lane. The houses became further apart, eventually blending into fields. It was dark now, but the sky still held some light from the sun as our world turned over to close its eyes. The air coming through the gap in the open window smelt of fresh grass and damp fields, and I breathed it in deeply. This smell always brought me calm and made me feel peaceful.

Haesel

A rabbit darted out of the hedges, lit up in the headlights, and ran an erratic line down the road in front of us, its white tail bobbing up and down before it bounded, in one leap, back into the safety of cover. I was looking for somewhere to pull over and spotted a wide farm entrance. Not far down the potholed track to the right, an area of concrete housed a couple of derelict hay barns. The halo from the car's lights lit up the barn, and I turned off the engine and locked the doors. Reaching into my bra, I produced the memory stick and wiggled it in front of Eve's eyes, which widened considerably as she inhaled a large breath.

"You still have it?"

I grinned. "Yep, I just hope getting it was worth it."

"Well, I'm gonna be straight with you, Haesel," Eve said. "I never, ever, ever want to do that again."

"Really?" I asked, faking genuine surprise. "That near-death experience didn't make you want more?"

"Never," Eve glared, playfully shoving my shoulder at the same time. I yelled out as my right arm bumped into the car door.

Eve's hand flew to her mouth. "Oh crap, sorry, Haesel."

"It's okay," I breathed through gritted teeth, twisting round to face Eve. "Could you get my bag off the back seat, please? I need to see if I can heal it."

Eve leaned between the seats to retrieve it, and I reached in, taking out a bag of mixed herbs that was among the others I had thrown in before we set off. I dropped it on my lap and groped around at the bottom of my bag between the pens, keys, notepad, tissues, and various other items. My fingers found what I was looking for and closed around a small pot of honey. I rolled back the short, capped sleeve of the uniform and checked out my wound. It was livid and angry looking. The torn and jagged flesh had stopped bleeding, but it was oozing and wet.

Opening the jar of honey, I smeared a thick layer from elbow to shoulder.

"Eww," said Eve, wrinkling her nose. "That will be all sticky, and shouldn't you have cleaned your arm first with disinfectant?"

"This is a disinfectant," I said, "and it's not ordinary honey. This is Manuka honey and has anti-inflammatory, antimicrobial, antibacterial, and antiviral properties. It's amazing at healing wounds and burns."

"If you say so...but really Haesel, I think we should just find a hospital."

"I'm going to add these herbs to it," I said, tapping the fine, sage green flakes out of the bag in a sprinkle over the honey. I stole a glance at Eve, who was busy attacking her fingernail with her teeth. "Don't worry, I'm fine, but if it doesn't work, I promise I'll go."

"Okay, good," Eve said, visibly relaxing with a satisfied smile. "What's in the herbs? No wait, let me guess. I've heard you go on about herbs enough before," she said, biting her lip, her eyes searching upwards for inspiration. "Ooh, I know one...lavender," she said, pulling her mouth into a thin line and jutting out her chin.

"Very impressive," I said, smiling. "I'll be dragging you into the shop if you aren't careful. There's also agrimony, comfrey, yarrow, and St. John's Wort," I said. "All good in their own way for causing the cells to proliferate and knit together."

Eve grinned, then her face turned serious. "Honestly, though, I think a hospital would be a better idea. That looks quite a mess now and is going to take a long time to heal."

"Well," I said, "hopefully not. Let's see if this works."

I hovered my left hand just above the gooey mess of red and green and thought of what Thea had taught me. I concentrated on the skin healing, the cells knitting and joining together, and a warm, orange glow appeared from beneath my hand, lighting up the skin. It grew brighter and brighter until you could barely look at it. My skin became warm to the point of being too hot and tingled and itched and crawled with a prickling sensation as the nerves slowly mended. Then the light slowly faded and died out on its own accord, I took a deep breath and felt renewed. Eve was staring open-mouthed as I pointed past her.

"Can you grab the pack of wet wipes from your glove box, please?" She duly obliged, and I wiped a small area at the base of the wound. The skin underneath was completely healed and back to normal. Eve gasped. I wiped the rest of the sticky green paste from my arm to reveal no sign of any injury.

16

Eve stared at my arm for a long time, so long, that I was beginning to wonder if she had gotten stuck, then she suddenly shouted out. "Bloody hell Haesel! You can do magic! But I mean like, real, actual magic. God I wish I could do that," and her shoulders drooped, although her eyes still sparkled with awe.

"Well, there is a bit of magic in there for sure," I said, "but we can all dig into our senses and be stronger than we think when we need to be." Eve shrugged, and I took hold of her hand. "You saved me in there today," I said, looking her straight in the eye, suddenly surprised to find mine filling up. "What you did was amazing. I didn't realise my powers would drain my energy so much. I hope that will strengthen with time, but Derek would have caught me for sure if you hadn't dragged me into the elevator."

Eve's face brightened, and she retrieved her hand to rub it absently over her forehead. "I can't believe I did that either," she said, leaning back and lifting her head up to rest it on the headrest. "But you win. If you weren't a witch with crazy powers, we would both have been brown bread."

I laughed at the slang comment, and then we both seemed to realise at the same time that we were in a car, in the middle of nowhere, in blood-soaked uniforms. I unhooked the pass, which was surprisingly un-damaged.

"We had better drop this in on the way back," I said, "but the uniforms are a write-off."

"I'll take them to my house and burn them," Eve said, sitting up. "I have a burn bin in my garden for rubbish. There won't be anything left."

"Okay, good idea. Let's get changed. I've a bag in the back that the uniforms can go in."

We grabbed our clothes from the back seat and discarded the uniforms.

"Ah, that feels much comfier," Eve said, getting back into the car. "What's the plan once we're back?"

"I was just thinking about that. I'm going to go home and print off everything on this memory stick and take anything relevant to Thea. I could use her input and advice on what we found. I'm hoping it will give us all the information we need on what Malicen is up to. Then we can go from there." Eve nodded. "We'd better go," I said, putting the car in gear and heading back down the farm track.

Eve rested her head against the side of the window and sighed, "I wish I could go with you."

"You wouldn't survive the journey, I'm afraid. The pressure of passing between the planes is too much if you don't have any powers to protect yourself. Besides, I need you here to tell me what's going on when I get back. Time is different there, I can be gone a week there and only lose half a day here, but a lot can happen in half a day."

"What's it like?" she asked. "It must be so amazing to go to another world."

"Alchemia is like here, but unspoilt by humans. It's pure. It's what Earth should be like if we cared for it, and there was no greed. The law of the land is to do no harm unless for defence, but there is little to defend it from. The Ancients have seen to that for centuries."

"Ancients?" Eve said, tilting her head to the side, frowning.

I hesitated, then leapt. "They're dragons."

Her expression matched what I had expected, with wide eyes and a slack, open jaw. I proceeded to tell her of Nithele for most of the journey back, answering the barrage of questions that interrupted me. We detoured briefly, hungry for a drive-through burger, then continued on.

It was near to four am by the time we arrived back. I dropped Eve at her house and said I would call her when I had some news. Exhausted, I made some tea to take up to bed, but I was asleep before I drank it.

My sleep was restless. In my dream, someone was playing some music, a repetitive tune of musical notes. I walked through the wood, trying to find where it was coming from, but I couldn't pinpoint it, even though I knew it was close. Thea appeared a little way ahead of me. "You have to try harder, Haesel," she said. "Focus on the sound." I was feeling more and more agitated. I was trying, but the music always stayed the same distance away. "Hurry, you're losing it." Thea was drifting backwards through the wood.

"Where is it?" I cried out and my eyes flew open. My chest heaved with ragged breaths, and my hands were releasing small crackles of shooting, white light. I sat upright, leaning forwards, and breathed in and out very slowly and deeply. The energy subsided from my hands, and my heart slowed its exaggerated beat.

Was it a sign? Maybe she was in trouble?

The song came again, and I jumped at the loudness of it. It was coming from the direction of my window. Quietly tiptoeing over, I held my breath and gently pulled back the curtain. There on the painted wooden windowsill in my room, perched a small bird.

"How on earth did you get in," I asked in barely a whisper. The bird tilted its head to the side, fixing me with its small, shiny black eye, then burst forth another volley of musical song before hopping closer to the glass, its little feet making scratchy sounds on the sill with every hop. It tilted its head in sharp, jerky movements back and forth before tapping its beak urgently on the glass. It looked back to fix me with another quizzical look.

"Come," I said, and I held out a finger, a smile breaking on my lips. "I'll let you out."

With a quick purring flurry of wings, it hopped onto my finger, gripping on tightly with its feet. It was so pretty up close, and I recognised it as a male chaffinch. His body was a beautiful deep rosy pink that contrasted sharply against the grey on his head, while black and white patterned wings folded neatly over the mossy green on his back that could just be seen through the wings.

I reached to unhook the window fastenings and opened the window wide. We both lifted our heads, the bird to listen for a warning of danger, while I breathed slowly and deeply to smell the ozone freshness of the morning air. With another quick burst of song that vibrated through my hand, a flurry of beating wings and speed saw him quickly and safely to the nearby silver birch tree in my garden. He sat, looking around, taking stock of his surroundings.

I smiled, watching him. Then a sense of foreboding crept up on me. I looked absently at the windowsill without seeing, as my thoughts processed. There was a saying that a bird in the house denoted a warning of being trapped. I didn't like the feeling that came with the thought, a tingling around my neck and shoulders that constricted my throat.

Shelving the thoughts, I checked the time on my phone,

which read 9:12 a.m. I felt completely alert and refreshed on just five hours of sleep, and considered that I must be repairing faster, now I was a witch.

After a quick shower, I headed downstairs, flicked on the kettle, and sat down in front of my laptop with the memory stick. The screen flashed to life as I lifted the lid. Sliding the memory stick onto the side connector, a window opened containing eight files. I hardly dared look. Apprehension ran through my body like ripples over a still pond. Taking a deep breath, I opened the first one with the title Bio-electromagnetics, and read all five pages from start to finish, then quickly skimmed through the other files.

My blood ran cold, and I physically shuddered, causing goosebumps to rise on the surface of my skin, tingling as the cells constricted and all the hairs lifted. My hand flew to my mouth. Oh, no, this was bad, worse than I could have imagined. I had to get to Thea now. If I was quick, I could get there, find out how to stop it, and get back before the SACL pill was rolled out later this afternoon.

I hurriedly pressed print on all of the documents. Then saved its contents to a file on my laptop before ejecting it. Grabbing a small plastic bag from a drawer, I wrapped the memory stick inside, then took out a bag of opened sugar from the cupboard and buried it in its contents. I'd seen that in a film. Hopefully, if anyone did come looking, they hadn't seen the same one.

Not having time for tea, I grabbed a glass of water while I waited for the wireless printer upstairs. Then, collecting the papers, I headed back down. I lifted my jacket off the end rail at the base of the stairs and, throwing my arms into the sleeves, stuffed the printed pages into my bag. I paused briefly, thinking that I should have something to eat, but my stomach was tight with knots, and I wasn't in the least bit hungry, so I quickly chucked some crisps and snacks into my bag instead.

Locking the doors, I hurried into my living room which was still as it was just thirty-six hours earlier. The coffee table lay splintered and broken in two halves on the floor, and I dragged the pieces to the corner of the room, sent a quick WhatsApp to Eve, and stood back, taking a few deep, shaky breaths.

Closing my eyes, I concentrated on the images in my mind, of Thea and her house and the clearing in the field.

Nothing happened. I tried again, but still nothing. What was I doing wrong? My palms started to sweat, and my chest felt tight. What if I couldn't get back? I squeezed my eyes shut and tried again, but other images kept flashing in, getting in the way. I saw Malicen's face and Eve's. Snapshots of what had taken place in his office. I saw Mick still lying on the floor in the lab. What happened to him? I hadn't had time to think about it or to find out.

I had to get through. Come on, Haesel. I willed myself to think straight, but the fear that I wouldn't be able to get back to Alchemia rose inside me. My heart drummed an anxious beat creating a loud, pulsed swishing through my ears. My hands glowed and crackled, and I held them up in front of me. "Stop it. Now is not the time." I sat on the edge of the sofa and thought of Thea, and her voice filled my head. *You can do this, Haesel. Just focus on the action you want to happen.* I thought only of my breath, in and out, sweeping through my body like a calming wave. Breathe in the good, breathe out the bad, in with the calm and out with the panic. My heart rate slowed, and the glow faded from my hands. I had to focus. I tried again. Nothing. I wondered if maybe my powers had been depleted when they were used for healing. There was a way I could try and make them stronger.

Standing up, I walked through the house and out into the

garden. The air smelt crisp and fresh in the cooler, light breeze, alive with nanoparticles of scent released from the flora by an overnight downpour. Jewels of water sparkled everywhere and clung to the ends of leaves and petals like diamonds. I marvelled at the border of nasturtiums that held on to large jewel-like pools in the centre of their superhydrophobic leaves, with scattered mini droplets of water balancing precariously on the flatter surface as though tiny Swarovski crystals had fallen with the rain.

They glittered sharply in the sun that burst brightly and suddenly at intervals through the clouds, and I bent to tip a leaf and watched it roll off. Under a microscope, the clever survival instinct of nature could be seen. Tiny nanostructures like miniature mountain ranges coated with a waxy substance covered the leaf, and air pockets filled the valleys causing the water to collect on the peaks. As the water rolled off, it took with it dirt and dust, keeping the leaf clean and allowing the plant to absorb light more effectively for photosynthesis. Scientists were studying it to work on producing the most water repellent material ever.

I, however, grew it for the vitamin C and iron found in the leaves and flowers, and the leaves also had an antibiotic effect that helped if you had an infection.

I grabbed a few leaves and continued down the garden, and my eyes sought out the herbs I was looking for, rosemary and sage. Back in the kitchen, I threw them into the mortar and ground them vigorously with the pestle for a few seconds to release the oils. Leaning over the bowl, I breathed in deeply through my nose and instantly felt the effect as the nanoparticles of oil infused in the air and hit my bloodstream. My focus sharpened as cognitive abilities were improved, increasing speed, accuracy, attention, and memory. The mental fatigue of the previous day disappeared, and my whole body buzzed with energy.

Haesel

I poured the contents into a plastic snap bag and stuffed it into my pocket, while walking back into the living room thinking of Alchemia.

The image that greeted me took my breath away as the scene filled the room. It was as though the image had been laid like a transparent covering on the surface of my eyes, the pixels bright, clear, and sharp. Nithele was in the clearing of the meadow field, looking out across the valley. She turned her huge head and walked towards me, wings bent, bedding into the soil. Lowering her neck, her head came close to fill the room, and her all-seeing eyes looked directly into mine from the void between us. The large yellow orbs narrowed as the words rumbled deeply, resonating up her throat.

"Come, witch."

The image slowly faded and was gradually replaced by another one. Rippling air centuries thick undulated and swam in front of me. It hummed with time, pressed together between planes. A gateway through.

I grabbed my bag and jumped.

17

Tumbling out onto the ground, I lay in a crumpled heap. This was something I was going to have to improve on, I thought, as I got to my feet and dusted myself off. I had hardly felt the pressure this time, and the dizziness wasn't so extreme.

I looked up to see Thea standing a few yards away, and we ran to each other, squeezing tight. I felt relieved to be back with her, with someone I didn't have to hide things from and could talk to without having to think about what I was saying first. Safe. Home. The thought took me by surprise, but I liked it.

"It's sooner than I expected." She pulled away to look at me, her smile broad and wide, the happiness it conveyed filling her eyes with light. "But I'm so glad. The forty-six days here have dragged…not that I've been counting each one of them at all," she said, looking up with a slow roll of her eyes.

I smiled back weakly, the burden of what was coming hovering, just out of sight.

"I've barely had time to breathe," I said.

"What is it?" she asked, her eyes searching mine as she sensed my anxiety.

"I've brought some information with me." I bit my lower lip. "I think it's really bad. I got it from Malicen's office, but I need to go through it with you to understand what he's doing." I turned to walk to the house, and then I remembered and stopped, looking around.

"Where's Nithele?"

"Nithele? She hasn't been here since you left," Thea said, her brow furrowed.

"She spoke to me, told me to come. I saw her in the clearing when I was trying to open the portal." I looked at Thea. "How did she know?"

Thea didn't answer. Instead, she reached for my hand and pulled me towards the house. "She must have seen," she called out as we broke into a jog. "It must be bad for her to use the insight and summon you like that. Nithele does not interfere."

We ran to the house and sat at the table, and I pulled out the documents I had printed.

"I've read them all, but start with this one," I said, handing it over to her.

Thea scanned it quickly, and her face paled as she read. When she had finished, she laid the papers slowly on the table and looked up. Her eyes stared off into nothing but darted around, looking at the projected images inside her mind.

"Thea?"

My voice snapped her out of her trance, and she looked at me quickly before looking down at the other documents on the table. "I'll look through all these first, so we have the full picture. It might not be as it seems," she said. But I had already glimpsed the fear in her eyes.

After half an hour of interjected mutterings and asking

me questions I could only theorise about, she sat back and looked at me. A deep line cut a valley between her eyebrows.

I stared back, and all was eerily quiet for a few moments before I spoke. "I don't fully understand this, but it's really bad, right?" A cold chill ran through me as the words left my body.

Thea's eyes were wide, and worry lines ran like wrinkles in the sand at low tide across her forehead. She sucked in her bottom lip, and her teeth drained the colour of her skin to white as she bit down and simply nodded. Not able to confirm it out loud.

I went into practical mode, the same as I always had when the kids were younger, and there had been a sudden injury. It must have something to do with a survival instinct that my mind cleared to deal with the situation, shelving all worries and everyday rubbish to concentrate solely on fixing the immediate threat.

"Okay." I laid my hands flat on the table. "I have to understand this properly, and this is your subject, right? Everything talked about here you know about in detail. So, let's go through it."

She remained still. I banged my hand loudly on the table. "Thea!"

She jumped and stood up. "It's okay. I'll make some tea. I can think better when I'm doing a mundane task."

"The SACL pill is getting rolled out tomorrow morning at 8 a.m."

She spun around. "That's too soon."

My shoulders slumped, "I know."

"Okay, let's go through it." She brought the tea and some bread, cheese, and salad leaves, and once again, we directed our focus on the papers.

I reached into my bag and pulled out the packet of crisps. Thea's eyes lit up.

"Oh my god, it's been so long since I had crisps," she said.

I smiled, handing them over. "Dive in. I'd rather have the salad." Between mouthfuls, I said, "So, let's put it in order. What's first? Oh, before we do that…" Delving back into my bag I held up the rosemary and sage.

"I have this. It will help to focus our minds on the information."

"Good idea." Thea went to retrieve an earthenware bowl from a nearby cupboard that had three chunky legs and stood four inches off the table. She poured a small amount of water into the bowl and added the herbs, then lit a candle beneath. I smiled. The oils from the herbs would warm and diffuse into the air as we talked.

"Right," I began, "we know about the graphene oxide being in the SACL pill, but why?"

Thea took a deep breath in and turned one of the pages over to make notes, then exhaled loudly. To anyone else, it may have looked like defeat. But I knew it meant she understood and was thinking how to explain it in layman's terms.

She wrote a word in large letters on the page, dividing it into three sections.

Bio/electro/magnetics.

"There seem to be several things at play here," she said. "All of these things have been studied for a long time now. For instance, graphene oxide particles, as nanoparticles, join to biomolecules, that's our cell matter, and become magnetic in the presence of millimetre wavelength frequencies. This is due to the nanoparticles of magnetite within the graphene."

She drew an arrow from the 'magnetics' part of the word and wrote graphene/iron oxide.

"Now, because these magnetic nanoparticles infiltrate every type of cell in your body, studies have been done in dogs that show, with the appropriate nanoengineering, such as tuning the composites, doping atoms or structures…" She glanced up and caught the vacant look on my face, and bit her lower lip. "Sorry, basically, the studies showed that movement or force can be achieved without the recipient being conscious. This is known as magneto-*mechanical* genetics."

My eyes flicked back and forth between hers and the page.

"So, the particles are controlled and move on their own?"

"Yes, exactly." She pointed at me with her forefinger. "Cells are genetically modified to incorporate ion channels." She circled the Bio and magnetics of the word she had first written. "It's using magnetism and genetics to control living tissue." She paused to look me in the eye. "That means it was possible, with certain wavelengths, to cause the muscles in the dogs, who were anaesthetised, to move on their own."

I opened my mouth to speak, but she held up her hand.

"Hold on, hold on…it is also a good thing. People who had lost feeling in their limbs could maybe one day wear a transmitter on their body that would cause their legs to move. It might lead to walking, but at the moment, much more study needs to be done."

"Well, that would be amazing," I said, "but you're going to tell me there's a downside, right?"

"Yes, I'll come to that." She picked up her cup and drank the remaining third of her cold tea, grimacing as she did so. "Okay," she continued, "so that would be the 'force' part, but there is also the 'heat,' and that's called magneto-*thermal* genetics. Part of the skin that allows us to sweat responds to millimetre wavelengths, much like an antenna can receive signals. Certain millimetre waves can cause people to feel physical pain via nociceptors or their pain receptors. They are free nerve endings located all over the body, including the skin, muscles, joints, bones, and internal organs. They play a pivotal role in how you feel and react to pain. "Now," she continued, "once you get to the higher millimetre spectrum of 75 GHZ+, the frequencies rapidly penetrate the skin, and it makes you feel like your body is on fire."

My mouth dropped open, and an involuntary shudder ran through my body. "That doesn't sound good. This is not actually a thing that is used, right?"

Thea nodded, pressing her lips together, turning them white. "It's already being used in Active Denial Systems, used for crowd control. You would definitely disperse if you felt it."

I drew a shuddering breath. "Okay, I understand, but how does this tie together?"

"Well, this is the bad part," Thea said, using her pencil to float over the words as she scanned them. She flicked through more pages, sucking in her top lip. "Where did I see it? Oh, here." She circled an area. "This is where it starts to link the different technologies to numbers, to code them. Here it refers to number 120 and links to the graphene, and here," she drew a circle on the paper again, "it refers to the number 145." She swallowed. "It says that 145 would be reset."

I shrugged and gave a quick shake of my head. "So, what's 145?"

Thea looked at me, then dropped her gaze. I could sense the anxiety coming off her in waves.

"I've read it several times because it's hard to comprehend such a thing, but on the next page," she said, turning it over and pinpointing it with her finger, "it clearly says that 120, over time, would result in an eighty per cent depopulation of 145." She sat back in the chair and rubbed her hand over her mouth. Her voice lowered, resigned. "145 has an asterisk and is explained at the endnotes as referring to humans."

My hands flew to my mouth and chest, and I jumped up, pacing the room.

"No, that can't be. Depopulation? So, you mean killing people? But that's mass genocide. No. No, I don't believe it." I shook my head in small movements to constantly back up what my voice was saying. "Surely there can't be enough graphene in a tiny pill to have such an effect?"

"You wouldn't think so, would you?" Thea said, rubbing over her forehead and allowing her hands to drag down her face before they fell into her lap. "However, fortunately, or unfortunately, depending on its intended use, graphene is the lightest, thinnest, strongest and best heat and electricity conducting material ever discovered. We are now able to make the strands so thin, one hundred nanometres or less, that they not only bend but dissolve in fluids or water. I think it's the joining link between the SACL pill and all the other technologies. The virus is being used as an excuse to have to take it."

"Oh, God," I said, remembering the speech Malicen said outside VialCorp. "Malicen said there would be another pill, maybe a succession. So, in that circumstance, would that be enough?"

"Yes, definitely. I imagine the deaths would be gradual as the vulnerable and elderly would be more susceptible. The increasing amounts in the subsequent pills would take care of the rest. The deaths wouldn't be linked to the SACL pill but blamed on the virus."

I leaned my elbows onto the worktop where I stood, and looked away. "I hardly dare ask, but how would it kill people?"

Thea sighed. "Severe clotting, all over the body, but in particular the brain and major organs. The wavelengths cause the magnetised graphene in the blood vessels to clump tightly together."

I turned, standing to face Thea. "It's hidden in plain sight. No one will suspect anything." My mind raced as I headed over to my bag. "I have to get back. I have to warn the kids not to take it, and Eve. I have to warn everyone and get this information to the right people." I grabbed the papers off the table, searching frantically. "I saw something mentioned about transmitters. That must be how he's going to control it."

Thea stood. "Yes, I think the obvious route would be to send the wavelengths through the mobile phone masts. There are already millions of those worldwide, and wi-fi is everywhere."

I looked up at her, still gripping onto the papers. "I don't know how much I can do, but I'll leave now."

"No."

The certainty of the word took me by surprise. "What?"

"Not yet. You have to go and see Nithele."

"No," I shook my head, squaring my shoulders, "there's no time."

Thea walked over and reached out, touching my shoulder with a firm, steady hand. "She might know what to do."

"If Nithele knows something, why wasn't she here when I arrived? She knew I was coming. She actually told me to come in the first place."

"Then she knows," Thea said. "Maybe she has to show you something."

My thoughts were all over the place. I felt torn to go and torn to stay. My hands started to glow with the confusion of mixed emotion.

"I will work on something while you are gone," Thea said, walking over to the table to scribble some notes on the back of one of the pages. "You have time. Nithele wouldn't have spoken to you without good reason. It was a message. You have to listen to it, Haesel."

I knew she was right, and I had to follow my path. My anxious state was born of my wanting to veer off. The glow from my hands faded at this thought. I had to trust my kids and Eve to make the right decisions. As hard as it was, I made a conscious effort to think only of the next thing to be done. Relaxing my shoulders as I breathed out, I looked up into her calm brown eyes. Thea was always sure, steady. It made me feel safe, and I realised that was something I had missed. I shook out my hands and straightened up. "Okay, what now?"

"Well, first, I've just had a thought," she said. "There is a chemical we make in our bodies that can help protect us from this pill. I brought some of my kit here that I stored before the fire. If I take a sample of your blood before you go, I can be working on isolating it while you are with Nithele."

"How am I going to use that?"

"I don't know," she said, standing up, "but Nithele might know a way, and you can tell me when you return."

Thea disappeared into her bedroom and came back after a few minutes carrying a metal case. She laid it on the table and flicked open the catches, lifting the top half to reveal syringes, needles, sterile wipes, and several other items, including a blood pressure sleeve and elastic strap.

"Right, sit down," Thea said.

I obeyed automatically, then stood up again. "Err, hold on. Why can't you use your own blood? Why does it have to be mine?"

"Well, that's easy. The younger you are, the more of this chemical you produce in your body. I'm after the amino acid that causes this to be produced, and I'll get a better sample from you. Plus, I think that your powers will enhance it and make it more potent." She smiled at me. "So…" she indicated the chair with her outstretched palm, "sit."

I blew out a puff of air and reluctantly sat. "I hate having this done…and please don't say, just a little scratch, because it's not," I said, glancing up at her, then did a double-take.

She was clearly trying not to laugh. Her lips were pressed tightly together in a line, while her chest and shoulders were making small jerky movements with the effort of holding it in.

A smile broke loose across one side of my face as her laughter escaped. I rolled my eyes, "Oh, just get on with it," I said, screwing up my eyes.

A few moments later, it was done, and I wondered why it had ever bothered me.

18

I borrowed a rucksack from Thea and packed it with anything I deemed essential. She had drawn me a rough map.

"It should take you just shy of two days to get to the Aaronly mountains, depending on how much you rest. There is a shortcut here," she indicated on the map, "which may save you some time. The terrain is mainly rough ground and grassland, so there is not much to get in your way, apart from the river."

My eyebrows shot up. "The river?"

Thea's mouth twitched, and she shrugged. "I don't know how wide it is there. I've never been."

The sun had reached its highest peak and was on its slow descent back down to the horizon. Gusts of wind brought with them a cooler freshness that felt invigorating, and billowing grey and white clouds had appeared from nowhere, chasing each other across the expanse of blue.

"Got it," I said, glancing down at the roughly drawn map in my hands. I folded it and pushed it into my pocket. "I'll be fine. I'll find a way. See you in a few days."

I set off down the path at a good pace, feeling light on my feet and determined to get answers from Nithele. I nodded to myself to settle the thought. She would be able to help. That must be the reason she asked me to come.

Heading past the beautiful cedar tree that Thea and I had sat under, I followed the way we had walked when we rested at the stream. I was to follow the stream as it steadily widened on its path from the mountains. I would cross it as it began to head south for several miles before it turned, meandering and widening on its way, as it grew nearer to its rugged source.

A rustling movement in the grasses to my right caught my eye, and two black patches bobbed around before disappearing from view. I stopped still to focus on the area, and sure enough, they appeared again. Ah, now I could see what it was. I waited as a large brown hare rustled its way through the grass and lopped casually onto the path in front of me, the black tips on his ears now mostly hidden as he pointed their oscillating, radar motion in my direction. He was huge as he sat back, steady on long powerful back feet, and stretched up, lifting his front legs off the floor, leaving them to dangle soft and light in the air. His jaw continued chomping sideways on the mouthful of long grass that was slowly getting drawn like a moving conveyor belt into his mouth. His nose twitched as he smelt the air and checked out my scent.

Then, turning his head slightly to get a better look, his large, innocent, but wary brown eye, which looked all the bigger due to the ring of cream fur that surrounded it, analysed me for a few seconds. Open to trust, but ready not to. His ears relaxed as he decided that even as a creature with binocular vision I was no threat, and he lowered his head, whiskers twitching, to lop kangaroo style into the same creamy-brown coloured grass as his fur.

My chest swelled with the honour of being accepted by this creature. I was reminded of Noi as I watched the long stems bend to allow him passage before returning behind him to offer complete concealment. I wondered what Noi was doing, and the thought of his happy, mischievous eyes brought a smile to my lips.

Haesel, you're back. Noi's childlike, joyful voice appeared in my head and made me jump. I spun around but couldn't see him. He chuckled a series of clicks. *Connected,* he said.

"Ah," I said out loud, realising what had happened. "Where are you?"

With Mama, Noi replied. *Where you going, Haesel?*

Can you see me? I asked, thinking the words this time instead of out loud. I turned in a complete circle, slower this time, to try and spot him.

A rhythmic light purring filled my ears as he giggled. *Fuzzy,* he said. *Only feel.*

I continued walking towards the river. "I have to visit Nithele, but I hope to see you when I return. I won't be too long."

No, no, sooner, he clicked and chirped.

I laughed. *"You're an impatient little one. Not long, I promise."*

I could smell the river and looked ahead. I needed to push on if I was to stay on schedule. The noise of the river grew louder as I approached, and I noticed the water line was higher up the sides of the bank. It was in a hurried state and pushed, leapt, and jostled in its haste to get downstream.

The air was cool and fresh and brought with it different scents of flowers and foliage. An almost iron-like mineral smell pushed towards me, carried in small flurries, gusting from the mountains. I looked up in the direction I was aiming for. The hills Thea and myself had climbed obscured the mountains, but above them, I could see the sky was darker. My hair blew across my face with a sudden puff of invisible breath, and I tucked it behind my ear and zipped up my jacket while I watched the wind ripple through the grasses in my direction. But this wasn't the wind, as only one area of the grass had moved. Something was there.

In my head, a purring giggle followed by a few tuts gave the game away.

I breathed out heavily, scanning the terrain. "Noi, I know it's you. Come out," I called, pursing my lips in a pretence at being cross, but the smile underneath was a giveaway.

Noi materialised in front of me, a big grin on his face, his eyes full of mischievous sparkle. "Sooner," he chirped, holding out his hands in a 'ta-da' fashion as he spoke the word.

I laughed a full breath until no sound came out. Gasping in a lungful of air, I reached out to squeeze his tummy in a tickle. "You're a little imp," I giggled.

His face fell instantly, his chin quivering in an attempt to hold back a sob. "I sorry, Haesel, I no mean it. I not bad." His shoulders crumpled, and all his leaves sagged as he hung his head while looking up at me through eyes filled with tears.

"Oh, Noi, of course not." I knelt down in front of him and took hold of his hands. "Whatever's the wrong little one? I'm not cross."

He bent his head, and a large tear rolled down his cheek. I reached to wipe it away with my thumb and cupped his face with my hands, lifting his face to look at me.

"Tell me, Noi, what's upset you?"

Noi sniffed deeply. I sat on the ground and pulled him onto my lap, wrapping my arms around him. He looked up at me, and the clicks and chirps translated.

"I not an imp, Haesel. Imps are bad, and I very scared of them. They do very bad things. They live in the dark world in the shadows." He took a stuttering breath and looked at me with wide eyes, his little forehead full of worry.

"Ah, I see. It's ok. I don't know of these imps you mention, but where I come from, an imp is thought of as friendly and full of mischief and trickery, but not in a bad way, just in the way of a playful child. That is all I meant."

Noi's face brightened, and his leaves did a little flurry up and down his body. "So, I not bad?" he said, looking around my face to read my emotions.

"I'm pretty sure you couldn't possibly be bad," I said. "Come on now." I gave him a final hug, and I hoisted him off my lap as I scrambled to my feet. "I really have to get going. It's very important that I speak with Nithele, and it's going to take me a while to get there."

Noi grabbed hold of my arm jumping up and down. "Mama take you. Faster. I tell her."

"Oh, no, that's ok little one. I just…"

"She here."

Before I could say anything else, Noi shot off further downstream, rounded the corner, and disappeared from sight behind an area of large shrubs and trees. Not ten seconds later, Loai came striding around the bend with Noi clinging on to her body with one hand and waving madly with the other. He was grinning from ear to ear.

"Noi, it's fine, really, please don't bother your mother," I said, my hands clenching at this delay.

He scrambled down her tall body and raced around, blurring into invisibility. Appearing next to me, he grabbed hold of my hand and leaned sideways to pull me towards Loai. The individual, deep cells on his hand sucked onto my skin and took hold, and I reluctantly walked the few paces towards her. She bent her head softly to look at me.

"I'm sorry I'm bothering you," I said, stretching my neck back to look up at her. "I don't want to put you to any trouble, and I really can manage on my own."

Loai and Noi exchanged a rapid series of clicks, chirps and

low whistles. Then Noi turned to me, ruffling his leaves in excitement. "Faster," he grinned. "Mama said it be honour to help."

I stepped back, my mouth opening slightly, my jaw slack as Loai stepped forward with one leg and slowly placed her other knee on the ground. She crossed one arm in front of her body and bent her head forwards in a low bow.

I felt a lump rise in my throat and pressed my hands to my chest as I swallowed. Closing my eyes briefly, I inclined my head to her, and when I looked up, her soft, large brown eyes were looking into mine.

I smiled. "Thank you. I truly appreciate your kindness." Noi voiced my reply in a series of clicks, and Loai extended her hand to the floor to lift me up.

She was softer than I expected and had a thin covering of hair. I could now see that the appearance of rough weathered skin was due to minute pigment cells that could change chameleon-like on demand. I clung to her arm as she stood, lifting me higher. Wrapping her arm across her stomach, she created a deep seat, and I rested against her body with my legs dangling. On closer inspection, the leaves that covered her were not leaves at all, but sensory structures that moved and felt the air, maybe smelt or tasted to some degree, but definitely provided feedback regarding her surroundings. A slow smile spread across my face and remained there, as my chest swelled with a warm, heartfelt glow at the trust afforded to me. Eve would love this, I thought.

Noi, deft and agile, climbed up his mother and came to sit beside me. They exchanged a few clicks and purring vibrations before Noi settled down and rested his head against my shoulder. "I glad you here, Haesel," he said, and I wrapped my arm around his shoulders to pull him closer.

Loai set off at a steady pace that quickly increased. It was a little bumpy at first, but then I hardly felt her feet touch the floor, a creature so in tune with the earth that it was almost as if she could feel the exact moment of contact. Millions of moving cilia beneath her wide feet propelled her along, creating a cushion of air as she flew over the surface. The gentle rocking motion quickly lulled Noi to sleep, and he cooed a soft murmuring sound on every exhale of breath. We reached the hills in just a few minutes and rose effortlessly over them. I gazed across the land towards the mountains and could see the weather front, clearly defined now as a sharp diagonal line across the sky. Beyond this line, clouds of deep steel blue-grey billowed and expanded, swirling and rolling over each other before deflating to build again. I was reminded of the bubbles in a lava lamp, but the clouds held a more ominous threat.

The land whipped by at greater speed, and Loai was across the river before I realised. The warmth on my face from the yellow afternoon sun started to wane, merging with the cooler air as we approached the mountains. Within the next ten minutes, we were in the cloud's shadow, and I was surprised as the wind dropped and the air became humid.

Before me loomed the mountains dark, hazardous and black, the jagged rocks a fortress of sharp edges, with the highest peaks disappearing into the clouds. Dragon screams split the air and sudden bursts of flame stood out vividly against the black backdrop.

Loai slowed and came to a standstill as the land started to incline steeply at the base of the mountains. The grasses had become sparse and patchy, replaced by denser rocks and soil that the roots could not push into. Her breathing was slightly heavier than normal, but apart from that, she showed no sign of weariness considering the distance she had just travelled.

She knelt to position me closer to the ground, and I eased away from Noi, who was still asleep and slid my way to the rocky floor. He stirred and laid down, turning over to snuggle up to her warm body.

I looked up at Loai, held my hands over my heart, then opened them out to her in a gesture of thanks.

She gave a small smile and inclined her head, closing her eyes briefly, then stood to tower above me before turning and setting off, back the way we had come.

19

The air was eerily still. I stood alone, looking at the expanse of rock in front of me. How do I find her? I could be on the wrong side, I thought and began walking up towards the higher rocks above.

My eyes caught a movement to my right, and I swung around, narrowing my eyes, scanning in small jerky movements. It was there. I could feel it. My muscles tensed as my eyes locked on a group of rocks that started to melt. My hands tingled, and a warm glow began to build from their centre. Very slowly, one rock slid over the other, and then the shape merged together as a whole image, and two wary orange eyes appeared. The dragon was much smaller than Nithele, almost entirely camouflaged against the blackish-brown rocks. It hunched low, scales on the side of its head flared, ready to take action, but I felt no anger from it, only defensiveness and curiosity. A row of small, sharp, pointed horns ran like a crown over the top of its head, and I deduced that it was male from the differences in bony structures on its face.

Slowly, I held out my hand. "It's okay. I mean no harm. I'm here to speak with Nithele."

The dragon started back with a low rumble at the sound of my voice and rose, puffing out his chest and beating his powerful wings before opening his mouth to release a searing burst of flame.

My hands rose instantly to counter it. Green, crackling light spread out and met the white-orange flame head-on, where they battled, at a stalemate to override each other. My initial surprise quickly turned to anger. I meant no harm, and he should know this, and I resented being attacked when I had been called here. I planted my feet firmly and drew myself up. My eyes focused as the green forcefield of energy changed into a jagged lightning shard towards him. His flames extinguished as my will hit home, and he screamed a piercing roar as thick, acrid smoke poured out of his nose in billowing clouds. The dragon lowered his neck and folded his wings forwards, planting the claws at the joint firmly into the ground. Red eyes glowed as his head moved slowly side to side, wary but challenged, while his long spiny tail thrashed wildly behind him.

My hands glowed and crackled by my side as I lifted my chin and glared back.

My eyes caught the slight narrowing of his dark, oval pupil the second he decided to try again. I raised my hands, and a wave of energy rippled towards him. He snorted, curling back his top lip to show razor-sharp teeth that slowly opened with a hiss, revealing the quickly brightening orange glow in his throat.

A deafening, screaming roar from above stopped us both in our tracks as Nithele swooped fast out of the sky. Her immense wings beat furiously as they fought to slow the speed of her giant body. The smaller dragon retreated to a safe distance at her appearance.

Nithele's legs stretched out to reach the ground, and claws gripped hold of the rocky boulders, exploding them as though they were made of cinder toffee, as she strode fast towards me.

"Stand down, witch," she spat, her lips in a snarl. She opened her mouth and released a powerful shock wave of energy. Its loud sonic boom reverberated and bounced over the rocks, disappearing into the distance. I was lifted off my feet and flew backwards until my travel was stopped dead by the unforgiving fortress of the mountain rock face behind me. All the breath left my body at the impact, my head smashing back onto the rock, and I cried out, grimacing at the searing pain as I slid to the ground.

There was no time to get to my feet. Nithele's large, scythe-like claw on her wing reached out at lightning speed and pinned me against the rock. The tip bedded into my upper chest below my collar bone and punctured the skin. I sucked in air through gritted teeth and glanced down to see my blood fill the indent like a lake before spilling over to run in a trickle towards my arm. I glared up at her through narrowed eyes, hard and defiant.

"You dare to come here and threaten me?" she roared. Her head was now hovering over mine.

My emotions were all over the place, but anger at this injustice rose above the others.

I screamed out, thrusting my hands upwards and releasing a blast of white-hot energy. It hit, catching Nithele square across her nose and cut a small gash across her upper lip.

Her head lifted a little, and her eyes widened briefly as deep red blood dripped from her wound to land on my face and chest, where it swirled and merged with my own.

Nithele released her grip on me and turned away. I jumped to my feet, then sucked in a sharp intake of breath, reaching up to cradle my head with my hands as it pounded in time with my heartbeat, and pain shot into the back of my eyes.

Gritting my teeth, I screamed at her. 'You called me here. Why are you so against me? Are we not both protectors, on the same side?"

She kept her back to me but turned her head slightly to glance back.

"Anger affords you enough protection, it seems," she snarled, her voice deep and rumbling, the sound amplified as it reverberated off the giant walls of rock.

I held out open palms, only to exhale and let them fall to hang limply by my sides. My shoulders slumped but needing to defend myself; I straightened up.

"My anger was defensive. I had no choice. The other dragon attacked me for no reason, and then you. I thought your law was to do no harm?"

Nithele had begun to walk away but stopped and half turned. She swung her head around, keeping her chest high, and peered down her nose at me. Her lip sneered, and she flinched slightly, then licked over the wound slowly. Her chest rose before she blew a full hot breath down her nose towards me. "Ethre is young. He has yet to learn and his instinct to protect is primary. Besides…" her eyes were scathing as they scanned over my face and body, "it appears there is no harm done."

She turned again and began walking over the rocks, heading around the base of the mountains.

Why is she behaving like this, I thought. It was like she didn't want to help at all. I started scrambling over the rocks after her, taking care to stay out of reach of her unpredictable, powerful tail.

"I came for your help," I called after her. "I saw you in my…"

"Enough witch!" She turned on me with speed, her eyes hard, pinning me to the spot, and she crossed the ground in seconds to place her monstrous, gnarled lethal head alongside mine. A loud growling rumble rose in her throat. "You are the witch of prophecy, but your belief and strength are pitiful. It's time you took charge of your fate and purpose. The times ahead will be tough and test you beyond your limits. You must accept it." I stepped back, and her head rose before me. Golden eyes full of secrets flicked to mine.

"I fail to see at this time how you will fulfil such a task. However, the prophecy is as it is." She moved her head back and closed her eyes on me altogether as she turned away. "Time alone will tell. Now come."

The rocks made speed difficult, and I struggled to keep up. A short distance ahead, Nithele stopped in front of a large solid area of rock that stood vertical, dominating with its presence. She inhaled a deep lungful of air and breathed a cloud of pale grey mist towards it. The dense, foggy mist swelled to cover the rock completely and hung in the air for longer than I expected. Then suddenly, she walked into it and disappeared.

I gasped and stood gaping for a moment. Nithele had gone. I straightened up, looking around, listening. I couldn't sense anything. My heart raced, and I ran towards the hanging mist. As I got closer, I noticed that although it was mist, it had a definite edge as it drifted up and down but did not break through its boundary. I couldn't see through it but held my hands out in front of me and stepped in. It was dense, wet, and surprisingly warm, and I hesitantly walked a dozen paces before the mist cleared, and I could see I was in a tunnel that went straight through the rock. I turned to look back, and the mist was gone, a solid rock wall in its place—a magical gateway in. For a fleeting moment, I considered that I was trapped, and my hands grew warm as adrenalin started to surge. The exit to the tunnel loomed wide before me, and I moved quickly now towards another brighter hazy mist. As I stepped through, the sight beyond took my breath away.

It was the most beautiful tropical oasis, a vast area humid and rich with plant life, trees, and foliage, alive with bright, vibrant colour. The mountains created a sheltered microclimate nestled in the centre of the high rocks. The rocks absorbed the heat from the sun, radiating it out into the centre, and the dragons' flaming roars kept the temperature high. Mist off the water gave permission for life to flourish, lush and plentiful.

From somewhere near the highest peak, a waterfall fell sparkling as it tumbled, frothing into an enormous, crystal-clear lagoon, rich with fish of all shapes and sizes. The water reached out to the edges, then spilt over to create the origin of the river as it gurgled over the black rocks through the tropical valley on its journey across the land.

Large caves were carved out of the steep rock high above. A couple of them were occupied by resting dragons basking in the late afternoon sun. The rays glowed bright with health-giving energy as they crept slowly up the rock face, determined to reach the top. I gasped and stepped back as a deep blue dragon with a larger crown of horns burst out of the water grasping an enormous, iridescent silver fish, half his size, firmly between his jaws. Razor-sharp teeth bedded into its flesh, and he beat his wings furiously, showering water everywhere in a bid to gain balance and height as the fish thrashed. Gaining momentum in this battle of power, he rose steadily and headed to a cave to consume his prize.

Nithele had stopped a short distance away. She lifted her majestic head and roared flames high into the air, and the other dragons followed suit. I covered my ears to the deafening sound. A curious paler green dragon with a yellow underbelly spotted me and froze, her eyes fixed on mine as her head lowered and floated slowly from side to side while she weighed me up. The decision made, she lunged forward, covering the ground quickly. Nithele turned and made a series of loud rumbling growls that echoed around the cavernous space and stopped the dragon's intention dead. She stretched her neck forwards, sniffing the air, then screamed an earsplitting high-pitched cry of frustration before retreating backwards, her head dipped and eyes lowered.

My feet suddenly felt very hot, and my clothes started to stick to my skin. I scooped my hair off my neck and took off my jacket, tying it around my waist.

Nithele had walked a short distance to a large cave where she sat with semi-folded wings trailing on the ground on either side of her, head held proud, surveying her domain.

I sat down across from her, just inside the entrance, leaning my back against the rock and sighed, deflating physically with my breath. My head was throbbing, and I needed a drink and something to eat, but I had flung my backpack to the floor when Ethre had appeared, and only now I felt its absence.

"Can we call a truce? Please? A few days ago, I was just an ordinary woman, a herbalist that loves plants and nature. Now I'm some witch of prophecy, and I'm just trying to take it all in. I could really do with a little help or advice, that's all."

Nithele continued to look ahead, but the set of her heavy shoulders and slight tension in her body made me think I was wasting my time.

"I cannot help you." She lowered her eyes, her voice rumbling. "To do so would change the lines of fate."

"Okay, well, don't help then. Just tell me what the prophecy is, and then I can figure it out."

Her shoulders dropped a little, and she turned her head to face me.

"I cannot do that either. It may change the decisions you make, which would alter the course for others. Fate is changed by small things, and the path is your destiny. It is how it should be and should not be interfered with." She hesitated. "This I know all too well." She dropped her gaze before turning her head away from me.

I sighed, clenching my teeth, and drew one leg up to pick aggressively at a muddy stain on my jeans. I knew she was honouring her position, but there was something else, and then I felt sorrow, the weight of it sudden and heavy on my chest. My irritation at her for not telling me what she knew eased.

"I'm sorry."

She tensed and looked around quickly, her eyes wide.

"I mean, it must be a difficult burden to carry. I didn't mean to push…but what if it's not me? The prophecy? What if it's another witch?"

Nithele's eyes flashed orange as they narrowed, and she rumbled a low growl, the cave magnifying the sound as it bounced off the walls. Her claws scraped pale lines into the rocky base of the cave, and the ground shook as she moved her huge, muscular body to face me. Her guard was firmly back in place.

"A nice try," she sneered. "You are empathic with emotions, I see. For your efforts, however, I will tell you this. There is a world where its beings are driven by greed and power. It will be their downfall. They are on a path to cause destruction of their world and themselves, ignorant to the fragility and balance of life…and in time, they will succeed. A witch will come from this world to save our realm from something I cannot yet foresee. You are the witch. You will be needed here."

She returned to her previous position, looking out of the cave, dismissing me as she did so.

I looked down at my hands and felt sadness deep inside. "We're not all like that."

"It does not take all," came her softly rumbling, truthful reply.

"So, is that it? That's what you wanted me to come out here for? To tell me it's down to me?"

"Patience. You were not called here for me." Her lips tightened, and it almost looked like she had pursed them as her body tensed in irritation. Her eyes flashed as they narrowed at me. "You humans always look inwards, so self-absorbed you don't see what is right in front of you—always thinking about what you have right now instead of the gifts you have been given, the possibilities. Your minds are closed. Instead, try to…" She stopped suddenly and turned, stretching her neck to look out across her domain, her eyes darting, searching. She shot me a glance and barked a final word, "Enough," as her stiff demeanour returned.

A flash of blue caught my eye, and I focused on it flitting quickly through the trees towards us. A gentle humming noise came with it and got louder as it approached, and a dreamy, floating song reached my ears. A euphoric calm descended, and I slumped a little as I let go of the tension I hadn't realised I had been holding.

The faerie hovered nearby, no more than six inches tall, she looked between us, assessing the mood. Her body shone and sparkled with the brightest pale blue light making it hard to see a defined edge. She drifted through the air and landed gently on the ground, folding her large, lacy wings, which reflected a myriad of colours, neatly down her back. The brilliant glow that radiated around her muted as her wings came to rest, and my mouth fell open as she grew in size to match my own, her form becoming more defined and substantial .

Haesel

She wore a close-fitting garment in earthy tones. Pointed ears protruded through her long black hair which shone with auburn tones and fell in soft waves around her strong, watchful face. Blue highlights, flashed as it moved gently in the breeze. On her head was a small rustic tiara that was entwined neatly with foliage, but glints of blue sparkled through as it caught the light. She stood strong and proud before me, then bent her head in respect to Nithele, who returned the gesture. When she turned to me, the sharp intensity of her pale blue eyes was mesmerising. I dipped my head in the same fashion, then, in my relaxed state, thought the whole scenario rather serious which turned to humorous, and I broke into a fit of giggles.

Nithele didn't move, except to raise one bone covered eyebrow and look down her nose at me sideways, her disdain clear when she spoke.

"This is Morrae, the guardian of your fate. She will endeavour to keep you on your destined path." A puff of smoke snorted out of her nose. "A mighty task by the look of it," she added, in a quiet rumble that rolled its way up her throat.

Morrae shot her a sharp glance. "She is young, Nithele. It will come."

"Oh, you're so amazing," I breathed, a lazy smile on my lips. "I'm Haesel. It's nice to meet you."

"Yes, yes, never mind, time is pressing," she said impatiently, and lifting a hand, she flicked her fingers towards me, sending a shower of glittering light in my direction. The spell broke, and all my senses returned. I shuffled hastily to sit up straighter.

"You are very important, Haesel," she continued, her face serious as her eyes locked onto mine "You must consider the path at all times, feel the pull of it to guide you, and the uncertainty when you drift from it." Her voice authoritative and urgent, sounded older than she looked. I thought briefly that there was something familiar about her.

I wanted to question her on my path, ask her what she knew, but when I opened my mouth to speak, she held up her hand and brushed my thoughts away.

"No, no, not now, lots to prepare," she said in a rush. "I simply wanted to assure you that you are never alone in your journey, although you may certainly feel so at times. This is just the beginning, and I will be near to guide you and help you when necessary. Now, it is important to remember your decisions hold great responsibility, and difficult decisions will have to be made." I noticed her glance at Nithele before her focus returned to me. "You may have to sacrifice what your heart says if the pull of your fate says to do otherwise."

My eyes darted back and forth as I considered everything she had said, and my chest tightened with unease.

"Now I must get going." Nodding briefly to Nithele, her wings sparkled as they rose behind her beating slowly as she shrank back to her small stature, then blurring in their speed, as she lifted into the air as effortless as a feather drifting on the thermals. My eyes couldn't follow as she flashed away brightly, sparkling here and there through the trees. A light breeze gusted across my face and faded words came with it. "Listen to the wind Haesel, it will lead you if you are lost."

20

The light was fading, and I got to my feet, brushing the dust from my clothes. I needed to be with Thea and make sense of everything. I felt a conflict of emotions, daunted, yet determined, anxious regarding my abilities, but trusting that my purpose would show me how. I had decided on one thing, and that was to protect my realm first. Malicen could not be allowed to succeed.

It would take me a while to get back on foot, but the light from the moon and stars would be bright enough to see for a while. I planned to shelter under a tree to sleep for a few hours before continuing.

I turned to Nithele, lifting my chest and chin. I wished to be on better terms with her, but maybe that would come once I'd proved myself. I knew she knew more than she was letting on, information that could help me, so right now, I still felt a little annoyed at her lack of help.

"Well...as thrilling as this has been," I said, rolling my eyes a little, "I really need to head back. I have so much to do and no idea of how or what yet. Can you at least tell me how to get through the wall when I reach it?"

My hint of sarcasm was noted, and her nose wrinkled into a sneer as she glanced away from me. "You can portal from inside the mountains," she grumbled.

My mouth fell open as the realisation hit that I could portal between places here. It had never occurred to me. I just assumed it was a gateway between realms.

Nithele glanced back when I didn't move, and her eyes widened before her lips twisted into a smirk. "You didn't know you could portal?" she asked, her eyes glittering with light, and for the first time, I saw them soften with a hint of amusement.

My mouth snapped shut. "Yes...I...umm. My bag is outside, so I was going to collect it," I stuttered as heat rose in my body, and I fought with it, not to show in my face.

Her eyes widened further.

I hung my head, poking at a piece of rock with my foot. "Okay, no...I didn't know." I felt like a child who had just been caught out by their parents, but there was also a need to justify my naivety. I held my head up, eyes wide. "But maybe that's because I'm not being told much," I said.

She turned away, and I sighed heavily. There was no point in feeling like this. She wasn't going to tell me. I had a feeling that whatever had happened in the past, she had paid a high price, and the least I could do was respect her integrity

Walking over, I stood between her ferocious-looking feet and reached up to place my hand on her chest. She stiffened, but I closed my eyes and felt the motion of her breath, the pulse of her heart beating through my palm, causing it to jump in a steady jerky movement. Her overlapping armoured scales were solid but felt almost soft in their smoothness.

I craned my neck to look up at her, and she, in turn, looked down her nose at me, the warmth of her breath fanning my face. Her expression was watchful, but that was all.

Haesel

"I will do this," I said. "Whatever I am meant for here, you won't be disappointed. I know I'm naive, but I'm also loyal and determined, so it wouldn't hurt for you to cut me some slack now and then." I stepped back a few paces and shrugged, holding out open palms. "You never know. We might even have a laugh." I turned and began walking towards the tunnel I had entered from, then half-turned, taking one last look at her magnificence. "Oh, and my bag really is outside on the rocks somewhere."

Nithele remained stoic, and I walked away.

"Haesel?" It was the first time she had used my name, and the growling rumble turned me on my heel. Her golden-flecked eyes held mine, and behind them were words she wanted to say but didn't know how. She blinked slowly, and when her eyelids rose, the hardened veil of self-protection had returned.

"The wall will let you through as you approach." Then she turned and made her way towards the others of her kind.

I stepped out of the damp, warm mist and shuddered as a breeze blew across the fine hairs on my arms. The afternoon was headed towards dusk, the sun hovering above the horizon, now a shimmering sphere of deep orangey-red that cast long shadows across the land. The leaves on the trees danced and shone brightly in the golden light, and I smiled as I closed my eyes and turned my face towards its healing, radiating warmth.

A myriad of nymphs, winged creatures and faeries danced in the rays. They were smaller and more disguised in nature than the kindred flock of faeries headed by Morrae. Some I thought were leaves floating on a gust of wind, but then one tumbled and rolled against my arm, unfurling for a few moments to reveal a tiny, pale face with large black eyes and wispy, stem-like arms and legs. It smiled and curled up again, rolling off my arm to float with the others on the breeze.

Making my way around the rocks, I spotted my bag where I had hastily discarded it and untied my jacket from around my waist, slipping my arm into the sleeve. My hand brushed against thickened skin below my collarbone—the wound from Nithele. I had forgotten all about it and now looked down to see raised, sinew-like, stretched, skin. A healed scar already formed. I ran my fingers over it, pins and needles tingled and faint, warm white light shone from within, but no pain. My reactions to situations I now found myself in had improved considerably, I thought wryly, along with my healing.

I turned to watch the sun deflate in a sigh as it rested neatly on the horizon, and was finally able in its deepening red glow, to look upon this giver and taker of life for a few moments. The fiery glow from the dragons' screaming roars now competed in flashes with its brightness.

I turned and thought of the clearing near Thea's house. The portal appeared before me, slowly spreading outwards as it floated and hummed. Small white bursts of plasma flashed, making a continuous crackling sound as they lit up the air around it. I took a final look at the sky, the high thin bands of cloud now turning an almost luminous cherry pink, and stepped through the undulating air. I was out again in an instant. This time I was ready for it, although emerging in a wobbly half run wasn't the elegant exit I had planned, but still, I remained on my feet. A win as far as I was concerned.

The small square windows in the house glowed and flickered with orange light, and I peered in to see Thea sitting at the kitchen table, furiously scribbling notes. An assortment of glass tubes, jars of liquids, and flasks now took up the rest of the space on the table. The flickering movement from the candles and lamps defined her features, which at this present moment were frowning heavily. All around the room, long shadows were given life as they twitched and danced with the movement of the flame.

She looked up as I entered, then stood quickly, tense, her hand gripping the pen she had been using. The frown she wore a few seconds before, turning swiftly to surprise, then back into a frown again.

"Haesel, you're back already. What happened?"

"Nothing," I said, walking over, dumping my bag by the table, and dropping heavily into the chair opposite her. The rush of air blew out the almost melted, squat candle on the table. "Nothing happened, literally. I met with Nithele, she wouldn't tell me anything, and then I came back."

"Already? How?"

"I opened a portal."

At least her open-mouthed expression was a relief to see, and told me I wasn't the only one who didn't know..

I took a deep breath, inhaling the relaxing smell of spent candle smoke. I loved that smell. It always made me feel happy, reminding me of birthdays, Christmas, and cosy winter nights. I proceeded to explain everything that had happened. When I finished, Thea stood up and, without a word, walked around the table, then reached out to pull my top aside and run her fingers over the scar left from Nithele. It gave off a faint warm glow at her touch, and she gave a small gasp.

"What? What does it mean?"

"I don't know," she said, sitting back down. "I just wanted to see it."

I glanced down at it, giving a slight shrug and relaxing back in the chair. "I don't feel any different."

"Well, that's probably a good thing." She smiled, but the smile didn't quite reach her eyes as she looked away.

Walking over to the worktop, she opened the lid of a large square metal centrifuge and reached in to retrieve a test tube of separated liquid. She turned and held the tube up to me before placing it upright into a holder.

"We're going to have to extract what we need from plants," she said, placing her hands on her hips. "You don't have the amino acid I was looking for, and it appears neither do I. It must be something to do with our powers. Maybe it's not necessary as we already heal so well, or, maybe there's a chemical produced in witches that causes us to heal more effectively."

I leaned forward, resting my elbow on the table and turned my head to the side, cradling it in my hand. I was invisible to her now as she paced the room, muttering her thoughts. Putting her hand to her forehead, she combed her fingers through her long, grey hair and pursed her lips, sighing through her nose.

"If I had the right equipment, I could study it in more…"

"Thea." My voice jolted her out of her musings. "Still here," I said, raising my other palm off the table in a lazy gesture. "What is it you're looking for?"

"Sorry," she said, scurrying quickly back to the table.

"I'm looking for cysteine."

"Yes," I said, sitting up, suddenly alert. "All the plant species of garlic, onions, and bell peppers contain cysteine. Why are you looking for that?"

"Well, along with two other amino acids, glutamine and glycine, they create the powerful antioxidant called glutathione. This is the body's saviour, a super protector, which can oxidise and bind heavy metal particles, eliminating the graphene oxide from the body. It strengthens the immune system by reproducing lymphocytes, a type of…"

"Yes, I know," I interrupted, my mind spinning fast. The herby aromatic smell of the rosemary and sage was still diffused into the room and focused my attention. "They are a type of white blood cell and include our natural killer T cells and B cells, our body's army."

"Yes, that's it." Thea's face lit up, her cheeks glowing, excited to talk about the subject she loved. I felt a tinge of sadness for her. Through her integrity and instinct to protect, she had been made to lose it all, including us. Without Malicen, she would have gone on to discover great things, but without her difficult decision, I would have lost her for good.

She continued in full flow, now able to help once again. "The lower the level of glutathione, the more prone to malfunction the DNA becomes, causing ageing and disease. Glutathione is amazing. It strengthens the immune system and is involved in nearly all the body's measures to heal itself." She grinned, her eyes alive in the reflected light of the candle. "It's not called the mother of all antioxidants for nothing." Drawing in a deep breath, she glanced down, and when she looked up, her expression was serious. "But… graphene oxide can be made to exceed glutathione by certain wavelength stimulation."

The realisation hit me, and I jumped up. "So, do you think that's what Malicen is doing? He's going to send out higher wavelengths and increase the effects of the graphene oxide in the SACL pill?"

"Yes, I think so. It will cause a cytokine storm and trigger the collapse of the immune system. If the initial clotting doesn't kill you, then the collapse of the immune system will. It will make the body unable to fight even the mildest infection. Any condition that already exists will take hold within days."

I walked to the chair and perched myself on the edge, thinking fast. "Okay, so this MagnanogenR4, it's a combination of technologies. I know there are herbs and ingredients in plants that can help remove heavy metals from the body, and I can draw on the properties of the plants that increase the cysteine, and therefore the glutathione, but that's it. Knowing how to protect the world population with this knowledge? Well, that's an entirely different thing." I threw my head back, looking up at the heavy wooden beams, hoping to find some inspiration.

Thea looked at me and just nodded as her eyes slid away. "I know."

I closed my eyes, pinching and stretching the skin between my eyebrows with one hand. "I should get back."

"Stay and rest here tonight. You'll be refreshed in the morning, and time or events will provide an answer."

"Yes, okay." I gave a resigned sigh and realised in that instant how exhausted I felt. Her suggestion gave permission to my underlying desire for sleep, and I felt comforted to not be on my own. I walked over to her and wrapped my arms around her hugging her close. She responded in kind. No words were needed or spoken. We cleared up the kitchen in silence, connected, even within our individual thoughts.

Lying in bed, I breathed in the damp smell of the air and turned to stare up at the stars through the open window—many more than were visible on Earth. I marvelled at how insignificant I was, even though the burden of my fate confirmed I was far from meaningless, no matter how small I felt.

A troubled sleep kept me tossing and turning, my mind refusing to let me rest.

21

I left early as dawn was breaking, fresh and clean. The air was earthy and cool, and I inhaled a full, deep lungful of the ozone freshness. A thin veil of mist rose and fell over the deeper pockets of the valley as the renewed sun peaked its head over the horizon, already too bright to view, spreading out golden fingers of hope and promise wherever it touched.

I lifted my face towards it, already feeling the warmth and power of its healing protection absorbing into my skin.

Wispy, ethereal clouds hung in the pristine, forget-me-not blue abyss, like the remnants of lost souls, dragging out their leaving in order to view the beauty of it for a little while longer, while small, brightly-coloured birds with long, wispy tails sang a heavenly chorus from their perches in the trees, welcoming in this new day.

Another day to start afresh. Another day that erased all negativity from the previous day. My heart felt lifted to be included in it.

I left Thea in the kitchen and walked to the clearing. The merest thought opened the portal, and I stepped in as naturally as if I had been doing it all my life.

I was stronger, my powers controlled and settled, and the travel was easy. I felt no sickness or dizziness, and my strength remained in the shift across realms.

I checked the clock on my living room wall. It was later than I expected at a little after midday. I remembered Thea saying the time wasn't an exact science. Time was something we could measure accurately on Earth, but who knew how far it was between realms or how time distorted across planes?

My phone connected to wi-fi and came alive with two-tone beeps, pings, and short musical bursts. Opening it, I saw a flurry of texts and WhatsApp messages. One from Jay and a few from customers at the shop, but four missed calls and six WhatsApp messages were from Rowan.

I opened Rowan's first.

9:48 a.m. Hi Mum, hope you're ok. Tried to call you x

9:49 a.m. By the way, just to say don't worry, I'm not going to take the SACL pill. (Smiley emoji) x

11:03 a.m. Mum, I'm coming home. Uni is closed due to the pill roll out x

11:24 a.m. I'm dashing to get the train. Kelly is borrowing my car as she is stranded. Can you pick me up please? x

11:37 a.m. Are you there?? I'm getting on the train now. If you're busy I'll get a taxi, see you soon x

11:58 a.m. Tried to call you again. Arriving 13.20 Are you ok Mum? (Heart emoji)

I quickly typed a hasty reply: Hi, I'm ok, sorry went to the shop and left my phone at home. I'll be there xx

I switched to Jay's message, which read: Hi Mum, all well. Don't take the SACL pill for the virus. Something doesn't feel right about it. Message me when you get this, Jay.

I sent a reply: Hi, I'm not taking it don't worry, busy now, I'll call you later. Love Mum x

Moving into the kitchen while still checking my phone, I flicked on the kettle and scrolled through the other messages from customers. Some asked if they could take the SACL pill alongside the herbs they were taking. Others wanted to know if I thought it was safe or knew what was in it. My instinct to protect these people right now fought with my need not to be exposed. I wrote a reply, then deleted it, then tried two more and deleted those too as my mind jumped back and forth trying to find a way to warn them. I wanted to tell them not to take it, tell them it was dangerous, shout it out across the world…but I knew this would only draw attention to myself, and I couldn't risk that. The media were whipping up a storm of fear and panic against the virus, and I knew my voice would be drowned out. So, I did the best I could for now and typed out a reply to all: Hi, the herbs you are taking are safe and have been studied for a long time. Maybe you should ask the doctor about the SACL pill ingredients, though? It's important you are informed of this and are aware of any adverse reactions before taking it. You could also check on the VialCorp website, which should list them. If you are worried, ask for further information. Haesel.

I drew in a long, deep breath and pushed send. At the very least, it might push them to ask questions.

I checked for further messages. None from Eve. I sent her a quick WhatsApp letting her know I was back and to call me when she was free, then went back into the living room, turning on the TV to get an update on what was happening.

My phone pinged. It was Rowan: There you are. Thank you x (heart emoji)

I sent back a thumbs up symbol with a heart emoji.

The train station was only fifteen minutes away. I threw the phone on the sofa and went to make tea. Taking it into the living room, I placed it down on the windowsill, as that was the only place to put it now I was minus a coffee table. I paced, fidgeting, absently picking at a rough fingernail and pulling on my top lip between my finger and thumb.

I don't know how to hide this, I thought. What do I say to her? If anything, I need to be thinking about what to do regarding the SACL pill, and I can't do that and be free to dash off if Rowan is home.

I switched the TV to the news channel and turned up the volume. The pill had been rolled out early. Everyone was to take two, and the second one would be available the next day. A national emergency had been declared, with other countries worldwide following suit. Details followed for emergency workers who could collect the pill after hours at their local surgery so essential shops could stay open. It was full-scale panic.

I gulped the last of my tea and jumped in the car early to collect Rowan. I had to be moving, doing something. My stomach was in knots, and my breathing was shallow. I switched between deciding to come clean and telling her everything or making something up about going away with Eve for a few days so I could delay it. I knew the invite to stay with Eve was always there whenever I wanted, which would be plausible. I felt an unease lurking in the background, and this thought increased the anxious tight sensation in the pit of my stomach as I drove.

Traffic was bumper to bumper as I reached the outskirts of town. Everybody was panicking, trying to get to the allocated outlets to get their antidote to the virus as fast as possible. I crawled slowly through the town centre, past my shop. My jaw dropped at the queue of people waiting to collect the pill from the local surgery. I followed it down the high street, around the corner, and it continued down the next street until just after the shops ended, and houses took over. Many more were walking to join on to the end, making it look like a giant mythical creature that was still forming. One of the figures I recognised was Rosa, always noticeable in her long brown coat. She was walking along the street ahead of me and skipping along faster than I was, my car now moving at a snail's pace. She's going to join the queue, I thought, surprised. Knowing her stance on natural treatment from our many conversations over the years, this would be out of character. I felt a need to talk to her. I wanted to ask her to be careful and ask questions, but as she neared the end of the throng of people, she continued walking and turned down the next road, disappearing from my sight. Not twenty seconds later, I rolled slowly by the end of the road and searched for her down the narrow lane, but I couldn't see her anywhere. A car horn sounded behind me, and I held up my hand in front of the mirror in acknowledgement. As I turned my eyes to the road ahead, a blue flash and a flurry of movement in my peripheral vision made me do a double-take. I scanned the area down the lane, but there was nothing. I pondered that maybe she had gone into one of the houses.

The car horn sounded again with several short blasts followed by a longer one. I glanced in the rearview mirror at the angry gesturing from the man behind and drove on, waving another apology in the mirror.

Eventually, the traffic became less dense as I took the back lanes to the train station. White, pillowy clouds had formed in the grey above and were racing across the sky as if late for an important meeting. Open fields on either side made me feel calm, and I relaxed, watching the different hedgerows and trees go by, the grassy banks at the side of the road, dotted now and then with brightly coloured wildflowers.

I arrived at the train station with just over half an hour to wait. I was ravenous even with the knotted tension, and the very basic Station Café now looked very appealing. The inside turned out to be not so appealing, with the overbright fluorescent tube lights giving everything a stark, hard edge. Reflected light bounced back into my eyes from the stainless steel chiller cabinet to my left. The grey linoleum floor was probably the original one, laid when the café opened many decades before. It was worn almost through in patches where it had sustained the heaviest footfall over the years.

I glanced at the tables, the red plastic gingham tablecloths showing visible remnants of hastily wiped over spillages and missed crumbs. Suppressing a shudder, I became aware that my disdainful expression was visibly showing my thoughts and looked up, hoping no one had noticed. An elderly lady with white, neatly curled hair was watching me. She sat with her same-aged friend, a flower brooch pinned to her burgundy jumper sparkled brightly in the onslaught of light. Between them on the table sat a pot of tea for two and identical scones that she was poised, knife in hand, to assemble. The jam and cream were supplied in tiny separate pots on the side of the plate.

I smiled at her weakly, and she scrunched up her shoulders, returning a broad, happy grin that crinkled her eyes almost closed before returning to continue her conversation with her friend. They chuckled heartily together, her friend throwing her head back as her companion laughed along with her. My smile deepened. They looked so content to be in each other's company, and I imagined they had been meeting here, regularly, for a long time. They certainly weren't bothered whether their meeting place was pristine or not. Walking to the counter, my eyes skimmed over the array of neatly packaged triangle sandwiches and slices of cake on plates, tightly wrapped with cling film. Nothing looked too appetising, but I chose a ham and cheese sandwich and tea to take out. I paid and went to sit in the undisturbed peace of my car, rechecking my phone. Still nothing from Eve. She must be busy.

I took the opportunity to dive into the rabbit hole of Facebook, scrolling through the posts of friends and friends who weren't really friends, but friends of friends, all portraying fun and perfect families.

What I really liked it for, however, was the groups. Now they brought people together. Amazing groups on everything you could think of, which was a valuable thing, connecting people with the same interests, likes, and dislikes. I turned to a group I belonged to regarding natural healing with herbs, noting a few interesting comments as I read through. A feeling of warmth spread slowly through my chest, and I turned to look out of the side window. Rowan grinned and waved excitedly as she walked towards the car, dragging her wheeled suitcase behind her.

I jumped out and embraced her in a tight hug, breathing in the smell of her hair, and my heart swelled, content and full. It didn't matter how old she was. Her smell was that of my child, and there was no feeling like it.

We broke apart, grinning. "Hey," she said, "sorry this is a bit sudden."

"Don't ever apologise for spending more time with me," I said, taking in her features.

Rowan took a deep breath and sighed, closing her eyes before opening them to look into mine. "It's so nice to be back early. I missed you."

The emotion I felt could only have come directly from my heart. I grabbed her again, "Ooh, I could squish the stuffing out of ya."

She laughed and rolled her eyes, shaking her head. It's what I had been saying to her since she was little.

"Come on," I said, automatically taking hold of her case and putting it in the car.

"Do you want anything to eat? The café isn't great, to be honest, or I can make you something when we get home?"

"No, I'm fine," she said, getting into the passenger seat. I got in beside her and started the engine.

"I got some take out food from the Costa before I got on the train."

"Home then." I smiled, absorbing a quick assessment of her features. Biased or not, she was naturally beautiful. Her dark blonde hair was tied up into a messy knot, straggly bits were hanging out, and the look was natural and effortless. Piercing blue eyes were fanned by thick dark lashes, and her full lips, naturally a deep pink, needed no external beautification, but her real beauty shone from within.

My concentration was distracted by conversation, and I drove slowly down the narrow country lanes asking her what had been happening at uni. She chatted animatedly about certain friends and funny conversations.

"How is the course going?" I asked, taking my eyes from the road for a split second to glance at her before returning them to the road.

"Good," she returned, and I felt the change of emotion prickle over my skin.

"Just good?" I prompted, raising my eyebrows.

"Yes, it's going really well." She looked down at her hands and studied her nails, rubbing over each one with her thumb. I waited. "Okay." She inhaled deeply. "There is something weird happening, like really weird. You're going to think I'm making this up."

"I most definitely won't," I said, looking directly into her eyes while thinking that I couldn't have meant that more with the week I'd just had.

Rowan placed her hands on top of her knees, her fingers spread wide. "Right, I'm not sure how to explain it, but... Oh, stop the car!"

"What?" I braked hard while checking mirrors, the car skidding a little in the dirt at the side of the road as we came to a sudden stop.

Rowan had undone her seatbelt in a flash and was

squeezing out of the passenger door that wouldn't fully open due to the grass bank.

I jumped out, joining up with her behind the car. I could feel a sensation of fear and loss, but it wasn't coming from Rowan. All I could get from her was an increase in anxiety, which was clouding my ability.

"Come on, she's just down here," she said, sprinting off. I followed on her heels.

"Who is? Rowan!" My sharper tone pulled her up, and she turned, placing her forefinger over her lips.

"Shhhh, just here…" She clambered up the grassy bank and bent to separate the thick hedging. I peered in behind her and froze as two large amber eyes of a female fox stared back at me.

"You can't have seen her from the road," I whispered behind her.

She twisted to face me from her crouched position. "I know. I didn't. That's the weird thing that keeps happening." She shook her head slightly and gave a little shrug. "It's like I felt her." Her brow knotted, and confusion emanated from her in waves that absorbed into my skin.

She turned her attention to the fox and reached out one hand. Wide, black-ringed eyes blinked, and a pink tongue flicked out below a jet-black nose to lick her fingers. It completely trusted her. Rowan put one hand on the fox's chest and the other around the back of the thick ginger-brown neck, pulling gently to encourage her out.

The fox dragged herself awkwardly forwards, pulling the rest of her body with her front legs, the back legs dragging behind as Rowan lifted her, gently soothing the fox with her voice.

"She's not long since had young ones as she's still producing milk." I crouched down slowly. Part of me was amazed that she could instil trust in this animal so easily, and part of me was unnerved by that thought.

She ran her hand down the fox's back. The fur compressed and then sprang back again, returning precisely as it had been once her hand had passed. She lightly felt over her legs and turned to me.

"The bones are broken. Maybe she was hit by a car?" From out of the thicket behind the vixen, there came rustling as three tiny kits came tumbling ungainly into view. A rasping series of barks came from one of them, and the mother called out to it with a fast, low, whining call. "They're only a week or two old," Rowan said. "A late litter too."

From across the road, through the trees of a small dense wooded area, my ears picked up the sound of another cub calling its mother. I turned to Rowan, "She must have been taking them across the road for more shelter. Maybe her den is there, and she got hit returning for the others."

The un-nerved feeling I had before was confirmed as Rowan turned to the cubs and made the same calling noise of the mother. The cubs spilt out of the long grass, pushing and jostling to get as close as they could to her.

I stood up. My chest felt tight. I reasoned with myself that it was a coincidence. Humans can make a vast array of different sounds. Maybe she had been doing that as part of her training to put the animals at ease? Yes, that was all it was. I was overthinking. My breathing relaxed. The vixen looked up at Rowan, then pushed a kit toward her with her nose. Rowan held out her hand. "She wants me to take them."

"We could take them to the shelter," I said. "She won't make it with her legs broken." My mind whirred with what to do. I was sure my powers could heal the legs, but to see that would freak Rowan out, and I would have to explain everything. A thought played out in my head. Maybe if I could drop Rowan home first, I could make the pretence of taking them to the shelter on my own, and heal the legs then. I turned to her.

"If you stay with the mother, I'll go and find the other kit, then I'll drop you home and take them to the shelter."

Rowan stood up. She turned to me calmly and took hold of my arms. "Mum, this is probably going to shock you, but try not to freak out. I promise everything is, and will be, okay."

22

I looked back at her and gave a brief nod, a small smile relaxing my brow. Alright, I have to just let this play out, I thought.

"It's okay, I'm ready. I promise I won't freak out."

I felt only calm radiating from her as we both crouched down near the vixen. Rowan stroked her hand from the tip of the fox's nose, over her face between her watchful amber eyes, and slowly ran her hand gently down her back, settling on her damaged legs. The movement seemed to instil a relaxed semi-sleep within the animal, and she laid her head down on the cushion of thick grass and closed her eyes, breathing deeply.

Rowan brought both hands together and moved them round in a circle, hovering just above the leg. A faint, pale yellow light glowed beneath her hands, briefly lighting the fox's fur to a brighter orange before fading to nothing. It wasn't enough.

So, it was as I expected. Rowan's powers were developing too, the chain of events and fate lines activated. Maybe this would be better to be out in the open, I thought. Rowan obviously has had time on her own to consider what was happening and was probably a little freaked out herself. Her kind nature had shelved her fears to help this animal.

I sighed and reached out to put my hand on her forearm. "Are you alright?"

She turned towards me, her mouth downturned but her eyes searching mine. They were filled with confusion as to why I was so calm.

That's it, I thought. Time to jump in with both feet. "Right, now it's time for you not to freak out, okay?"

I pulled her up to stand in front of me and opened my hands wide. Energy coursed through my body like lit gunpowder lines leading to explosives. I drew to me the microscopic healing elements of the plants that nature provided, Comfrey, Mullein, Self Heal among them. My hands glowed a bright orange as white light swirled in patterns around us both, the energy magnified. Rowan's jaw dropped, and her mouth formed a perfect oval, but she showed no fear.

"Try again," I said, indicating for her to crouch down with me. I sprinkled the fine powder over the vixen's legs, then she placed her hands over the top, and I cupped mine together and held them over hers. Blinding white light radiated from beneath our hands then faded quickly to nothing.

Rowan released the breath she had been holding, her chest heaving. Her eyes were sparkling intensely green and darted around as her mind tried to piece together what had just happened. She felt the legs, now showing no trace of injury and moved the joints that were now unbroken.

"How?" She looked at me, then stiffened, her eyes round and staring. "Whoa, your eyes are really bright green."

"Yours are too. They'll fade as the energy dies down" I smiled at her. "And to answer your next question, get ready…

we are witches. Descendants from a long line of witches actually, that included your Nan."

Rowan gasped. She sat back on the grass cross-legged and was quiet for a while. I gave her the time. Her eyes stared blankly as her mind pieced together all the things that had been happening to her, and then looking up, she said matter-of-factly, "Well, that explains it." Three snuffling kits tumbled into her lap, clambering over each other and bringing her attention to the current situation.

"Eww," she said suddenly with a shudder, and looked up at me anxiously, "I just had a thought. Please tell me we don't use parts of animals to make potions in cauldrons." She bit her lower lip.

I laughed. Relief at her reaction and how she had handled it flooded through me. It struck me that maybe the younger you were, the easier it was to accept information that may be difficult or frightening.

"Not as far as I know," I said. "I think modern-day witches have moved on a bit from that." A yawn escaped me suddenly, now able to release itself as the tension melted.

"Come on, let's take the mother and kits over to the woods to be reunited with the other one, and hopefully, she will look both ways next time," I said, rolling my eyes.

I checked my phone quickly, still nothing from Eve. Where was she? I wondered, concern now starting to creep in.

Rowan reached over to lift the mother fox, and her touch woke the animal who was on her feet in a flash. She bent her head to her body and licked at one of her legs, then rubbed her head against Rowan.

"You're welcome," Rowan said, smiling. "I'll take your kits safely across."

With the family back together, we watched them head off into the woods and then got back in the car.

"So, how did you know? How long have you known? Do you think Nan knew? What can we do? What other magic things…"

"Whoa." I held up my hand. "Slow down, let's take turns. Okay, I've only known this for the last week. You?"

"Same. When I said I couldn't come home for the weekend, I needed to have some time on my own to try and recreate a couple of things that had happened and check that I wasn't going crazy. I didn't have a clue how I was going to tell you."

"Same," I said, checking my mirrors before glancing at her. "I mean, it's not every day this happens, right? I think it's a chain of events that started with me and was meant to happen at this time." I paused and reached over to rub her leg gently. "Were you scared?"

She breathed out heavily through her nose, pulling down the corners of her mouth while her eyebrows raised. "That's the weird thing," she said, with a small shake of her head. "I felt more excited. It felt…err…" Her eyes looked upward and searched around, looking for the right words. She gave a small shrug of her shoulders. "Natural, I suppose like this is what all the unsettled feelings were. Finally, it made sense, and it just felt right." She threw her head back and laughed. "Oh my god, that's the most bizarre thing I've ever said."

I laughed along with her, relief fixing itself on my features with a smile that remained long after the laugh ended.

We drove through the quiet, rambling country lanes, everything looking so ordinary and normal. Fields stretched out on either side, the barley still green but now showing the path of the sprightly, mischievous wind as it skipped erratically across its surface. Patchwork squares of rapeseed dominated, intoxicating the eye with its bright yellow flower now in full bloom. The sun, fighting to be seen for brief intervals through the racing clouds, lifted it and gave it life, as it expanded the colour to a luminous swell that restored my wellbeing, before cloud obscured it once again, instantly breaking the spell and dropping the golden bounty back into the field. The heady scent of the pollen found its way through the air vent filters.

"So, what witchy things can you do?" Rowan asked, then snorted heavily through her nose and looked up at the roof of the car, her hands wide. "Oh man, another surreal question," she said, with a higher-than-normal laugh.

I told her of my powers and asked her what she knew of hers as we drove. I didn't detail Alchemia or Thea. That was going to take some thought, and right now, I had no idea how I would approach that.

"Right, we can both heal," she said, her manner relaxed and matter of fact, and I marvelled at the ease at which she had accepted this was happening. "You seem to have powers to do with nature and plants," she continued, "and I seem to have a particular way with animals. They understand me, and vice versa. The first time it happened, I was…" Rowan's voice faded as my eyes urgently sought out my phone. Its insistent tone and vibration demanded instant attention. I checked the road, then glanced down to where it was lying on the central console. The screen displayed—Eve one new message.

"Rowan, sorry, sweetheart, I was listening, but could you just open my phone and read the message from Eve, please? I've been waiting to hear from her, and it could be important."

"Sure, don't worry," she said, picking up the phone and swiping it open. "I'll tell you properly when we get home. I've got loads I want to tell you." She swiped to open the screen.

"You really should password protect this," she muttered as she brought up the message and read it out loud, "Hi, sorry for the delay. I'm at the old Airfield, postcode below.

I've got some exciting news, too long to explain. Could you get here ASAP? I'll wait for you. Heart emoji."

I knew that airfield. Specifically built in 1939 for the military for use in the Second World War, it had been abandoned almost twenty years ago and had lain derelict ever since. It was recently up for auction, its original use to be preserved, and turned into a historical museum of wartime artefacts.

My mind remembered pictures I had seen of it in my news feed, and the memory triggered a sudden, bright light behind my eyes that made me gasp out loud. I involuntarily gripped the wheel tightly with both hands. Snapshots of images flashed before my eyes. High windows with bars. Broken glass. Patterned floor tiles…and then dark. No wait, the dark was moving, a figure.

"Mum." Rowan grabbed the wheel and tried to turn it against my fixed hands. The images disappeared, and the road ahead came into view—the wrong side of the road. My reflexes reacted as a silver car came, too fast, around the corner ahead. I swerved back out of its way just in time and braked hard, the other driver's horn blared a long blast, and my heart raced. Pulling over at the entrance of a wide gravel driveway to one of the massive houses furthest from the village, I sat back in my seat and pressed a hand to my heaving chest. The high, black iron gates were an ominous threat in front of me and made me think of prison bars.

"Bloody hell, what happened? Are you okay?" Rowan's eyes were wide as she leaned forwards to look at me, placing one hand on the dashboard. I could feel the electrical build-up of energy from our heightened senses fill the confined space. I wound down the window to release it, breathing in the forceful gusts of mixed warm and cool air.

"I'm okay." I turned to her. "Sorry if I scared you. I have visions, well, premonitions, actually. They happen when I least expect it but are extremely real."

"What did you see?"

"Not much, patterned flooring, broken windows."

Rowan shifted her position to flop back against the seat. Her eyes blinked rapidly as she looked straight ahead, each blink linked to a change of idea or thought. "Does it have something to do with Eve?"

I had to play this down. I didn't have time for explanations. "It's hard to say, but I doubt it. I'm going to drop you back home and go check it out."

"I'm coming with you."

I shook my head and glared at her. "No, you're not, Rowan. I have been working on some research, and there must be something that links it to the airfield. That's all it is. Her message didn't sound worried."

"Try and call her and check."

I sighed heavily, picked up the phone and tried her. It went straight to voicemail.

"See," she said.

"Okay, Watson, that doesn't mean anything. There's probably no phone signal there."

"Watson? Don't you mean Sherlock?" she asked, looking at me like I'd lost the plot.

"Nope, I'm Sherlock, so you're Watson, and I say there's no problem."

She laughed. "You're a slice short of a cake; that's what you are."

I nodded in agreement. "I can't argue with that."

I started the car and pulled out of the driveway. A little way further and around the next bend, outskirt businesses began to appear, the funeral directors and solicitors among them, and then in another half a mile, it was mayhem. Cars blasted their horns and blocked the road, everyone trying to park as close to the end of the queue as possible. The road's double yellow lines had now become obsolete as angry drivers shouted and cursed. There was no way through.

"Okay, plan B. I'll have to back up and go the long way. I'll come into the village from the other end beyond our house."

"Then I'm definitely coming with you. It would be silly to go home before heading off again," Rowan stated. I started to reply, but she cut in. "Come on, I don't want to sit in the house on my own... I'll wait in the car," she added after seeing the look on my face. "It will be lovely to see Eve again. Maybe she could come back to ours for a catch-up, or we could go and get something to eat after?"

Her eyes looked hopeful as I turned the car around in the road and headed in the opposite direction.

"We might be ages," I said and turned to see her face fall briefly before she recovered with a slight nod and a smile. I tried to order the thoughts swirling around in my head. On the one hand, it seemed a chain of events had started, but I didn't know where or what they would lead to. Unbeknown to Rowan, Eve's message was definitely fake, which worried me a lot. On the other hand, I had missed Rowan, and she seemed to be capable and calm about what had just happened, although this would be adding some emotional worry for me if she came along.

I cleared my head and remembered what Morrae had said about feeling the correct path, and everything was fated, and I thought only of the events that had happened. Rowan had been fine with the magic, and I was now turning around, unable to drop her home. The path had been laid.

My forehead released its tension, and I smiled across at her. "Okay, you can come."

Eyes sparkled as her face lit up, and she grinned a wide grin with her teeth clamped shut. "Thank you," she said. Drumming her feet up and down excitedly in the footwell of the car. "I won't be any trouble."

"Well, I'm not sure that's something you can stick to, but I do need to stress a couple of things." I glanced over to her, briefly holding up one finger. "First, there is a lot…" my eyes grew wide in emphasis, "and I mean a lot of stuff that I haven't told you, and now is not the time." I lifted another finger. "Second, because of this, you have to do what I tell you because there is magic involved. This is not about you being my daughter or being younger or any of that crap. You just have to. Okay?"

Rowan fixed her eyes on mine. "I will," she said, with a slight jerk of her chin, her mouth twisted up on one side in a cheeky half-grin. She held up her closed fist with just her little finger raised like a hook. "Pinky promise?"

I hooked my little finger around hers, sealing the deal. "Pinky promise," I said, although my stomach lurched uneasily.

We spent the half-hour drive to the airfield describing what initiated our powers, what triggered them, and how we felt. Rowan was unsure as they had not gained strength yet, but I knew being around me had started that ball rolling.

23

Open fields turned into heathland ten minutes from our destination. The bright yellow flowers of the gorse bushes peppered the terrain and gave a beautiful contrast to the lilac and deep mauve heather. I turned right down a wide, rough concrete road that cut an unnatural scar through the unspoilt countryside. The concrete had been laid in sections, now mostly green with moss. The edges had disappeared into overgrown bracken and weeds, and both sides seemed to be competing to be the first to reach the centre. As I continued, the thick lines of grass that had grown between the dividing sections caused a repetitive double thump as the car tyres rode over them. Rabbits dived into the bracken at our noisy disturbance of their peace.

I became aware of the knot that had formed in my stomach, and the lack of oxygen from holding my breath now demanded my attention. I opened the window, inhaling a lungful of the fresh, fragrant air, and took in the sounds of nature all around me.

It was as though all the birds had got together to discuss something important—their many different songs were competing over each other and blending in collective, nonstop chatter.

"Look," I said, pointing to a large group of sika deer that were grazing off to our left. The beautiful white spots on the russet coat would forever remind me of Disney's Bambi. The largest of them turned its face towards us, ears and eyes fixed on our approach whilst nonchalantly chewing.

"Oh, they've got babies," Rowan cooed as little ones flung themselves into the air in joyous leaps, relaxed and happy to be alive on this day.

I followed a bend to the right that ran behind a dense area of trees, and the colossal aircraft hangar came into view. Pulling up in front of the old, dilapidated building, I checked my phone. No signal, just as I thought.

"Stay in the car," I said, turning to Rowan. "I mean it," I added.

She nodded. "Okay, but if you're not back in thirty minutes, then I reserve the right to come looking," she said.

I rolled my eyes and huffed. "I'm only meeting Eve, not getting kidnapped," I said, making light of it and playing down the situation.

"That may not be the case," she said. "Where's her car?"

My irritation grew. Rowan was not stupid, and she could argue for England. "Just wait for me, okay? You pinky promised."

"I will. I will...unless I think you're in trouble, then that breaks the pinky promise. You know that, right?"

I glared at her and got out of the car. "I'll be back in a bit with Eve," I said and shut the door.

I shouldn't have brought her. Now it seemed clear that my instincts were telling me I should have dropped her at home. Great, I thought. This would be a damn sight easier if someone could just bloody tell me my fate.

To the side of the hangar, there was another smaller

building that could have been a reception. I headed over, turning a full circle as I walked. Where was her car anyway?

The sun had come out again, but the wind had free rein across the flat, open landscape, and it lashed my hair across the back of my jacket with a sudden strong gust. A tingle ran down the back of my neck and continued down my arms to my fingers. Nothing felt right about this.

The rotten wooden door had dropped on its hinges and wedged against the frame at the bottom. I gave it a hard push with my shoulder, thinking at the same time that Eve couldn't be in here.

Suddenly, the door gave way, and I entered with a giant step that forced my eyes to look down. I gasped as my vision merged with reality. The tiles weren't tiles, after all, but a red and blue circular-patterned carpet. I followed the path of my vision and looked out of the broken window to the hangar beyond, and the high rows of broken glass windows braced with bars. My ears picked up on a sound and led my eyes to movement. I focused, squinting. It was a small bird flapping furiously against one of the unbroken panes—the warning of a trap.

Energy coursed through my veins as time caught up with itself and the vision ended.

She must be in the hangar. My heart rate increased more than the short walk required as I approached the dominating building. The yellow brick was weathered and crumbling, stained green in parts by algae, and thick with ivy that clung to all the easy to hold crevices now the cement had fallen out.

The huge khaki green corrugated iron doors were bent, rusted rivets causing panels to hang sideways. The paint had peeled so much it was now showing more of the natural metal grey colour than the green.

A lopsided, hanging section of panel beckoned me inside, and I peered in.

It looked empty but was gloomy and dark, and my eyes had not adjusted. I looked back at the car and signalled a thumbs up to Rowan. She raised her hand, wiggling her fingers in return.

The flapping sound of the bird grew louder as I walked in, and I looked up just as it became exhausted and sat resting on the sill, its tiny chest heaving frantically.

The hangar was empty except for a few large shipping crates to my right, which I made my way towards. Broken equipment and old parts of aeroplanes had been cleared and stashed along the left-hand wall, along with a wheeled platform ladder that was rusted to the point of disintegrating.

The light was dim despite the windows. The panes of glass that remained unbroken had turned a greenish-brown with moss and algae that had found a new home, and they allowed in little light.

He was here. My skin crawled and itched, repelling the feeling of hatred directed at me and my stomach churned and bunched, finding the merest essence of him abhorrent. I looked towards the crates where the energy was focused, and Malicen stepped out from behind them.

He was dressed immaculately in dark grey trousers and a matching shirt that complimented his neat greying hair. His black, full-length, belted trench coat hung open, and his hands were plunged deep into the pockets. He cut a striking figure, one that was powerful, confident, and determined.

The only sound came from his sure footsteps on the concrete floor as he walked a few paces towards the centre of the room. His eyes fixed hard on mine as he removed his hands from his pockets and pulled on tight black leather gloves, one side of his mouth twisted up in a semi-smile that twitched with the effort to hide his irritation.

My body surged with energy, and I inhaled a deep lungful of air, tightening my stance. A white glow spread out from my hands, and the air around them cracked with the build of emotion. I consciously tried to keep calm.

"Ah, Haesel," he said with slow deliberation. The light from my hands reflected off his narrow, rimless glasses, but behind them, I could see his pale, blue eyes glitter coldly as they absorbed it. "Your powers seem to have gained some momentum…and control, I see. Very interesting," he said, nodding slowly. His eyes hardened.

I ignored him. "Where's Eve?"

"Oh, she's safe…for now, but that depends on you." He lowered his head and peered at me over his glasses, his forehead wrinkling up in tight lines.

"What do you want, Malicen?"

He paced slowly back and forth, clasping his hands behind his back. "Oh, simple things, really. Power, recognition."

My brow furrowed. "You already have that."

He threw his head back, and a loud, short laugh burst from his chest, which echoed around the cavernous building.

"Yes, yes, I suppose I do," and he pulled his mouth down at the corners, rocking his head back and forth as he faked pondering this notion, before turning to me, his lips now pressed into a hard line.

"But not enough." He spoke through gritted teeth as his hands clenched slowly into tight fists by his sides. "I have had to fight my way here, and it's taken years. I have been knocked back again and again by one pretentious upstart after another, along with your meddling, of course," he said, flinging an arm in my direction.

His breathing became heavier through flared nostrils as he lowered his head and paced. "I'm not getting any younger, and this position is delicate. It can be taken from me in the blink of an eye by another clever-arse scientist with a bright idea." He paused and regained control of his breathing, twisting his head to the side to glare at me with squinted, focused eyes.

"You can't win, Haesel, despite your little break-in at my office, and the fact that you now know what is to come, there are other very powerful people involved in this, and the plan will continue, with or without me.

I tried not to show the fear that trickled over my skin at hearing these words and lifted my chin, feigning confidence.

"However," he continued, wagging his finger as he walked, "the power of magic is something no one can compete with, and now, you are going to give it to me." He spun around to face me. "Thanks to your mother, I learned enough of her secrets and worked out how to create the portal. And now…" He plunged a hand into his pocket, and the wide grin that spread across his face revealed perfect white teeth.

My eyes grew wide, and I stepped back as he withdrew a syringe full of liquid. He brandished it in front of him, standing taller in his crazed triumph. "Now, I have the missing link. I have that!" He pointed to my glowing hands, then held up the syringe close to his face, where it shook slightly in his gripped fist. "In here, I have all I need, your DNA and your blood. Oh…" his lips curled into an insincere smirk, "thank you for leaving that behind, by the way, while you were rifling through my private things."

My chest tightened further.

Malicen's eyes flashed with the expectation of what was soon to be his. "Your blood behaves quite unlike anything I have ever seen, and it's the key that gives your magical abilities their strength. I've studied, tested, and isolated the cells, and finally…" his lips spread into a wide, manic grin that showed almost all of his teeth, "you can be witness to my transformation."

"It won't work, Malicen," I said, my voice booming around the room as I remembered Thea's words and hoped above all things that she was right. "Your body will reject my DNA, and your immune system will attack any blood that it sees as an imposter."

"Ah, yes, good point," he nodded, tilting his head to the side, his eyes looking around the ceiling. "Ordinarily, that would be true, but I have already taken a cocktail of drugs that proved in my trials to counter all that. So, all in all, I think we're good to go."

I straightened my stance, my eyes fixed on his, and shook my head. "No. It will kill you. Mick's already dead, but if you do this, you will be next, and all your work will have been for nothing."

My voice was confident and calm in my attempted bluff, and I felt the slight change in his energy as he absorbed the tiny seed of doubt.

He looked momentarily surprised before his face hardened. "Mick's not dead," he spat. "I thought he might have been, but when I returned sometime later, he had gone. Ran away like the coward he is. He's weak, and he thrived on the attention I gave him."

Malicen's lips twisted into a half-smile that settled, smug on his face.

"It was easy to manipulate him to lure you to the portal, though. My little pretence that your expected powers would help so many people worked like a charm."

My breath caught in my throat. So, Mick wasn't dead, and he had genuinely thought he was doing a good thing after all.

"Now, where were we?" Malicen snarled.

My hands glowed and sparked, and I looked him in the eye. I wouldn't let him do it.

His eyes flicked to my hands and back to my eyes again. "Ah yes, there is one thing I would like you to see first."

He reached into his pocket and pulled out a small electronic device that fitted into his palm. His eyes glittered and narrowed as he held it up. All his feelings of hatred and bitterness hit me like a wave as a muffled cry sounded from behind the crates.

"Eve!" I lunged forward.

Malicen dashed to block my path, holding up his hand. "Not so fast, Haesel. You wouldn't want to be the cause of your friend's death, now would you?" His eyes flicked to look to his left momentarily.

Breathing heavily, I walked around him in a slow, wide circle until Eve came into view. I gasped, my heart pounding in my chest. "Eve, don't worry, I'll get you out," and determination rose like a gigantic wave in my core, drowning my anxiety.

She sat in a heavy, metal-framed chair, her mouth covered with duct tape and her wrists and ankles bound to the arms and legs of the chair. Fear and confusion filled her eyes, and mine grew wide as they took in the scene, settling on a machine positioned on top of a singled out crate. Wires ran from the machine across the floor and ended at a syringe taped to her arm, the needle embedded deep into her vein. She glanced down at it and tried to yell out, and her face turned a deep red as she thrashed around against her restraints.

This had to stop. My anger swelled, and my hands glowed brightly as I aimed a bolt of crackling energy straight at Malicen. The sound renewed the fight in the exhausted bird, and it rose in panicked determination to beat its wings against the glass pane with renewed vigour.

Malicen was ready and jumped quickly to the side, but not quick enough. The blast caught his leg just above the knee and he stumbled, releasing a cry of pain, as blood expanded like a flower opening into full bloom through his grey trousers. He straightened and fixed me a hard stare. There was no fear, and a cold chill trickled down my spine.

I looked at Eve, who was shaking her head vigorously while her large black pupils stayed fixed in position.

"Be very careful before you go any further, Haesel," Malicen said through gritted teeth. "There is a concentrated liquid version of the SACL pill in that syringe, embedded in your friend's arm, and I only have to push this button for the whole lot to be pumped into her body. Then I simply turn on the transmitter…" He waved his hand flippantly. "You know the rest. At least the end will be quick," and his mouth twisted into a smirk.

My eyes darted back and forth as I tried to understand. "Why bring her here? You could have injected yourself without all this, and no one would have known."

"Ah, good question. I knew you would get to it eventually." He shook a finger in the air. "Well, firstly, I'm sure that your interference would at some point have caused me further problems. And secondly, I might just need you, Haesel. You're my plan B. If this doesn't work, then I will need you to heal me. I saw the regeneration ability of your cells at the lab, and I intend to study you further. You will comply to save your friend, won't you? Otherwise, poor Eve here is no more."

It became clear to me at that moment that he would never stop, and no matter how powerful he became, it would never be enough.

I felt our paths of fate come together. I was the one destined to stop him. This was it.

I eyed Malicen's hand, his thumb on the button, ready.

His smirk broadened into a smile. "Ah, I know what you're thinking, Haesel. You're wondering if you can get there to save her quicker than I can fill her veins with poison, or, if you could strike me fast enough to get to this remote."

He paced slowly further away from Eve, closer to the entrance, leaving me in the middle, between him and her. "Go ahead, try." He gestured towards Eve with his left hand in a whimsical manner, still gripping the remote device. I turned to Eve. "Oh…you can't, by the way." My head swung around again as he continued. "I've done numerous calculations, and it's quite impossible." A gleeful chuckle escaped him.

I turned back to face Eve, torn with what to do first. She locked her eyes onto mine then gave an almost imperceivable nod of her head. It was the permission I needed, and my heart grew stronger with her faith in me.

"You will be okay," I said. "Don't worry."

Eve's mouth gaped suddenly and her eyes stared through me. My heart leapt and thumped loudly. What was happening? Had he pushed the button?

She thrust her head forwards repeatedly, her wide eyes indicating for me to look behind me.

I swung around to see Rowan walking across the cavernous room in our direction.

Malicen saw me draw a full breath and turned to see what was behind him.

"Rowan, run! Get out!" I yelled. Adrenaline surged and flooded my muscles in seconds.

She froze, her eyes darting between Malicen and me. She started to back away, then stopped. I held my breath as I watched the precise moment her mind decided, for whatever reason, to be by my side. Before I could call out, she was running towards me in an arc around Malicen.

He suddenly dashed towards her, faster than I was prepared for, and my breath caught in my throat as he lunged and wrapped his arm around her neck.

"Mum!"

Her scream triggered the reaction from my body as the

energy headed at speed, down my arms. Like a large body of water heading for the waterfall, events had been set in motion.

"Don't move, Rowan, just stay calm. It will be ok." I lifted my hand, now glowing orange and spitting sparks and narrowed my eyes at Malicen.

"Are you accurate enough not to hit her, Haesel?" he spat. "I don't think so. Open the portal, and I'll let her go."

I felt a calm come over me. Looking directly into his squinting desperate eyes, I sensed the uneasiness from him. He wasn't sure of his precarious situation and what I would do. I shook my head slowly. "I won't do it."

He gritted his teeth, spittle forming in the corner of his mouth. Then he grinned a strange, fixed smile, and featherlight fingers ran across my shoulder blades as I felt him shift from uneasiness to determined confidence. My heart upped its pace in my chest. He had come this far, and now it was all or nothing.

Rowan cried out as he tightened his grip before plunging the syringe into his leg, releasing the cocktail of my blood and DNA into his body.

24

Nothing happened at first. Then Malicen's face seemed to lose all its muscle tone. His mouth fell open, and a line of saliva escaped over his sagging bottom lip before running down his chin to drip onto the floor.

Rowan struggled out of his grip and twisted to face him, stumbling back, her eyes wide.

He made a choking sound, and his body jumped and jerked as though being punched from the inside. A gurgling noise escaped from his throat, then his head lolled forwards, and he stood suspended and limp, a puppet still held up by its strings.

All my muscles tensed, ready to act. It didn't work. It can't have. Then all the hairs rose on the back of my neck an icy cold chill shot through my body from head to toe. Malicen was glowing.

No, that can't be, I thought. My blood ran faster around my body, and I felt my strength intensify. I had to do something. I couldn't allow him to have this power. I focused my energy as white light leapt from my hands, crackling and swirling around me as it built in its force. I narrowed my eyes and sent it spitting and blinding towards him. My energy hit…and disappeared.

I gasped. What had happened? It didn't have any effect at all. It just seemed to soak in. Then the realisation hit me and all the air left my body in one giant rush. Oh God, that's exactly what had happened. My power had simply been absorbed.

The red haze surrounding Malicen grew steadily outwards and intensified in its brightness, and he came back to life. Drawing a huge, shuddering breath, his chest heaved as he dropped the syringe he was still holding, thrust out a hand, and sent a blast of red crackling energy straight at Rowan.

"No!" I reached out. A golden wall of protection spread through the air at speed between them. But not fast enough. The blast hit her, and I watched in horrified slow motion as she crumpled and fell to the floor.

"Rowan!" My terrified voice didn't sound like mine as all my senses focused on her. She lay still, but I could still feel her, and I could see the green glow of her eyes behind her almost closed lids. She was okay.

I was rooted to the spot, unsure what to do. If I fought him, would my energy just make him even stronger? Doubt crept in. I wasn't ready. I wasn't strong enough.

"Yes!" Malicen screamed. He turned to face me with crazed eyes that were darting in all directions. He looked down at his hands, clenching and unclenching his fists, then back at me. "I did it. I really did it." He pulled back a sleeve, turning his arm to check his skin. A second of elation raised his eyebrows as his mouth fell open before his features shifted to satisfaction and the realisation that he now had the power he wanted. It had worked. He threw back his head and let out a cry that released all the years of accumulated effort, anger and frustration.

I glanced at Eve, whose eyes were wide with fear. What

could I do? I had to save her. Then everything became calm and took on a strange, surreal feeling.

A sudden strong gust of wind took hold of the sheet of corrugated iron where I had entered the hangar, and the remaining rivets gave in to the rust. It flipped and fell to the floor with a loud rattling crash. Malicen spun to look in its direction.

I saw a brief flash of blue before a light breeze worked its way across the hangar and blew gently across my face. A voice whispered, *Use how you feel, trust it and intensify the feeling.*

What feeling? I thought. *Doubt?* What did it mean? I didn't have time to think.

Malicen raised his hands, drawing on his power, and in front of me, the portal started to open. I stared, stunned. How could he open it when he had never been through? Had never seen?

Then I felt it, a pulling sensation. He was drawing on my power to enhance his own and open the gate to the other realm. Could he see all that I could see now? I felt dizzy. The surge of pheromones emanating from him assailed my nose and smelt strong and aggressive. Would he go to Alchemia? Fear spread out from my heart and began to radiate through every cell.

I watched the portal open, unable to stop it. It looked different this time as turbulent air, thick with menacing clouds, swirled within the gateway that now hovered, complete before me.

"It worked!" he screamed before staring open-mouthed at the portal. Then he turned to me. Grasping his glasses, he threw them across the floor as his eyes flashed, and the crazed grin of a madman spread slowly across his face. My fear increased.

He threw a glance at Rowan before turning back to me. Holding up the remote controller in one hand, his other aimed at Rowan, his shoulders shook as a jubilant, high-pitched laugh escaped him.

"Who will you save Haesel?" And he pushed the button.

A muffled cry to my right made me spin around. Eve's eyes were round and wild, flicking back and forth between me and the liquid that was starting to pump slowly into her vein. Her nostrils flared as she panicked, rocking the chair, struggling to breathe with the tape across her mouth.

"Eve!" My chest heaved as the rhythmic swishing sound of my blood assailed my ears.

"Mum!" My head swung back. Rowan was sat up, leaning back on her hands, her eyes fixed on Malicen. I inhaled a deep lungful of air as fear prevailed and surged in a cold chemical rush that flooded my body. *Use how you feel*, the words repeated in my mind. That was it, use my fear.

Time slowed, almost to a standstill. Who do I save? In the stillness of time, my thoughts ran at breakneck speed back and forth through my head. Every action has a reaction. Rowan was my daughter. She was my first choice always. But Eve couldn't defend herself in her trapped state. Rowan had powers and could heal. Eve could not. It would kill me to lose Rowan.

My power reached out, and this time my golden, crackling wall fixed itself in place as a divide between Rowan and Malicen. Then I ran to Eve through air that felt much thicker, like that of a dream when you are trying to run but aren't getting anywhere. The movements of Eve and Malicen were in slow motion, inching forwards.

Rowan's voice came through the fog. "Mum, what can I do?" I glanced back to see her on her feet heading towards me, the time freeze I had created not affecting her.

"Just stay back behind the wall," I yelled, reaching Eve and pulling the syringe from her arm before any more of the toxic poison could enter her bloodstream. I held my hand over the entry wound and spread my fingers, concentrating on drawing the graphene oxide particles to me. A thin, barely visible grey line snaked out of her arm and swirled before me. I aimed a blast of energy, and it flashed brightly, crackling in the air before disappearing. Pulling the tape from her mouth, I quickly freed her hands, then swung around sharply at the distorted roar that came from behind.

Malicen had fought against the time freeze with his newly found power and rigid, claw-like fingers reached out inches from my face, his lips were curled into a snarl that exposed his gritted teeth, while his face was crimson with the effort to break through. I reeled in shock at the vehemence in his unearthly, glowing, red eyes.

In a flash, I grabbed the syringe. It was still three-quarters full. Then swinging around, I held it up and stared Malicen straight in the eye. His face changed in slow motion, his eyes widening and mouth dropping open with the realisation of what I was going to do. He thought to back away, but the time freeze didn't allow for speed, and his eyes grew large and swivelled sideways to show the bulging, red-veined whites as he stared at my hand.

I hesitated. This went against every part of my being. I had never injured anyone before, let alone killed them. I fought the feeling. I had to do it, this was my fate, and if I didn't, he would kill billions. Launching the needle into his arm, I released the toxic contents.

The sudden relief hit me, and my shoulders sagged. The fear eased, and with it, the slowing of time ended. The wall in front of Rowan vanished, and Malicen fell towards me, his hand grasping air as I reeled to the side.

"What have you done?" His voice came out in a high, screaming whisper, eyes wildly darting. His fear of death was intense, emanating into me, and my eyes teared in an involuntary response that I had done this to another.

Behind him the portal swirled and thrashed in angry torrents like a tortured creature. Then I suddenly became aware that it was still open, but how? It should have closed by now. Malicen began to stumble backwards towards it and I watched, stunned, as the realisation dawned on me that he was being drawn to it. Something dark and sinister was pulling him in from the other side.

He staggered as his body convulsed and jerked, and he let out a high-pitched scream. The chemical poison mingled quickly with his blood, and his body raged as it fought itself. I imagined the fight, the graphene attacking, grouping, and squeezing the blood cells, reducing the oxygen and blocking the vessels. A cytokine storm would ensue as his immune system collapsed...but I was not ready for the horror that happened next.

The convulsing stopped abruptly, and he began tearing wildly at his clothes, shedding his coat and shirt, his breath coming in rasping bursts as he shrieked. "Stop! Get it off! Get it off!" He let out a scream that did not sound human.

A thin, white t-shirt that had been under his shirt, revealed arms that were blistering and bubbling as his newly found powers reacted with the chemicals.

The look of pain and fear on his face made my blood run cold as a black swirling mist emanated from his body, circling and growing before engulfing him, thrashing and screaming. A sulphurous smell reached my nose, and I gagged. Bending forwards, I wrapped my arm around my face, breathing through the material in the crook of my elbow.

Behind him, the portal convulsed in violent waves as crackling bursts of plasma shot out into the writhing mass, now the only thing that could be seen of Malicen. It shook and vibrated with immense power and I stared open-mouthed as it gradually grew darker through all the shades of grey before it matched the deep black colour of the seething shape before it.

Rowan was transfixed. She was close, too close, unable to move—rooted by the horror that unfolded before her.

A blood-curdling scream made us both jump, and I reacted instinctively. Energy surged as I reached out to protect her.

An ugly, gurgling laugh erupted from within the writhing darkness as a deep red light glowed from its centre. The portal's energy began to feed off Malicen, as he was dragged towards the monster of angry turbulence.

I cried out and braced myself to hold and strengthen the orb of safety that surrounded her. My muscles strained and burned, fighting the pull of the portal. Then a blackened, elongated hand shot out of the swirling ball that was now Malicen. It sliced through my power as though it was plunging into water and grabbed Rowan, pulling her into the blackness.

"No!" My heart stopped, and my legs crumbled. Quick as a flash, the wreathing mist from the portal shot out and joined with Malicen. A blood-curdling cry came from within. Then the whole mass was sucked back into the portal and was gone.

The last thing I saw was a flash of green from her eyes as she disappeared.

25

Eve screamed from where she was hiding behind a crate, but it was a long, drawn-out sound that reached my ears slowly in my shocked state. I knew what I had to do and my mind flashed through my last thoughts at high speed. It didn't matter that the world would be lost, that Eve would die, that I might die too. I briefly thought of Jay, torn, as the pain in my heart deepened. But this child had gone, and our invisible bond, along with my parental instinct, left me with one thought only. I had to save her.

My whole body surged. Crackles of electricity shot out from around me as chemicals reacted and muscles bunched. The portal would close. I didn't have long.

I ran forwards and leapt, diving towards the shrinking darkness, and hit an invisible force that slammed into me head-on, knocking me to the ground. A heavy weight landed on top of me for a moment, and I could just make out a blurry transparent outline as my eyes homed in before it pushed off me and shot across the floor. Beyond, the portal collapsed in on itself and was gone.

"No! Rowan!" Tears sprung into my eyes, and I spun my

head around to locate the distorted patterns of air. All of my hatred focused on this thing. It crossed the hanger at speed, scaling the high brick wall and coming to a stop halfway up. It sat, pulsing, breathing, and I was on my feet, ready. Green and white light came together, swirling and sparking around me as I lifted my hands and focused.

Then it moved, two glowing green eyes looked into mine and I felt the invisible bond that tied me to my child. All the bonds that held me together fell like heavy rain as the breath left my body.

"Rowan!"

"Mum? What the fuck?" The shaky voice killed my energy but swelled my heart, and tears ran freely down my cheeks and clogged my throat.

I ran over on legs that barely held me up.

"Rowan, it's okay," I choked. "Try and stay calm. It's your fear response. Can you work your way down?"

Slowly she appeared, glimmers of colour deepening as her emotions calmed, until she was entirely visible again. Then she let out a shriek as she fell off the wall, twisting to land lightly and easily on all fours in front of me. I grabbed her, pulling her to me and held her tight, kissing her hair and breathing her in as I choked back the sobs.

"Oh, thank you, thank you, thank you," I muttered under my breath, my eyes squeezed shut. I released her to look at her face. "It's okay, sweetheart, you're safe now. I've got you."

Rowan remained still, but I could feel her whole body shaking. "My hands," she said, in barely a whisper. Then she looked at me, her eyes wide and her brow wrinkled with a mixture of worry and disgust. "What's wrong with them?" She shuddered. "Urghh, it feels awful."

I looked down at her hands. A blue glow was visible, shining through her veins. It was slowly disappearing, moving from her wrist towards her fingers. Her hands were swollen and puffed out with millions of overlapping scales.

I reached out to touch one, and they lifted, sensing my presence, and swept towards the movement like coral swaying within sea currents—the tiny buds grabbing hold of my finger.

"Urghh," Rowan exclaimed again. "It's so disgusting. It's making me feel sick. I really don't like it. Please get it off." She grimaced, clamping her jaw shut and breathing through her teeth.

"It will go," I said. "The quicker you calm your emotions, the quicker it will go. Close your eyes and take some deep, slow breaths in and out."

I smiled as I suddenly understood, and Noi's sweet face popped into my head. When we had connected, I had only received the telepathic part of his magic because my senses were my strength. But when I was healing the fox with Rowan, we had connected, and it must have passed over his other attributes, sensing her affinity with animals. Now she could climb and had invisible cloaking abilities like Noi.

"Look, it's almost gone."

Rowan opened her eyes and looked at her hands, breathing a huge sigh of relief as the last few cells disappeared into her skin and it returned to normal. Wide-eyed, she stared at me.

"So, what in the fucking, fuckedy hell just happened?"

A laugh burst out before I could stop it.

"Not funny," she glared at me. "Really, Mum. Not."

"Sorry, it's just the relief that you're okay and not dead." I sighed. "It's a long story. I'll explain everything on the way home. How did you get out of the portal? What happened to Malicen?"

"I don't know. I think it was just speed that got me out. I could suddenly move really fast."

Ah, yes, that made sense with her having Noi's abilities, I thought.

"I didn't see what happened. I was too focused on getting out."

"That's okay, let's hope he's gone for…"

A sudden whimpering noise made us both whip our heads around in the direction of the crates.

"Oh no, Eve," I said. We ran across to the crates to find Eve bunched up in a ball on the floor, her head on her knees and her fingers in her ears. She was rocking back and forth, repeating over and over again, "It's okay. It's okay. It will be okay."

"Eve." I touched her shoulder, and she screamed, scooting backwards, making us all jump.

"Haesel?" Her whole body was shaking, and she stared at me briefly before her eyes darted quickly around the room.

"It's okay, Eve. It's all over. He's gone." Her face crumpled, and I went to her, wrapping her in my arms.

"I knew you would save me," she cried, sobbing into my neck.

I swallowed the lump in my throat and squeezed harder. "Come on, let's go."

Eve let go, and Rowan stepped in, grabbing her and squeezing her tight. "Oh Eve, I've missed you. I haven't seen you in ages. Did you see me? I scaled that wall," she said, pointing. Now recovered a little, she obviously thought her ability was pretty cool.

Eve just stared at her and gave a thin smile. "That's great, Rowan… I think," she added, turning to me, her face confused.

I realised she must have missed that part with her eyes shut and her fingers in her ears.

"Rowan's a witch, too." I shrugged. "Remember? It's passed down through generations."

She nodded. "That makes sense," she muttered, still shaking and looking as white as a sheet. I took hold of her hand and turned to set off across the echoing hangar. A flapping noise made me look up to see the bird fly further down the building and out through a broken window. It never gave up and was now rewarded with its freedom.

"What did Malicen mean?" Eve said suddenly.

"About what?"

"When he said there were others that would carry on, with or without him? That you can't save the world. Are we all going to die?"

"What?" Rowan said.

"What did you find out with Thea, Haesel?"

"What?!" Rowan interjected again, her eyes round. "Nan?"

I shot a look at Rowan and held up my hand. "Later, I promise."

Eve grabbed hold of me. "You can heal, Haesel. That's your strength. You drew the poison out of my blood. You must be able to do something?"

She was right. I could draw healing elements to me, but how could I use that for so many people? It would take too long. I absently rubbed at an itch on my chest, and my fingers felt over the scar left by Nithele. It tingled and grew warm, and my mind raced. It all made sense. This is where Nithele injured me, and her blood had merged with mine. I thought of her words.

Your minds are closed. You don't see what's right in front of you— the gifts you have been given.

She had given me a gift, something I needed to save everyone. She did help me, after all.

I could see the warm orange glow spreading out and growing brighter through my clothes. I slipped off my jacket, exposing the scar above the neckline of my top, and the light grew intense, shining up onto the corrugated ceiling.

"Whoa," said Rowan. "What does that do?"

"I don't know, but I think I should be outside. Whatever happens, both of you stay back. I'll be okay, but I have a feeling this is going to be big."

Rowan took me at my word for once. "I'll take Eve and wait in the car."

I smiled at her, "I love you."

I hadn't failed. As soon as I was outside, the power took over. Enhanced by the blood of a dragon, I became a vessel through which my healing powers could pass.

Shades of white, gold, and green light swirled out from the scar like an ethereal mist and wrapped in swirls around my body. I opened my hands and thought of all the chemical properties of the herbs that would bind to heavy metals and help clear the graphene oxide from the body, a process known as chelation.

Then I drew them in from far and wide.

Suramin from the scots pine and dandelion, blueberries and garlic. The fine microscopic particles in the air were drawn to me and multiplied through my magic. I drew to me all the foods that contained cysteine, glutamine, and glycine, the three amino acids that made the powerful antioxidant glutathione. Onion, ginseng, oats and sunflower seeds, spinach, parsley, poppy seeds, and more.

The magic coursed through my veins, multiplying the properties in the ingredients as they landed in my hands. Then the energy balled in my centre, and intense heat radiated out, turning to flame as it drew the healing elements upwards in light-filled streams. I tilted my head back to watch it being carried up, high into the sky by the dragon's power. Once it reached the jet stream, it would be carried around the world and impregnate the air for all to breathe in and counter the toxic pill's effects.

I wasn't tired. Both mine and the dragon's magic kept me strong as I stood, drawing in what I needed, the power sending it upwards in pulsing waves. Eventually, after what seemed a long time, the energy subsided, and the magic died.

My arms dropped to my sides. I was content that I had fulfilled my fate. I felt light, a weight lifted, and I walked over to the car where Eve and Rowan were now chatting. Rowan wound down the window, and I leaned in. They both twisted around to face me.

"Wow, that was awesome," Rowan said, her face lit up in awe. "Are you okay?"

I smiled at her, nodding. "Very okay, actually."

"Do you think it will be enough?" Eve asked, sucking in her bottom lip, her eyebrows drawn together.

"I don't know. I'm sure it won't save everyone. There will be vulnerable people, who are sick or elderly, or both who don't have the strength to counter it. But hopefully, it will help the majority."

A nagging thought prodded my mind. Malicen had gone, but I didn't know where, and I had to check that Thea was okay. I straightened up. "I'll just go and grab any evidence and tidy up, so nothing looks suspicious. I won't be long."

Rowan opened her door, "I'll come with you."

"No, stay and chat with Eve," I said, backing away. "I'll be two minutes, and then we'll go and get something to eat."

To my surprise, Rowan smiled and closed the door, resuming her conversation with Eve.

Once back in the hangar, I quickly opened the portal and jumped through. When I was ejected out the other side, my eyes darted around quickly. My energy surging, ready. All looked calm, nothing out of place. I checked the house and found Thea out back in the allotment. My shoulders dropped with a large exhale of breath.

Malicen wasn't here. Was he alive? I felt an unease that I knew would not go away until I found out what had happened.

I briefed Thea on what had happened.

"He will have been taken to Lucerin, The Dark World," she said, pressing her lips together. "The Dark World will hone in on evil intentions, and it sounds like he was drawn there."

"Yes, it did look like that."

"We should be safe enough," she said. "There are laws that even evil obeys. The result of breaking those laws would be catastrophic for all."

"Well, let's hope it stays that way." I smiled, but a tiny seed of doubt still irritated my core. "On a lighter note, I have some news I think you'll be pretty excited about," I said, my smile genuine this time and spread fully and relaxed across my face.

"Oh?" Thea lifted her chin, her eyes sparkling with anticipation.

"I will be bringing a visitor to see you."

Her hands flew to her mouth as tears of joy magnified the sparkles in her eyes. "No...not?" She couldn't say the name just in case it wasn't true.

"Yes," I nodded. "I'll bring her next time," and I told her quickly of Rowan's magic.

I left her in the allotment, happily tending to the plants, and took one last look around, inhaling several big lungfuls of fresh air before opening the portal. It gleamed pure white and frothy in the sun, and I felt more sure of myself than ever before.

Back in the hangar, hardly any time had passed. I watched the portal close, then picked up the syringes, machine pump, wires, and any evidence that showed we had been there. I wrapped them in Malicen's discarded shirt and coat and would dispose of them properly once home.

I glanced back for one more quick check and turned to leave, but something caught my eye. Light reflected off an object tucked into the corner of the crates by the wall. Walking over, I saw what it was and bent to pick up Malicen's glasses. I shuddered to even hold them in my hand.

Passing a rusty bin on the way to the car, I dropped the glasses inside and looked out over the heathland. The wind had dropped to a warm light breeze, and the evening light held a hopeful promise as the suns healing rays stretched across the land. The smell of gorse and grass drifted on delicate waves of air, filling my nose with its sweet scent. For now, all was calm.

Eve had jumped in the back, and I got in and started the engine. My Phone pinged and I retrieved it from inside the central arm rest. It was from Jay, and simply read;

Mum, I'm coming home, all OK but we REALLY need to talk x.

I replied; *OK, I'll call you in a bit. Can't wait to see you.* xx, and replaced the phone back in the arm rest.

I felt the unease, something was amiss, but I was ready. Nothing could be as bad as what we had just gone through and I felt excited for us all to be together again.

"Right," I said, looking at two now weary faces. "Let's go and get something to eat. I need wine."

"Ooh, yes, me too," Rowan said leaning back with a sigh.

"Not as much as I do," Eve stated, "I need a whole bloody bottle after that." Rowan laughed, and I reached back for Eve's hand, squeezing it tight. Then throwing the car into gear, I headed for home.

THANK YOU FOR READING!

I hope you enjoyed reading Haesel, my first book of the *Conspiracy of Fates* series. If you did, please leave me a review on my Amazon page. I would love to hear what you liked about it. Who is Rosa? Did Nithele feel menacing? What character could you identify with?

Would you like a little freebie from me?

Please go to the link below, leave me your best email address, and receive a free short story character insight on the making of Julius Malicen.
https://www.subscribepage.com/malicenfreeshortstory

Join me and follow on Facebook
Keep up to date with new releases, book snippets and more.
http://www.facebook.com/AuthorHJRobertson

ABOUT THE AUTHOR

My love of books began when I first learned to read and has continued ever since, but my imagination was truly captured by dragons, faeries and all things magical and mythical. I was the one hiding under the covers with a torch so my mum didn't see the light on, and sat in the classroom reading a book in the lunch breaks at school.

I write urban fantasy novels with a touch of sci-fi. My first series - Conspiracy of Fates - starts here with Book 1.

Interested in receiving updates on release dates, upcoming book snippets, and more?

Sign-up on my landing page:
https://www.subscribepage.com/malicenfreeshortstory

Join me and follow on Facebook:
http://www.facebook.com/AuthorHJRobertson